# BLOOD BEACH

Led by the rebellious Captain Corrigan, Assault Troop form part of the 'Iron Division' during the 1944/45 European campaign. Although the men are relatively inexperienced in battle, Corrigan is determined to instil his own fighting spirit into them. Sent over to France before the main invasion force on D-Day, they have the task of breaking through the German beach defences, linking up with the paratroops and then carrying out a recce into Caen, Monty's primary D-1 objective. When the landing goes disastrously wrong, Corrigan sets out without permission to join the hard-pressed Red Devils and to proceed to Caen.

# BLOOD BEACH

# BLOOD BEACH

*by*

Ian Harding

**Magna Large Print Books**
Long Preston, North Yorkshire,
BD23 4ND, England.

British Library Cataloguing in Publication Data.

Harding, Ian
  Blood beach.

    A catalogue record of this book is
    available from the British Library

    ISBN   978-0-7505-2670-8


First published in Great Britain in 1983
by Century Publishing Co. Ltd.

Cover illustration by arrangement with
P.W.A. International Ltd.

The moral right of the author has been asserted

Published in Large Print 2007 by arrangement with
Eskdale Publishing

Magna Large Print is an imprint of Library Magna Books Ltd.

Printed and bound in Great Britain by
T.J. (International) Ltd., Cornwall, PL28 8RW

''Twas on a summer's day – the sixth of June.
I like to be particular in dates.
They are a sort of post-house, where the Fates
Change horses, making history change its tune.'

Lord Byron, *Don Juan*

# 21 ARMY     GROUP

# PERSONAL MESSAGE
# FROM THE C-IN-C

*(To be read out to all Troops)*

1. The time has come to deal the enemy a terrific blow in Western Europe. The blow will be struck by the combined sea, land, and air forces of the Allies— together constituting one great Allied team, under the supreme command of General Eisenhower.

2. On the eve of this great adventure I send my best wishes to every soldier in the Allied team. To us is given the honour of striking a blow for freedom which will live in history; and in the better days that lie ahead men will speak with pride of our doings. We have a great and a righteous cause.

   Let us pray that 'The Lord Mighty in Battle' will go forth with our armies, and that His special providence will aid us in the struggle.

3. I want every soldier to know that I have complete confidence in the successful outcome of the operations that we are about to begin.

   With stout hearts, and with enthusiasm for the contest, let us go forward to victory.

4. And, as we enter the battle, let us recall the words of a famous soldier spoken many years ago:—

   > 'He either fears his fate too much,
   > Or his deserts are small,
   > Who dare not put it to the touch,
   > To win or lose it all.'

5. Good luck to each one of you. And good hunting on the mainland of Europe.

   **B. L. Montgomery**

   General, C.-in-C.,
   21 Army Group.

5 June, 1944.

# ONE: A CALL TO ARMS

# ONE

Whistles shrilled alarmingly.

Right on cue, the flight of Spitfires howled in straight from the sea, racing over the edge of the cliff at 400 mph. Instinctively the observers ducked, as the planes zoomed towards their target. Brazen lights flared the length of their wings and like angry red hornets the tracer shells zapped towards the line of bunkers. The morning rocked as the missiles hit. A minute later they were howling upwards into the hard blue of the spring sky, trailing startling white contrails behind them.

Now, out of the billowing white smoke-screen sent up by the destroyers offshore, the first blunt-nosed barges began to emerge. Immediately the gunners dug in halfway down the cliff took up the challenge and the air was full of the angry snap and crackle of small arms fire. Heavy machine-guns chattered ponderously like angry woodpeckers. All around the slow-moving barges, the water erupted in vicious little spurts and here and there there was a hellish howl as a slug ricocheted off their sides. Now the gunners in the bows of the barges started to return the fire. Smoke erupted from their heaving decks and tracer zipped lethally towards the high white cliffs.

The first barge ground to a stop in the shallows. Its front flap crashed down with a metallic clang. Shouting, bellowing khaki-clad men dropped into the water, weapons at the high port, and raced up the shingle towards the cliffs, the bullets chipping up stone all around their flying heels, the sweat streaming down their ugly red faces. Another barge slapped into the shingle and discharged a mass of soldiers, who pelted up the beach after their comrades.

Now they were dropping to their knees at the base of the cliff, forming a defensive perimeter, weapons at the ready, while two NCOs with frantic, fumbling fingers set up the rocket-launchers. Above them, another flight of Spitfires came racing in at cliff-top level, dragging their shadows behind them across the green surface of the sea like evil black hawks, harbingers of death.

'*Fire!*' someone cried hoarsely.

A soft belch. A puff of bright white smoke. And another. The smoke clouds burst open. From them emerged two great, gleaming steel grapnels. At tremendous speed, they hurtled towards the top of the cliff, quivering lengths of stout white rope snaking out behind them. *Whack!* The first steel hook slammed into the stone. Its sharp prongs grated on rock. Next instant the other one slammed home.

Like monkeys, the soldiers started to scramble up the cliff-face, their chests heaving frantically with the effort, oblivious to the slugs peppering the rocks all around them and showering them with stones. Below them, more barges were grinding to a halt in the shingle. Ramps were slapping down and heavy motors roaring into life. White scout cars, packed with troops, were now beginning to emerge. It seemed as if the whole coast was alive with the noise of the battle.

Now the first flushed faces appeared over the edge of the cliff. Men flopped down on the cropped turf, weapons at the ready, eyes keenly peering through the smoke.

A sergeant appeared. To the observers on the hill, he seemed a pretty old man for this kind of thing and he wore the ribbons of the Old War on his chest. But he was fighting fit. Now he ran back and forth along the edge of the cliff, shouting at his gasping soldiers, chivvying, cajoling, pushing them into a skirmish line for what was now to come – the assault course.

They were off. Spread out well at five-yard intervals, they pelted forward, firing from the hip as they ran, eyes wild and staring.

A line of concertina wire, six foot high, curled and cruelly spiked, appeared ahead of them. The old sergeant didn't hesitate. He ran smack into it, arms outstretched, as if he were plunging from a diving board. The observers winced. The NCO's wizened, bronzed face contorted with pain as the barbs bit into his body. 'Gildy, you pregnant penguins! Come on! *At the double now!*' he cried through gritted teeth.

A young solider ran forward, clambered up the older man's body and dropped panting to the ground. Another followed, and another. In seconds they were all over the human bridge and the NCO was tearing himself free to somersault expertly over the wire, landing on his feet with the agility of a trained acrobat.

'By God, that noncom is first class!' cried the Brigadier, watching from down below. He had to yell to make himself heard above the roar of the half-tracks and scout cars which were now thundering up the beach like primeval monsters in search of prey. 'Damned good chap! We could use a few more like him in the Iron Division when the time comes!'

Now the assault troopers were crawling up a muddy slope criss-crossed by knee-high barbed wire. Hosepipes were turning the ground into a glistening, clinging morass, and the men were slipping and cursing, ripping their hands on the wire, deafened by the thunderflashes exploding on all sides and the deadly white Morse of tracer bullets hissing just above their heads. At last they were through. In front of them loomed a great wall of planks, some twenty yards high. They staggered towards it, leathern-lunged and gasping like asthmatics, uniforms drenched in mire.

Yet still the old NCO gave them no rest. 'Come on,' he snarled. *'Come on! At the double now! Too much five-against-one in yer bunks at night, I'll be bound... Load a' soft nellies! Couldn't fight yer way out of a bleeding paper bag! At the double, Assault Troop!'*

Madly they clambered and grappled their way upwards, deafened by remorseless machine-gun fire, rough timbers ripping and tearing cruelly at their hands. Over they went, head first, to plunge into 'Smoky Joe's', a dark, cavernous wooden hut filled with smoke and tear-gas. Choking and cursing, they groped their way through the smoke-filled gloom and clambered through the roof, harassed and kicked all the way by that little whippet of an NCO. The man had absolutely no mercy on them. As they exited, tears streaming down their faces, stumbling blindly onwards, he was there again, still screaming at them. 'Into the water... Into the bleeding water... *Bash on, Assault Troop!'* And before they knew it, they were plunging into an ice-cold, waist-deep torrent with thunderflashes flying through the air thick and fast and exploding on all sides.

17

On and on went the torture for the gasping, crimson-faced youths in khaki. For now the armoured vehicles had reached the cliff-top through one of the gaps in the cliffs and could clear the way for them, as they would on the day.

'Tanks... *Enemy tanks!*' the little NCO screeched. As one, the men dropped into the prepared holes. Out of the smoke came rumbling three bren gun carriers. At thirty miles an hour they bumped over the rough country, heading straight for the holes. The Brigadier held his breath. He had never liked this part of the course, but he knew it had to be done.

Churning up a great shower of earth and pebbles, the little armoured vehicles swung to left and right. Next moment they were rolling right over the holes in which the petrified young men crouched in fear of their lives, the tracks racing just over their ashen faces, showering them with earth and filling their nostrils with the stink of petrol. Then they were gone.

From his vantage point, the brigadier heaved a sigh of relief. Each man had popped up from his hole. No one had been hurt this time.

'Final test, sir!' his chief of staff called, above the roar of the advancing assault armour. 'Attack on enemy gunpits at three o'clock, left of that clump of yellow gorse –

hundred-yards dash under live fire. Marksmen standing by at each end of the field. They'll use crossfire. As long as the chaps keep moving, everything will be all right. Closest we could get to the real thing, sir,' he added apologetically.

Meanwhile the old NCO rallied his men of the Assault Troop for the last lap. 'Come on now,' he called firmly, seemingly inexhaustible. 'Let's be having you lot o' pansies!'

Swaying as if they might collapse at any moment, eyes blank and unseeing, huge pearls of perspiration gleaming in their eyebrows, the young men in their tattered khaki formed up. Weapons held at the high port, they began to advance again, plodding forward slowly like weary farmers returning after a hard day in the fields.

Almost immediately the marksmen on the bren guns to left and right opened up. The air on both sides of the slow-moving line was sliced by hurrying spurts of vicious white-and-red light. Slugs ripped the turf to front and rear. Dirt and pebbles spurted everywhere. Now the air was full of the fury of the machine-guns, the whine of slugs ricocheting off rocks, the curses of the frightened soldiers, and the roar of the engines following them.

And then it happened. A bullet howled off a concealed boulder. A soldier screamed shrilly. His rifle fell from suddenly nerveless

19

fingers. Slowly, very slowly, as if in slow motion, something grey, hideous and steaming began to crawl from the ragged hole torn in his guts. The boy stared down at his protruding intestines, his face contorted with agony, horror and utter disbelief. Next instant he fell writhing to the ground, howling pitifully like a trapped animal.

'Oh, my God!' the brigadier gasped. 'That chap's hit!'

'Got to expect casualties, sir,' the chief of staff said hastily, his face suddenly ashen. 'It'll be much worse on the day.'

Now the men of the Assault Troop were falling to the ground, hugging it fearfully. Only the NCO remained standing. Now he fumed and raged, heedless of the tracer cutting the air all around him. 'Get on yer feet this instant!' he screamed, face brick-red with fury. 'By Christ, if you're not on yer plates o' meat in a minute, I'll have every last one of you sodding nancy boys on a fizzer! Yer feet won't touch the frigging ground on the way to the guard room!' He aimed a savage kick at the ribs of the nearest soldier, cowering at his feet.

To no avail. The men were too terrified to move.

The brigadier, watching, tugged at his old-fashioned moustache. It was exactly what he feared would happen on the day. He had seen it all before in the Old War. The men would go over the top confidently enough, but once the Boche opened up and they began to take their first hits, all the fight would fly out of them like air from a balloon. Thank God, the Commanding General wasn't here to see this fiasco! And there were only days to go before the real thing...

'*Corrigan!*'

Suddenly a wild cry broke into the brigadier's gloomy thoughts.

'*I say – that's Corrigan!*'

As one, the observers of the Brigade staff swung round. A tall, lean figure had flung itself over the side of the leading half-track. Now the man was pelting across the pitted turf towards the pinned-down infantrymen. Although he was an officer, he carried an infantryman's rifle and was helmetless – which was against King's Regulations. Spare bandoliers of ammunition bounced up and down across his chest and over his broad athlete's back he carried a bag of grenades.

Swiftly the Brigadier swung up his glasses. A hard, handsome, bitter face swung into the centre of calibrated gleaming glass, the lips drooping a little in the corners like those of a man who had been disappointed in life. But there was no mistaking the purpose and determination stamped on those harshly handsome features. It was the face of a man born to lead and command.

Through his binoculars the brigadier

watched as the officer reached his men. Completely ignoring the tracer, he shouted something to the soldiers lying on the earth. No response. To one side the little NCO was shrugging his shoulders, as if he could do no more with his frightened troops.

Corrigan's face twisted into a bitter smile, as if he had been expecting this to happen all along. He grabbed a grenade from the bag on his back. Angrily he put the deadly little egg to his lips and ripped out the cotter pin with his teeth.

'God Almighty,' the brigadier breathed incredulously. 'Surely the fellah's not going to–'

His words were drowned by a great roar of rage from the lone officer. Next instant the brigadier saw Corrigan hurtle the grenade directly to the rear of his men.

It exploded ten yards behind them in a ball of angry yellow, whirling fire. Razor-sharp gleaming shards of steel howled through the air. Yet Corrigan seemed not to notice. '*Up,* you damned young fools,' he bellowed angrily. '*Up!* you'd be sitting ducks on the day! Up I say!'

It worked. His men sprang to their feet. More frightened of Corrigan's blazing blue eyes than they were of the flying tracer, they rushed the 'Jerry gunpits', whooping like drunken, crazed Red Indians, while at their side the wizened NCO, Sergeant Hawkins, once more urged them on. '*That's* the stuff to give 'em, lads! Knew you wouldn't let me down! Get in there. Frigging well give 'em the point!... *Bash on, Assault Troop.*'

''Pon my word,' the brigadier said weakly, mopping his brow with a silk handkerchief. 'Never seen anything like it in all my born days. Throwing a live grenade at his own chaps. 'Pon my word!'

Behind his broad back, the chief of staff grinned. That kind of thing was typical of Captain Jim Corrigan, MC, the commander of the Iron Division's Assault Troop. Corrigan had never believed in going by the book. That was why he was still a captain.

## TWO

The men were sprawled out on the cropped grass, collars open, puffing at their Woodbines or drinking tea from their awkward square mess-tins. A few munched the iron-hard rock buns served by the girls of the 'Sally Ann's' mobile canteen. Here and there a man lay face down on the grass, rifle thrown carelessly to one side, too exhausted even to smoke.

Sergeant Hawkins, seemingly tireless, moved from man to man, checking them

23

out, his voice now surprisingly gentle and concerned after the rasping commands he had barked out on the assault course. 'All right, son. Any complaints? Feet okay?'

'Sure, Sarge. Fair dinkum,' Slim Sanders replied when the NCO finally worked his way round to the pint-sized Aussie. 'If me heart was as tender as me feet, I'd be the kindest man alive.'

The men laughed, and Sergeant Hawkins held up a dirty middle finger. 'Well, yer know what yer can do with that, Trooper.' But there was no rancour in his voice – even though Slim Sanders caused him some of the worst headaches of the whole damned Troop.

'Sorry, Sarge,' said Sanders, lazily drawing at his cigarette. 'Already got a double-decker bus up there.'

Now the effects of the assault course were beginning to wear off, and some of the men were already in the mood for singing. Young Wolfers, the giant of the Troop, struck up that old favourite: *'Drunk last night. Drunk the night before, Gonna–'*

*'–Gonna get drunk tonight like we've never bin drunk before,'* the others joined in heartily. *'For we are the boys of the R-E-C-C-E...'*

Corrigan, however, did not share his fellow-officers' amusement. That old song had caused more bar-room brawls than the Iron Division had had days in combat.

The little scene was typical, Corrigan

24

reflected angrily. It was nearly four o' clock, time for tea. So tea they had – as if the Germans would stop the war just to let them brew up and drink that precious damned char of theirs!

After four years of waiting for the Big Day, they were still *playing* war, with tea-breaks and company smokers, drill parades and ceremonial guard mountings – all the stupid bull of the pre-war Regular Army. Corrigan shook his head in dismay. It was sickening. The poor young sods didn't know what they were in for. They'd have to learn the hard way – just like the other poor sods at Anzio Beach that January…

'Gentlemen, gather round, please.' The voice was that of the brigadier. He was squatting on his shooting-stick, fat face wreathed in a ruddy smile, pausing to take a little tot of whisky from his silver flask. 'Well, gentlemen,' he said as soon as he had the attention of the assembled officers, 'that was it. The last exercise!'

For a moment the message didn't seem to sink in. Then the bored young faces were suddenly animated, eyes sparkling and ex- cited. 'You mean – *we're going in?*' someone cried.

The brigadier, a wooden-faced, unimagin- ative man, smiled, pleased with the effect of his announcement. 'Yes, gentlemen. The orders came through from Second Army early this morning. The Iron Division starts moving south at twenty hundred hours tomorrow night, as soon as we have the cover of darkness. We're going into the cages. It's on – and that's official.'

Immediately excited chatter broke out among the officers. Here and there men shook hands solemnly. Others slapped one another on the back, huge grins on their faces. One or two of them simply stood there, their faces entranced, as if they couldn't believe that at long last it was really going to happen.

Corrigan, still helmetless and carrying the Lee Enfield infantryman's rifle, felt strangely out of it, apart from their excitement. He could understand, of course. Some of then had been run out of Dunkirk four years before and had returned home beaten and weaponless. Then they'd had to watch farmers sharpen their pitchforks, and Home Guards parade with pikes, and coastguards patrol the beaches with knobbed sticks. Others had still been schoolboys at the time of Dunkirk, and had learned of the events of that terrible summer of 1940 from their radios and newspapers.

Four years had passed since June of that year. At first they had waited for the enemy to appear on English soil; then when he did not, they had trained to take the war back to the

Continent. All those years, training had been an end in itself. Now at last, however, they were facing the real thing, leaving behind their uneventful, almost peaceful existence, broken only by the occasional air-raid, and venturing out across that dark-green sea to meet all the unknown terrors of battle.

It had been a different war for Corrigan, though. First in Norway in '40; then Greece and Crete, '41; then the Western Desert in '42. Defeat after defeat, year in, year out – and all because the officers hadn't been ruthless and aggressive enough and the men insufficiently hard. Of course, in '43, things had begun to change a little. There had been victories in Sicily and Italy. Yet still they hadn't brought about the final defeat of the Germans. How bitter he had been at the waste, the inefficiency of it all!

Somehow Anzio had brought it all to a head. It was as if something had snapped inside him. He breathed out hard at the memory. That day he had only just escaped being cashiered by the skin of his teeth. *'If it weren't for your record and your gongs, Corrigan,'* the divisional commander had snapped at him angrily as he handed him his posting back to the UK, *'I would have tossed you out of the Army on your ear. My God! To do a thing like that in an Allied army, commanded by an American general…'* At that point the crimson-faced general had been

27

unable to speak another word; his head was somehow twisted to one side as if he were choking. Finally he had stuttered, *'Now in heaven's name, Corrigan, go – get out of my sight!'* ...

'Gentlemen,' the brigadier's somewhat fruity voice broke in upon Corrigan's reverie. 'It's time we saw about getting the chaps back to camp. I hear on the QT that the cooks are preparing something special for them tonight. There's much talk of fried eggs – eggs from *real* chickens – and other such delicacies.' He beamed at his young officers, and they beamed back at him.

'The whole division is being stood down after tea till eight hundred hours tomorrow morning. Don't tell the chaps why – let them have a bit of a fling. It'll be the last chance they get. Once we're in the cages we'll be sealed off from the outer world until the...' he paused, as if he could hardly bring himself to utter that overwhelming word: '...until the Invasion. Thank you.'

As one, the officers clicked to attention and saluted. Corrigan was about to walk away with the rest to carry out the Brigadier's order when the latter snapped, 'Corrigan ... Captain Corrigan – one moment, please.' The warmth had gone from his voice now.

Hastily the staff colonel moved out of earshot. He could see Corrigan was due for a rocket and he did not want to be a witness to the scene. He rather liked Corrigan, but he dared not tell that to the brigadier, or to any others of the staff of the Iron Division. It was well known that the tough, bronzed captain with the bold, angry eyes was at the top of the staff's personal shit-list.

'Sir!' Corrigan said, standing stiffly to attention, rifle held rigidly at his side and gaze fixed on some distant horizon, like the most junior private in front of a drill sergeant.

It would have been normal military courtesy to tell him to stand at ease, but the brigadier was not feeling very courteous towards Corrigan this May afternoon. 'You know, Corrigan,' he rasped, 'I value the handful of officers like yourself in the Brigade who have had recent battle experience.' He flashed an angry look at Corrigan's sand-coloured Africa Star, the purple-and-white ribbon of the Military Cross and the red, white and blue of the American Distinguished Service Cross. For a moment he almost seemed to blush. 'General Montgomery specifically asked for officers of your kind, so that you could pass on your experience in Africa, Italy and elsewhere to the rest of the men.'

Corrigan stood his ground. In the background the harsh voices of the NCOs could be heard barking commands at the men: '*All right, get fell in, in threes now! Come on, you dozy buggers, let's see yer move them legs. Don't worry – nothing will fall out...*'

The brigadier suddenly fixed Corrigan with a glare. 'But I really can't have you seriously endangering the lives of the chaps like that,' he snapped. 'That business of the grenade was exceedingly foolhardy.'

'Train hard, fight easy, sir,' Corrigan answered, gazing calmly at the brigadier's heavy, flushed middle-aged face and wondering if *he* would last the hard battle to come. 'That is the Germans' motto, sir, and it pays dividends.'

'You might think me old-fashioned for saying this, Corrigan,' the brigadier said icily, 'but we aren't Germans.' He stopped, as if he half-expected the tall harshly handsome officer to reply. But Corrigan said nothing.

'All right,' he continued, 'now just remember this.'

Across the way, the first long khaki column was moving off, rifles slung, lustily singing: '*Now this is number one, and I've got her on the run. Roll me over, in the clover... Roll me over in the clover and do it again...*'

'You've blotted your copybook – for a regular army officer, at least. But you've got a chance to try and improve your record. So do it, Corrigan.' The brigadier stared hard at the other officer, but Corrigan's face was

30

impassive, revealing nothing – not even contempt. 'But I warn you, one slip, the merest mistake, and I'll be down on you like a ton of bricks.' In irritation, as if he already knew his words would have no effect on the silent man facing him, the brigadier waved his cane, 'Now be off with you ... dismiss.' And he turned his back on him.

Down the road they were singing, *'Now this is number two, and he's got it up my flue... Roll me over and do it again...'*

Corrigan grinned.

## THREE

'You know what it'll be like, sir,' said Sergeant Hawkins. Outside the troop office, the bugle sounded sweet, clear and somehow haunting, followed an instant later by the harsh crunch of heavy nailed boots on gravel as the new guard marched off to their posts. 'As soon as the NAAFI opens the wet canteen, they'll be in there like a shot, getting pissed and matey. Then they'll get more pissed – and randy. But they won't be able to get their oats in this one-horse town – not unless they're a ruddy Yank or an officer and a gentleman.'

Corrigan sat on the edge of his desk, toying

31

with a 36 grenade, it's lever stuck down with insulating tape. He grinned. With his collarless khaki shirt and ruddy cheeks, 'Papa' Hawkins looked the very image of an English working-class Dad. But looks were deceptive. This troop sergeant, who dyed his hair with cold tea to conceal his age in order that he could go into combat again, was in fact a very shrewd and competent NCO. He ensured stability among the men, fathering them, schooling them in the chaotic conditions of the battlefield. More than one eager young subaltern had won his 'good gong' thanks to the devotion and reliability of sergeants such as Papa Hawkins.

'So, because they won't be able to find any crumpet,' Hawkins continued, 'they'll get angry. And if they're really pissed, they'll start taking things apart – including each other.' Hawkins sighed like a man sorely plagued. 'So I'll have to see they don't do any serious damage. A black eye or two, a thick ear, a bloody nose – but no broken bones. I don't want any of 'em staying behind, in hospital, not after I've trained the buggers all these years.'

Corrigan laughed softly.

Outside, a group of men leaving the camp on pass were standing in front of a full-length mirror next to the gate, which bore the legend: ARE YOU A CREDIT TO YOUR REGIMENT? They were carefully checking their appearances before braving the provost marshal, who, they knew, would send them back into camp if they didn't meet his high standards of military turnout. 'You know they call you "Papa" Hawkins behind your back?' smiled Corrigan. 'I'm not surprised. You fuss over those young soldiers like a mother-hen.'

Hawkins grinned almost proudly. 'Somebody's got to look after 'em, sir. Most of them had never been away from home before they joined the Kate Karney.'

'And what about you, Sergeant? What have you got planned for your last night before we go into the dreaded cages?'

Hawkins shrugged and sucked idly at his evil-smelling old pipe; it was unlit, for he had already used up his weekly tobacco allowance. 'Oh, I suppose I'll have a couple of quiet gills over at the sergeants' mess before the fun starts in the NAAFI. Then it's the wanking pit for me. It's been a rough day, one way or other.' He looked meaningfully at the tall, lean officer.

'I know, you old rogue, I know. You mean with the grenade? Don't tell me. I've already had a rocket, personal and hand-delivered by the brigadier himself. But what if they'd gone to earth like that on the day? It would be a massacre, Hawkins.'

The old noncom slowly took his pipe out of his mouth and looked thoughtful. 'I know what you mean, sir. But perhaps, you...' He stopped and hurriedly changed the subject. 'And you, sir – how are you going to spend your last night of freedom?' Without waiting for Corrigan to answer, he lowered his voice and added, 'They tell me there are some very obliging young ladies to be found at the Royal in town. *Very* obliging... It's even been rumoured that they've *helped out* British soldiers now that all the Yanks are moving south.' He winked knowingly. 'Could be worse ways of spending the night, sir...'

Corrigan looked at him in mock-amazement. 'My God, Hawkins, you're even trying to mother me now! I'm ashamed of you – a married man with three children in Barnsley, trying to set your commanding officer up with ladies of ill-fame! I'll certainly have to talk to the padre about you and your immoral ways.' He straightened up and reached for his cap and stick, then tucked the grenade into his blouse pocket as an afterthought. 'No, Hawkins, not tonight – though thanks for the recommendation. The colonel's ordered all officers of the Reconnaissance Regiment to dine in tonight.' He sniffed and frowned, as if suddenly he had decided he didn't much care for the idea. 'So I'd better get on to that Australian rogue of a batman of mine, Trooper Slim Sanders, and check whether he's found time in his busy schedule to polish my Sam Browne.'

Hawkins returned his grin. 'God knows how we ever got landed with the Aussie, sir. But I'll say this for the little bugger, if you'll forgive my French: he's a cunning one, that he is.'

Corrigan paused at the door. Outside on the parade ground, a red-faced, sweat-lathered jankers man was lumbering up and down, carrying two heavy firebuckets filled with sand, urged on by a bellowing regimental policeman waving his stick. Obviously *he* wasn't going to enjoy his last night of freedom.

'You can say that again, Hawkins. Slim Sanders certainly wasn't born yesterday – nor the day before, for that matter.' Casually he touched his hand to his cap, set at its usual bold non-regulation angle, and was gone, marching across the parade ground.

Thoughtfully Sergeant Hawkins watched him go, sucking at his empty pipe. There was no hope for Corrigan. In a quarter of a century of soldiering all over the world, he had seen quite a few Corrigans: the hard, impatient loners who tried to buck the three-hundred-year-old traditions of the British Army. But in the end the system always broke them.

Hawkins tapped his pipe on the heel of his boot. He was thinking of flogging this week's chocolate ration for an ounce of baccy in the mess; then he remembered the kids back home in Barnsley and thought better of it.

'Strewth, digger,' Trooper Slim Sanders breathed in awe, as he and Wolfers pushed through the heavy blackout curtain and entered the noisy, smoke-filled lounge of the Royal Hotel. 'Will yer take a gander at all that gash!' He gulped hard. 'Holy cow, I could eat it with a knife and fork!'

Towering well above the little Australian at six foot four, Trooper Wolfers nodded nervously and licked his lips. For a moment or two, the pair of them stood and gaped at the scene: everywhere there were giggling girls and brawny Yanks, the latter puffing at big black cigars and swigging from bottles of whisky which these days cost at least five pounds on the black market – more than an eighteen-year-old trooper of the British Army earned in three months.

Wolfers groaned. 'The place is full of Yanks, Slim,' he protested, 'we ain't got a chance!'

But the smooth little batman with the cynical eyes was undismayed. By way of reply, he tapped the captain's stars which he had 'borrowed' from Corrigan's dresser and hastily sewn on his tunic an hour before, and said confidently, 'What do you think these are, you big dope – Scotch mist? I'm an officer and gent, ain't I? And you're my batman!'

'Yes, b-but...' Wolfers stammered, blush-

36

ing a deep red; for in spite of his enormous bulk and tough exterior, he lacked his companion's worldly *savoir-faire*. 'But ... I mean ... what if they find out?'

Slim winked knowingly. 'But they *won't,* will they? Listen, cobber, I promised you we'd get a bit tonight. Can't have a young bloke going into action for the first time and still a virgin...'

At this, Wolfers blushed even more and thought with a gulp of the dozen French letters he had stuffed in various parts of his khaki battledress, ready for this momentous occasion.

Meanwhile, Sanders started to push his way through the drunken, happy throng towards the bar. 'The Yanks might have their nylons and chocolate bars, but yours truly is an officer – and *that* makes a difference. Just you watch out for my steam.'

So saying, the Aussie jabbed a big fat American master-sergeant in the back, causing him to choke on his beer. 'Sorry, old chap,' Slim chortled in his best British officer's manner – and neatly took his place at the bar.

Once there, he held up a hand for service, and called out: 'I say, Gladys, two very large whiskys for me and my servant, if you please!'

Next to him, two brassy blondes were deep in conversation at the bar. Their skirts were short, bosoms strapped high beneath their chins, faces bright with rouge and white powder. Both looked flushed and feverish as if in the last stages of TB.

'Heard about the new government utility knickers, Doris?' said one to her companion. *'One Yank and they're off!'*

Her neighbour cackled with laughter.

Slim beamed at the two whores and took the plunge. 'I say, ladies,' he said in his best stilted tones, 'that really is most amusing.'

The blonde nearest to him glared down coldly at the little Australian. 'We don't talk to Limeys,' she said icily, 'so piss off!' And with a sniff she turned back to her port and lemon.

A sweating, red-faced barmaid placed two glasses in front of the two assault troopers. 'Ten bob,' she said defiantly, as if fully expecting a flood of protest at this exorbitant price. 'That's what the Yanks all pay.'

Slim, however, did not bat an eyelid. Casually he placed one of the four five-pound notes he had removed from 'A' Squadron's safe that afternoon on the bar, and said, 'Have a drink yourself, dear. You look as if you could use one.'

Wolfers gulped again. Ten bob for two drinks! That was the sum total of his weekly pay!

'Cheers!' Slim said. Just then something seemed to catch his eye. With a jerk of his head he indicated two ATS girls standing alone at the end of the bar, morosely sipping at small glasses of shandy. 'Get a load of them Sheilas, sport,' he said. 'They're ours – even if they do wear khaki knickers. Come on.' He took a quick swig of his whisky.

Hastily the giant trooper did the same, hoping the spirits would give him the courage he would need for what was to come, and followed the little Australian as he began to push his way towards the girls.

'Good evening, young ladies,' Slim said, his voice at its fruitiest. 'All alone?'

Seeing the captain's pips on Slim's shoulders, the taller of the two girls made as if to stand to attention. But Slim was *noblesse* itself. With a wave of the little officer's swagger-stick he had borrowed from Corrigan, he said airily, 'No rank at the bar, my dear. Off-duty the British Army is very democratic. After all, I am in the company of my own batman, another ranker like your two charming selves.' He beamed at the ATS, and indicated the red-faced young giant next to him. 'Yes – that's the modern British Army. Democracy in action.'

'The British Army is a crock of shit!' said a drunken voice, full of menace, behind them.

A sudden, heavy silence seemed to fall on their section of the bar. The ATS girls looked worried. Slowly, very slowly, Slim Sanders began to turn his head, his winning smile still glued to his thin lips. Wolfers did the same.

Three hulking paratroopers in jump-boots stood before them, the one who had spoken, an ugly, broken-nosed sergeant, swaying drunkenly. His combat jacket hung open and numerous five-pound notes were poking out of his breast pockets. His garrison cap was shoved to the back of his cropped bullet head, and there was a stump of a cigar in the corner of his mouth...

Slim waited some time before he spoke. Finally he looked up at the American sergeant and said, 'Were you addressing me, my man?'

The sergeant blinked several times, as if he were having difficulty in focusing. Behind him, one of his companions, his broad chest heavy with multi-coloured medal ribbons, grinned at the two troopers: 'How's ya war going, Limeys? Still losing?'

His comrades laughed mightily.

'Don't worry,' the drunken sergeant choked, tears of laughter streaming down his brick-red face at this witty sally, 'the American Army's here. We'll win it for you... When the Krauts hear we're coming, they'll high-tail it back to Berlin in double-quick time!'

''Ere!' said Wolfers, his anger rising, suddenly doubling his fists like two small steam-shovels.

Slim laid a restraining hand on his companion. 'Leave it to me, Trooper Wolfers.'

His tone was all sweetness and light, even though the three paratroopers were now leering down at him more threateningly than ever. 'I see you chaps have a large number of campaign ribbons.' He indicated their chests with his cane. 'Or did you get them for coming over here in the *Queen Mary?* Or maybe for eating brussels sprouts? Recently I heard of three of your chappies who went to see a war film at the local fleapit. One fainted straight away at the sight of blood and won the Purple Heart: the other two were awarded a medal for gallantry in action above and beyond the call of duty – for carrying him out!'

'What did the little Limey jerk say, Al?' the drunken sergeant asked, brow creased in a puzzled frown. Suddenly it dawned on him that he had just been insulted. 'Why, you goddamned creep!' he cried in rage. He made a grab for Slim's blouse. 'Holy mackerel, I'm gonna murder you for that, you little–'

But it was not to be. Slim's cane shot out. The brass point caught the big paratrooper sergeant right between his spread legs, just as he drew his fist back to punch the little Australian. Caught off-guard, he screamed shrilly and collapsed to the littered floor, moaning and whining and clutching his crotch in utter agony.

Now Wolfers swung his massive fist. The

second paratrooper with the chestful of medal ribbons caught the punch right on the point of his chin. His eyes crossed immediately. With a soft moan, he settled gently on the floor, cap falling over his eyes, back against the bar. Slowly his teeth began to fall from his gaping mouth, dropping to the floor one by one like pearls.

'A fight ... a fight!' cried an excited voice to their rear. 'The Limeys are fighting, guys... Come on – let's get a piece of the action!' A woman screamed. Another yelled, 'Get yer frigging hand from under my skirt!' A civilian behind the bar shrilled an urgent blast on a police whistle. Somebody slung a bottle at him. It missed and smashed against the big mirror, which shattered into a thousand pieces. In a flash, all was confusion, screams, yells, howls of pain and the solid thud of flesh slamming into flesh, as fighting broke out on all sides.

As always, Slim Sanders, veteran of a life of crime on three continents, was master of the situation. He grabbed his empty glass from the bar and flung it at the lights. They splintered with a series of loud electric plops. Immediately the confused mass of screaming, cursing men and women was plunged into darkness.

'Okay, cobber,' he yelled at Wolfers, 'head out to the pisshouses in the yard. I'll follow yer, mate.'

Above the chaotic din, the wail of the US military police sirens could now be heard, growing ever louder; the 'snowdrops' were already racing to the scene of the riot. It was time to be gone. Now Slim turned his attention to the ATS girls. 'Come on,' he said excitedly, grabbing them both by the hand. 'This is no place for a couple of nicely brought up young ladies like you. I know a nice, quiet little air-raid shelter close by, where we can discuss – er, *things* – away from all this noise and roughness. Come on.'

Herding the two girls in front of him, Slim headed for the exit, pausing only to grab a bottle of Johnny Walker from the bar and to deal the still-prostrate paratroop sergeant a vicious kick in the ribs. 'So long, sucker!' he chortled. And then he was gone...

Now the great binge was coming to an end, and at last the camp was settling down for the night. Across the square at the NAAFI, a good-humoured voice which Corrigan recognized as that of Papa Hawkins was saying, *'All right, my lucky lads, you've had a good skinful now... Off you go to yer wanking pits... That's it... On yer merry way... Christopher Robin and Sergeant Hawkins still loves yer...'*

Somebody blew a wet kiss. Another attempted a drunken verse or two of an old song before breaking off suddenly with a hurried gasp. Judging by the frantic retching which followed, the unfortunate soldier was coughing his guts up.

Lying in his bunk, Corrigan grinned as he heard Hawkins slap the trooper on the back: *'Come on, son, get rid of it... Get it off yer manly chest – yer'll feel better for it in the morning...'*

Then at last all was silent in the camp, save for the steady stamp of the sentries' boots and the faint wind in the trees. From far off, Corrigan could hear 'lights out' being played at the Brigade Signals camp. The bugle call carried by the breeze was somehow unutterably sad and wistful.

He put down *No Orchids for Miss Blandish*, the only book he had been able to find in the mess, and listened to it, hands behind his head.

It reminded him of his days as a cadet at Sandhurst before the war, a callow youth who had joined the army straight from Harrow, determined to serve King and Country loyally, just as his father, his grandfather, even his great-grandfather had done before him. He thought of Anzio and a similar bugle call being blown over those mass graves, the sound wafting out to sea, echoing and re-echoing as if for ever. And as the memories came flooding back, he couldn't help thinking what a frightful balls-up he had made of everything...

# FOUR

Moonlight flooded the dead-straight, white road that led to Campoleone. Up ahead, the Italian sky glowed pink as the German artillery pounded the positions of the trapped British battalion – or what was still left of it; for the 1st Battalion of the Sherwood Foresters had now been cut off at the point of the Anglo-American advance out of the Anzio beachhead for a full thirty-six hours. If they were not relieved soon, there would be little hope for them.

On both sides of the road, Major Corrigan's armoured cars and half-tracks waited for the order to roll. Meanwhile Corrigan himself exchanged a whispered radio conference with the colonel commanding the US tanks, who were to follow the Recce men in once they had made the breakthrough. Quietly, Corrigan's veterans smoked, hands cupped around the glowing ends of their cigarettes, each man shrouded in his personal cocoon of thoughts and forebodings.

Corrigan put down the radio. 'All right, Sanders,' he whispered to the little Australian, whom he had picked up the previous year during the confused fighting of the

North Africa campaign. 'Off you go.'

Sergeant Sanders nodded. 'OK, mates,' he hissed to the troops, 'hit the trail. Let's get us some Jerries!'

Obediently the handful of assault troopers vanished into the shadows, their weapons slung, pick-handles and sharpened entrenching tools held in their hands instead. Behind them, armoured personnel stubbed out their cigarettes and prepared for the order to move out. Corrigan flashed a glance at the green-glowing dial of his wristwatch. He would give the little Aussie fifteen minutes. To his front another German flare hissed into the night sky and exploded in a burst of brilliant white light, illuminating all below for a few seconds in its incandescent glare. The Germans were getting nervous. He began to count off the minutes.

As the first German guard tried to unsling his machine-pistol, startled by the sudden noise from the shadows, a dark figure detached itself from the olive trees. A flash of silver. The next moment Slim Sanders had his arm crooked around the sentry's neck, silencing his cry of alarm. Slim's cruel knife slid in between his third and fourth ribs, once, twice, three times. The sentry's back was tautened. He heaved. He seemed about to drag himself free. Then quite suddenly he went limp in the Australian's arms. Gently, very gently, Sanders lowered him to the cobbles and wiped the blood off his knife on the dead man's tunic.

'One down, two to go,' Sanders hissed to his companion, who was busy strangling the life out of the other sentry with the strap of his own coal-shuttle helmet. The German's eyes bulged wildly out of his head like those of a madman. His spine curved like a taut bow. Then he, too, relaxed into death. The kill had been swift and silent.

Like grey timber wolves, the little group of assault troopers crept up each side of the road. From somewhere to their right, Slim could hear the sound of spades slicing into sun-baked earth. A new German outfit was probably digging in there to meet the new Allied threat. With a quick jerk of his head, the Australian indicated they should veer to the left.

Two more German sentries guarding the road that Major Corrigan's armoured spearhead would follow were dealt with as speedily and cruelly as the first pair. 'Easy as falling off a bleeding log,' Slim commented softly, wiping his knife clean once again.

'You ain't half a bloodthirsty little git, Aussie!' one of the assault troopers commented, slightly awed.

'Less of the Aussie, cobber,' Slim said warningly, stealing a little hand inside the dead German's pocket and pulling out his watch. 'Them's three stripes I've got on my arm, remember.'

Suddenly there was a soft *plop*. 'Freeze!' Slim commanded. A German flare zipped into the night sky and exploded. The raiders stiffened, even the toughest of them praying that they hadn't been spotted. After what they had just done to the sentries, Jerry would be taking no prisoners. For an eternity they stood there, bathed in the flare's icy white glare, tensely waiting for the first hoarse cry of rage and the angry chatter of an enemy Spandau. Nothing happened. Finally the spent flare began to descend to earth like a fallen angel.

Slim glanced at one of the four looted wristwatches he had strapped to his right arm. *'Out!'* he hissed. *'We ain't got much more time left.'*

Obediently the troopers doubled forward once more, their sock-covered boots making hardly a sound on the cobbled Italian road. Suddenly Slim stopped and dropped to one knee. Without a command, the assault troopers instantly followed suit, tense and alert, each man peering into the gloom to left and right, searching for the enemy. Slim took his time. He raised his head and sniffed the night air like a wild dog seeking his prey. To his front the heavy guns rumbled again, and far off the sky was already flushed a faint pink. There was no sound. Then the little Australian seemed to pick up the scent. It was that typical ugly stink of coarse, black German tobacco, and it was coming from the right-hand side of the road, a little further up. It was the last German outpost barring Corrigan's way.

Crouched low, knife clasped firmly in his right hand, he started to steal forward. Behind him the others followed. Slim paused and sniffed again. The stink was coming from a cunningly camouflaged dugout some ten yards away, and he could now see the long, slim, deadly barrel of a dug-in 57mm anti-tank gun covering the road. He grinned wickedly. 'Yer never gonna use that pop-gun again, mates,' he muttered under his breath, and crawled on.

'*Wer da?*' Suddenly a harsh challenge shattered the heavy stillness, making even Slim jump.

Behind him, one of the assault troopers reacted quicker than he did. Taking swift aim at the dark figure in the coal-scuttle helmet, he hurled his sharpened entrenching tool through the air like a tomahawk.

The sentry screamed shrilly as the razor-sharp blade cleaved deep into his chest. His rifle clattered to the ground and he sank slowly down.

'*Get the buggers!*' Slim hissed. '*Before they sound the alarm!*'

His assault troopers needed no urging.

They swarmed forward.

Startled, the German anti-tank gunners, who had been enjoying a quiet smoke in the trench, struggled to their feet, grabbing for their weapons. Too late! The troopers burst in on them. Entrenching tools flashed. Bayonets stabbed. Loaded sticks thwacked down. Now it was every man for himself, as Tommies and Jerries engaged in fierce hand-to-hand combat. No quarter was given, and none was asked. As soon as a man went down in the midst of the mêlée, hard, cruelly-nailed boots slammed down on his upturned face, smashing it into an unrecognisable pulp. Slim crouched over a prostrate German, slashing at his exposed throat with his knife. Hot blood spurted up in a thick jet and soaked his hand. Another German tried to tackle the little Australian before he got to his feet. His rifle-butt was upraised ready to smash in the back of Slim's skull. In the nick of time Slim dodged to one side. The rifle came crashing down into nothing. The German lost balance and fell on one knee. Slim didn't give him a second chance. He flung his knife. It thudded audibly into the German's chest. He staggered back, croaking horribly, trying to pluck out the killing blade, the blood flooding his clawed hands. Next instant he fell flat on his back, dead, his false teeth bulging stupidly out of his gaping mouth.

Slim clambered to his feet and pulled out

the bell-shaped signal pistol which Corrigan had given him. He raised it in the air and pulled the trigger. The green signal flare exploded above his head, casting its unreal, glowing light on the macabre scene below. The road to Campoleone was open.

The assault troopers, now packed into their vehicles, tore down the road towards the beleaguered Foresters' position at a crazy speed, racing to link up with the trapped battalion, while the surprised German defenders pelted the long column with everything they had got. Tracer zipped back and forth. Spurts of bright crimson flame stabbed the white smoke. Anti-tank rockets howled through the air, followed by trails of fiery red sparks.

Carried away by the mad blood-lust of war, the troopers in their rattling, shaking half-tracks, fired to both left and right. Ahead of them the 37mm cannon of the armoured cars leading the mad dash boomed and boomed, their thin barrels swinging from side to side like the snouts of predatory monsters seeking out their prey.

A ricochet howled off Corrigan's helmet. He slammed against the steel side of the half-track, the impact making his head spin momentarily. To their right a German machine-gun was spitting fire from the upstairs window of one of the bullet-pocked cottages which lined the link-up road.

Bracing himself on the swaying deck of the racing vehicle, Corrigan gritted his teeth and pressed his trigger. The tommy-gun leapt at his side like a wild thing. Tracer curved viciously towards the open window. The German gunner screamed shrilly. Next moment he was falling, to land with a smack on the cobbles below like a bag of wet cement.

Beside him, Slim swung back his hand like his hero, Don Bradman. A phosphorus grenade flew through the air. A second later it exploded inside the house, scattering white, smoking pellets in all directions. In seconds the place was aflame. Screaming wildly, their uniforms already ablaze, even their faces smouldering where pellets had embedded themselves, the Germans jostled in panic, fighting to get outside. The assault trooper manning the 50-inch machine-gun on the top of the cab next to the driver swung his weapon round. A stream of slugs slammed into the Germans as they poured out of the building, cutting them down without mercy. The column rattled on at top speed, leaving the bodies piled in a crazy heap, twitching and burning at the same time.

Now, from the right, an anti-tank roared, sending an armour-piercing shell tearing through the glowing darkness. To Corrigan's front, the high Humber reeled violently, as if struck by a tornado. Next moment it was careening off the highway to smash into the ditch, thick white smoke pouring from its ruptured engine, its wheels spinning in the air. Something rolled out of the open turret to disappear under the flailing tracks of Corrigan's vehicle. It was the commander's head.

Frantically the crew of the German gun tried to reload, tugging madly at the breach, the loader trundling up the big brass shell. Corrigan gave them no second chance. 'Get him, driver!' he screamed, yelling to make himself heard above the snap-and-crackle of small arms fire: *'Quick!'*

The driver responded instantly, swinging the wheel round. The half-track thudded down from the road, forcing the assault troopers to cling on for dear life. Now they were ploughing across an uneven rice-field, spraying up water behind them. Ahead of them, the German loader had dropped the shell and grabbed his Schmeisser. Panicked beyond measure, he stood there, fingers glued to the trigger. Slugs howled off the metal sides of the half-track. And then with a huge, rending crash, the eight tons of flying vehicle hurtled into the gun, bowling its barrel to one side, churning the crew beneath its tracks into red pulp, and smashing blindly on through the German positions.

Ahead of them, Corrigan could faintly distinguish tiny, ragged figures climbing out of their fox-holes and waving their arms in the air. As the half-track thundered on towards them, he could just hear their voices. They were crying hoarsely, 'Thank God... *Thank God!*'

They had reached the trapped Sherwood Foresters.

Corrigan slowly clambered out of the half-track. Behind him, German signal flares were streaming into the ugly dawn sky. They were summoning help, he knew. Soon the little corridor would be cut off again.

Everywhere there were bodies – bodies piled up like heaps of logs in the churned-up earth, or sprawled out like bundles of tattered rags. One soldier lay impaled on rusting barbed wire, arms extended in agony, like some khaki-clad Christ figure. In all his four years of combat Corrigan had never seen so many corpses.

A corporal of the Foresters, head and leg bandaged, limped to meet him, his uniform caked with dry mud and blood. All the same, he managed to swing an immaculate salute.

Corrigan returned it gravely. 'Could you take me to your commanding officer, please?' he asked. Such politeness was unusual, yet there was something about the man that commanded respect. Corrigan was awed, too, by the lunar landscape all around him. Death and destruction were everywhere, and a dreadful silence had settled on the battlefield, broken only by the moans of the wounded and the low hum of conversation between the Foresters and the Recce men. 'I *am* the commanding officer, sir,' the corporal said, standing stiffly to attention. '"A" Company came in with a hundred and sixteen men. Now there are sixteen of us left. All the officers and senior noncoms bought it except me, sir.'

Now Corrigan could see the wounded lying in the big open pit behind the corporal. They lay in two rows, caked in mud, their field or shell dressings wet with new blood. Those with head wounds snored ferociously. Those who had been hit in the guts lay curled up, legs drawn up to their chests, sobbing for breath. The lung wounds stank. Others turned and twisted, unable to settle, moaning and groaning in semi-oblivion. A man gone mad sat tied to a shattered tree, laughing uncontrollably, his whole skinny body trembling violently, baring his teeth like a trapped animal.

Suddenly the anger boiled up within Corrigan. These men had gone through too much. They had to be evacuated at once. Let the Americans take over. It was their commanders who had got the invasion force into trouble in the first place, sitting on their fat arses in their shell-proof bunkers back at Anzio beach after an unopposed landing, all the time allowing the Germans to bring up their forces at leisure. 'Where's your wireless?' he snapped urgently. 'I'm going to get you and your fellows out of here.'

'We could probably hold out for another twelve hours, sir,' the young corporal said bravely, but Corrigan could see that he was at the end of his tether. His lips trembled and his eyes were covered with a kind of wet sheen, as if he might break down and weep at any moment.

Corrigan clasped a hand on the boy's skinny shoulder. 'You've done enough already. Now where's that radio?'

But Corrigan was in for a shock.

The metallic, disembodied voice at the other end was distorted by the heavy radio traffic in the area, but its message was clear enough. 'No can do,' the American armoured commander answered. 'The Krauts are closing the corridor rapidly. I can't risk my Shermans up there. They'd be sitting ducks for those damned Kraut Panzerfausts. Sorr-ee.'

'But the infantry up here are exhausted,' Corrigan protested. 'They won't hold the line longer than this afternoon! We need your armour, Colonel– We've *got* to have it.'

But all he had received by way of answer to his desperate appeal as the first German mortar bombs started to howl down on the tattered remnants of the Sherwood Foresters, was a casual 'No can do,' followed by that almost mocking, long-drawn-out 'Sorr-ee.'

Lying there on his narrow bed, listening to the faint hiss of the wind and far off on the Great North Road, the rumble of endless convoys heading for the cages, Corrigan remembered that terrible morning back in Italy.

After the American tank commander had refused to bring up his Shermans, Corrigan had been wild with anger. On his own authority he had assembled what was left of the Foresters; eight officers and two hundred and thirty men out of the thousand who had gone into action thirty-six hours before. Somehow he had managed to pack them on board his vehicles, with his assault troopers abandoning their half-tracks to them in order to act as covering infantry. Then he had ordered them to abandon the hill-top position. Somehow or other – even now he didn't know how – he had fought his way back down that corridor, still littered with German dead, taking and inflicting casualties, until finally the exhausted men had reached their own lines. There, now almost beside himself with rage, he had ordered Slim Sanders to take the wheel of one of the half-tracks, its steel sides now pocked with bullet-holes, and together they had gone racing into Allied Headquarters in Netruno.

'Hold it right there, buddy.'

Sanders and Corrigan had been about to

stroll into the bunker housing the command of the US Armoured Division, when a rasping American voice restrained them. Looking round, they saw that it belonged to a cigar-chewing white-helmeted MP.

Corrigan, white-lipped with rage, nodded to Slim Sanders.

'With pleasure, sir!' murmured the Aussie, and raced over to the cab machine-gun and swung it round. Next moment a burst of tracer ripped the dust just in front of the guard's immaculate boots. Almost swallowing his cigar, the brawny MP fled for cover.

Inside the bunker, Corrigan noticed that all the American armoured commanders looked like peas out of the same pod: big, heavy, middle-aged men with generous paunches, dressed in riding breeches and custom-made blouses. Although they were safely six yards below ground, all wore immaculate black lacquered helmets.

They had turned as one from their deliberations, as Corrigan, still dirty and blood-stained from the front had come bursting in, wild-eyed and bareheaded, his .38 clasped in a bandaged fist.

'What the Sam Hill is this?' cried one of them, a fat heavy-set man, with the two silver stars of a major-general on his helmet. He rose to his feet, his chubby face suddenly crimson with anger.

Corrigan ignored him. 'Which of you

swine is the commander of the division's Combat Command "A"?' he rasped, his eyes narrowed to slits.

'Why, me,' replied an easy-going, roly-poly colonel, toting a long ivory cigarette-holder. 'Now feller, what's the–'

'Shut your mouth!' Corrigan rasped, advancing on him, revolver held high. He would have recognised the voice anywhere. It was Mister Sorr-ee all right.

Suddenly fear flickered across the colonel's face. Pushing back his chair, he retreated, holding out his pudgy hands as if to ward off the advancing Englishman, this crazed apparition from a world that he wanted no part of. 'Now listen, pal,' he quavered. 'I don't–'

Corrigan dug the muzzle of his revolver into his fat gut. 'Out of the door!' he barked, voice cold with fury.

'But why–'

Corrigan dug his revolver into the fat gut once more. 'Out, I said. Move it – smartish!'

At the head of the table, the general gasped. 'He must be crazy... The Limey's gone Section Eight... For chrissakes, get me a medic in here, and–'

But already Corrigan was out of the door, pushing and prodding the ashen-faced colonel towards the waiting half-track, while Slim Sanders, who was enjoying every minute of the spectacle, gunned the engine.

'Kindly look at them – *look at them, will you!*' Corrigan commanded, as Slim brought the half-track to a halt before the pitiful survivors of the Sherwood Forester battalion. 'There are the soldiers *you* were going to leave to their fate – and all because of your precious tanks.'

The colonel stared over to where the ragged soldiers sat slumped in the dirt, gazing apathetically at their mud-caked boots. 'Gee, I didn't know–' he stuttered.

But Corrigan didn't give him a chance to finish. He gave the American another savage dig in the ribs. 'And there – look at the wounded,' he cried, his rage getting the better of him again. *'Look at them!'*

Helplessly the American stared at the hundreds of wounded men, draped in the soaking greatcoats of their comrades. Most of them, mercifully, were now unconscious, but a few stared back at the fat American with ghastly livid-white faces, shivering and shocked, some of them mumbling incoherently like madmen.

The colonel licked his lips uneasily and turned away. There was a look of pleading in his eyes now, as if he couldn't stand much more of this. 'But you must understand, Major. I'm not heartless… But armour is a tricky thing…'

Suddenly Corrigan's wild Irish temper flared. He had had enough of the incompetence of the higher-ranking officers, the lack of fighting spirit, the waste of human lives the whole bloody useless farce. His red-rimmed eyes flamed with an almost unbearable rage.

Slim Sanders saw the signs: the tightening of the jaw, the doubling of the fist. He yelled in alarm, 'Don't do it, sir! For fuck's sake – *not that!'*

Too late.

'*Sorr-ee!'* Corrigan shrieked hysterically. He knew now that his career was ruined and he couldn't give a damn. Next instant his hard fist exploded right in the middle of the colonel's pudgy face...

## FIVE

'Ring the sodding bell!' said a dumbfounded trooper, *'there's real sheets on the beds!'*

'Ay,' chimed in a broad West Riding voice, 'and 't NAAFI's open all day!'

'A redcap outside the wire just smiled at me,' said another, in total disbelief. 'Catch me, lads, I'm going to swoon!'

'The condemned man ate a hearty bloody breakfast,' said a fourth, in a hollow sombre voice. 'A bloke who's bin in the cage since the day before yesterday just told me that

61

the cookhouse-wallahs here dish out two fried eggs apiece for breakfast – *and yer can have seconds as well!*'

There was a stunned, awed silence at this latest news; for most of the men, two fried eggs at one sitting was an unheard-of luxury.

Confused and bewildered, they looked around at the vast tented camp on the cliffs that was their new home. It was surrounded by high, barbed-wire fences, and on them hung notices warning the few remaining civilians not to talk to the soldiers. Armed redcaps patrolled the perimeter. It was clear the Brass were taking no chances – those guards were not to keep the civvies out, but to keep the soldiers in!

Sergeant Hawkins smiled to himself. At the moment he was stripped to the waist in the June sunshine and scrubbing his false teeth with a nail-brush. The big, gaunt Geordie who had said the 'condemned man ate a hearty breakfast' was right: they were being prepared for the killing to come – and Hawkins knew it even if the rest didn't. Popping his teeth back into his mouth, he set about scrubbing his torso. It was a relief to wash off the dust and muck after the twenty-hour drive down to the cage. For a moment, before putting his shirt back on and covering his skinny, battle-scarred body, he paused and took stock of his new surroundings.

Everywhere hung newly-erected signs

directing the men to the 'MI' Room, the 'NAAFI', 'B' Mess, 'A' Mess – military shorthand, unintelligible to a civilian, but to which Hawkins and his men had become accustomed over these last years. There seemed to be long queues at all hours: queues for latrines, queues for the showers, queues for food. They said that the cook-houses served food twenty-four hours a day, and that if you got in the wrong queue you could end up having mutton stew and tinned peaches in the middle of the night. As for the latrines, hessian-screened 'thunderboxes', it took at least half an hour to secure a place, and anything up to eighty men at a time squatted and strained there, while their comrades called and threatened and pleaded impatiently outside. It was said that the brigadier had placed an armed guard outside his own personal thunderbox so that no one but himself could use it.

Out in the green-tossing Channel below, shipping of all kinds lay at anchor, packed tightly as far as the eye could see. Flat, long ships carrying a forest of what looked like pipes – rocket-ships, the latest secret weapon; Liberty ships; flat-nosed barges; anti-aircraft cruisers; Motor Torpedo Boats; huge concrete caissons as big as five-storey blocks of flats, complete with anti-aircraft guns mounted on top and crews' quarters – these, it was said, could be linked together to form a kind of artificial harbour once the beachhead had been secured.

Sergeant Hawkins' smile vanished at the thought. Yes – that was what it was all about: the beachhead. Slowly he put on his shirt and gazed at the assault troopers – 'my boys', as he always called them proudly when he was at home with Mabel, back in Yorkshire…

They had come to him as callow eighteen-year-olds back in '40 and '41. Most of them had never been away from home before, and on that first night as he made his rounds of the barracks, he had heard a few of them weeping softly to themselves, overwhelmed by the strangeness of this new life so far away from everything and everyone they knew and loved. At first he had been hard on them, very hard. It had been the only way. He had flung all the usual contemptuous phrases of the drill sergeant at them: *Pregnant penguins… Showers of shit… Lily-livered nancy boys…* And so on, deliberately trying to break their spirit, brutalise them – above all, make them think as soldiers, *British* soldiers.

He had introduced them to 'bull'. 'If it moves, salute it,' he had barked, 'and if it don't, *paint* it.' He had demonstrated how to turn the dull surface of their new ammunition boots into black, gleaming mirrors by the application of polish and a hot spoon. He had shown them how to keep their uniforms neatly pressed without the use of an iron, by

64

greasing the creases with soap and sleeping with them beneath the mattress. He had taught them how to cover their webbing equipment and packs with blanco, until the barracks reeked of the stuff.

Slowly the puppy fat had disappeared, and with it had gone the pallor of days spent in offices and nights whiled away in pubs and cinemas. His boys had begun to exalt in the clean, vigorous life, the hard effort, even the danger. They had felt more alive than ever before. Finally they had become soldiers, contemptuous of their former soft life in 'civvy street', proud of themselves. At last they were 'assault troopers', the cream of the Reconnaissance Corps, able to march fifty miles in a day, run twenty in four hours, swim rivers in full marching gear, spring from trucks moving at fifteen miles an hour, run up the fronts of advancing tanks, allowing the steel monsters to roll over their slit-trenches – a hundred and one different skills.

They were better trained than any soldiers he had ever had – and yet… Sergeant Hawkins gazed out across that rolling green sea with its vast armada of ships towards the dark smudge beyond which was France. They still had not seen the real thing. They had not yet been bloodied. He bit on the stem of his old pipe. Training was one thing; war was another. How would they measure up on the day?

As if to match with his sombre mood at that particular moment, grey clouds came scudding in from nowhere and blotted out the June sun. Abruptly, a great black shadow fell, and all was darkness out to sea...

But if Papa Hawkins' mood was uncertain, the brigadier's was not. As he faced the Brigade's officers, crowded into the big tent, his broad, bluff face positively radiated confidence. The staff colonel called for silence from the excited officers, and the brigadier stepped forward to the little rostrum. 'Well, gentlemen,' he said ebulliently, setting down his cane, 'this is it!'

He nodded at the staff colonel, who drew back the canvas covering the plaster model, and for the first time they saw what they had been training for for the last four years: a stretch of coast, flanked by high, white cliffs, set between two rivers – and all labelled quite clearly with French names: names of villages and hamlets, rivers and streams. The secret was out at last!

'*Voila!*' the brigadier exclaimed above the excited whispers and gasps of surprise, extending his hands like a conjuror who has just successfully produced a rabbit out of his top hat. 'Our Corps' objective is this stretch of Normandy beach between the Rivers Orne – *here* – and Seulles – *here!*' He tapped the sand-table relief map with his cane. 'Our aim is to capture the city of Caen – *there!* That will be the task of the good old Iron Division, while the Canadians will head for the airfield at Carpiquet – *here* – some eleven miles from the coast.

He paused to let the information sink in, noting that the faces of his listeners had flushed crimson. Being a very unimaginative man, he put this down to excitement.

'Opposition?' he barked, and immediately answered his own question: 'Intelligence reports that on the coast itself there are three battalions of the Boche 716th Division, closely supported by several other battalions of unknown quality, mostly impressed men – Russians, Poles, Ukrainians and the like.'

The nations and races he listed were supposed to be Britain's allies, but their nationals, it seemed, were quite prepared to fight for Nazi Germany and repel the Allied invasion. This strange paradox, however, did not seem to worry the brigadier. He went on:

'To the front of Caen – *here* – is the German 21st Panzer Division, and to the rear of the city – *here* – their 12th SS Panzer Division. However, I don't think we'll have much trouble from the SS johnnies. They've never been in action before and they're mostly sixteen- to eighteen-year-old kids. Even the Boche themselves call the Twelfth the "Baby Division". Apparently their officers won't let them drink beer, only milk!' He guffawed loudly at the thought. 'Still on the titty, what?'

The battalion commanders laughed. Battalion commanders always laughed at the brigadier's jokes – but not those who knew the SS, like Captain Corrigan. For his part, he frowned and stared hard at the relief map.

Already he could see several inherent weaknesses in the great plan. With two German armoured divisions around Caen, one of them SS, and no British armour to speak of on shore that first day, the capture of Caen would require considerable luck. Boldness might pay off – a quick dash from the beaches before the Germans had recovered from the shock of the landings, maybe. But he couldn't see the heavy-set, red-faced brigadier taking that kind of risk. So far, the brigadier had shown himself to be little more than a wooden-headed plodder, happy to let others take the initiative. Somehow he guessed the brigadier and the other brass-hats like him would be well satisfied if they managed to secure a beachhead that first day; then they would order the men to dig in, drink their wretched tea, and wait to see what the morrow might bring.

'Now, the role of the Brigade,' the brigadier continued, tapping the map with his cane. 'We have the honour of going in first. The South Lancs will go in *here,* and the

East Yorks – *here* – running along the right bank of the Orne. Once they have cleared the beaches, they will head for the Periers Ridge – *here.*'

For all his dislike of the brigadier, Corrigan could not help but admire his no-nonsense, unthinking style. The man had no qualms, no nerves, no doubts whatsoever about the successful outcome of the mission given to his Brigade. For him, it was simply one more of those endless schemes and exercises that he had run these last four years.

'As soon as the Periers Ridge is taken,' the brigadier went on, 'three exit gaps will be cleared for your Recce squadrons, John.' This last was addressed to Corrigan's CO, Lieutenant Colonel Peters. 'Your "A" Squadron will take the first exit and head north-east to link up with the paratroopers of the Sixth Airborne, who will have been dropped during the night on the other side of the Orne. Once they are away, your "B" and "C" Squadrons will follow via the other two exits. You will recce the roads leading to Caen to the south-east, probing all the way until the division can follow. By the way, we hope to have tanks ashore by the evening. Clear?'

'Clear,' the Reconnaissance colonel snapped back, in the same confident manner.

Again Corrigan frowned. They were all so damned *certain.* Don't they know what it's like on the battlefield? Aren't they aware that if anything *can* go wrong under fire, it *will* do? Nothing in war has ever turned out the way the tacticians planned it.

'Well, gentlemen,' the brigadier said genially, rubbing his hands like a shop assistant who has just made a sale, 'for years now you've been attacking the spots marked on the models. But, of course, you didn't know that. That was all part of the great secret. Now at last you know the real names of your objectives.' He beamed at them. 'So I shall now leave you to study your individual objectives for a while, then afterwards you can give the chaps a quick briefing.' He glanced at his old-fashioned fob watch which hung by a silver chain from his battledress pocket. 'I'll expect you all over at the Brigade Mess for a farewell drink at seventeen hundred hours. I know it's a while before sun down, but we'll break with routine just this once.'

'Just a minute, sir,' Corrigan cut in almost brutally. 'How long have we got?' Suddenly he was angry at the air of cosy optimism that seemed to have settled over the gathering.

The brigadier frowned. That Corrigan fellow making a damned nuisance of himself again. At the first possible opportunity he really must transfer him out of the Brigade...

'Twelve more hours,' he replied frostily. 'We begin to embark the men at eighteen-thirty hours. The Senior Service wants them on board before dark.'

'*Twelve hours!*' somebody echoed, and there was no mistaking the shock in the officer's voice. 'Is that all?'

'That is all,' the brigadier repeated. For one, brief instant the bluff, unthinking confidence seemed to have gone from his fruity voice. It was almost as if, for the very first time in all these long years of training and waiting, he had just realised the enormity of the task that lay ahead...

## SIX

Wolfers was still in a daze as he wandered around the crowded tank landing craft. He hardly heard the cries of surprise and amusement as yet another of the self-heating tins of soup exploded and went sailing up into the darkening sky. Wolfers' thoughts were entirely on the events of the previous night. *He'd had it,* he told himself for the umpteenth time. *He'd really had it! He was a virgin no more!*

It had been a 'knee-trembler', as the other blokes called it, up against the wall of the air-raid shelter – a pretty vile little hole that smelled of dog piss and human fear. He'd been a bit shy at first, but the ATS girl had pulled down her knee-length khaki bloomers and told him it was the only way. Apparently you didn't get pregnant if you did it standing up. He had been so excited and nervous that he had forgotten all about the dozen French letters he had concealed about his person.

Afterwards, the ATS girls had sobbed a little and said she hoped he would not think too badly of her. It turned out her boyfriend had been killed in Sicily in '43 and she had been a bit 'wild' ever since. Besides Wolfers was going overseas himself soon – he would need a little souvenir of England, wouldn't he?

Even now, dazed as he was, the big ugly soldier was touched to the heart by that simple, tearful statement – even though it had been whispered to him in the back of a smelly air-raid shelter, to the accompaniment of animal grunts and excited little screams respectively from his companion, Slim, and the old ATS girl, who were raucously making love somewhere in the darkness.

*A souvenir of England...* Suddenly it dawned on him as he stared out at the Solent, at the grey-blue hulks of the battle-ships at anchor, the landing ships camou-flaged in crazy zig-zags, the myriad craft bobbing and ducking at anchor in choppy green sea, that he was leaving his country for the very first time. He realised too that all over England, there were young men just like him – soldiers, sailors, airmen, commandos, paratroopers – all waiting, just like him, for the signal to move out. Hundreds of thousands of them, barely out of their teens, soon to cross that twenty-one mile stretch of water... Suddenly, he shivered at the thought of what was to come.

'Penny for them, mate,' said a familiar voice at his side.

Wolfers turned, a little startled, and looked down at Slim Sanders. A small bottle of whisky protruded from his back pocket, an enormous bacon sandwich dripping with grease was clutched in his hand. Without waiting for an answer to his question, he offered it to Wolfers. 'Here yer are, son. Tuck that inside yer before we get moving. Got it off one of them greedy so-called cooks.'

'Thanks – thanks,' Wolfers stuttered. For some reason, Slim, who wasn't liked by anyone else in the troop, had taken to him. Why, he didn't know. Even Papa Hawkins, who seemed to like everybody, didn't particularly care for the cocky little Aussie. He took a big bite, the hot grease dripping down his heavy, jutting chin. 'I was just thinking, like.'

Across the water, a first ship was now beginning to move slowly out, a small, dull-grey landing craft with a fat, silver barrage balloon tethered above it like a great slug.

'Thinking, mate! Shouldn't do that. Bad

fer yer head. Leave thinking to the officers like that cocky bastard, Corrigan – they get paid for it.' Suddenly his voice became subdued. 'Worried?'

'A bit,' Wolfers answered, tucking into his sandwich. Funny – he never seemed able to get enough to eat. He'd been hungry all his life.

'Don't let it get yer down, mate. Everybody is.'

'What's it like, Slim?' Wolfers finished the last of his sandwich and wiped a heavy-knuckled paw across his mouth.

The little Australian looked up at Wolfers, unusually solemn for him. 'Listen, sport, I had a kid brother once, like you. A big, ugly bastard, proper digger type – not handsome, like me. Sometimes I wonder about my old ma. Well, he bought it in New Guinea in '42. Forgot to keep his silly great noggin down, I suppose. Eighteen he was, like you. Volunteered, too. A right mug.' Suddenly he looked up at Wolfers, his cunning eyes blazing with fierce intensity. 'So I'll give it you straight, kid: over there, it'll be a right bleeder!'

Across the Solent, another landing craft was beginning to move out at a snail's pace towards the horizon under a dark, lowering sky.

'Aw, hell!' Slim cried, as if in sudden disgust. 'I'm going below to see if I can take a quid or two off them greedy matelots at

Housey-Housey. If I can get into the galley again, I'll bring yer another bacon sandwich. Sod it, eh? What a bleedin' life...'

And with that he was gone, leaving Wolfers to stare after him in bewilderment. Still, maybe Slim Sanders wasn't as crooked as he looked.

Corrigan snorted and spat on the armoured deck, trying to get rid of the stink of diesel fumes which still lingered after his hour-long stint down in the hold, manoeuvring the scout cars, half-tracks and jeeps into their correct position for the assault landing. Now at last he was satisfied. With Sergeant Hawkins at his side, he made his way through the tall, steel chasm of the hold, making one last inspection of the supplies with which the vehicles were laden. Cans of water and petrol. Crates of compo rations. Belts of machine-gun ammunition. Verey pistols, tarpaulins, hand grenades, 'Tommy Cookers', battery-charging motors, crowbars, shovels, spare bogie wheels – a hundred and one mundane items nonetheless vital to the success of the landing.

'All we need now is the bleedin' kitchen sink, sir,' Hawkins said, reading the officer's mind.

'You can say that again, Hawkins.' Corrigan paused by his own jeep, with the newly-painted five-pointed white star of the

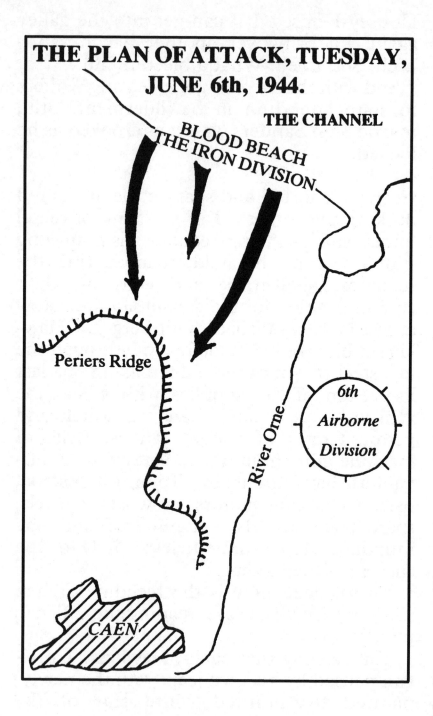

invasion force on its side. 'But you know what it'll be like over there. It's no use relying on anybody else to do your packing for you.'

Hawkins nodded. 'Don't you think you should let me off first with the half-track?' He indicated the blunt-nosed steel monster parked directly behind the jeep. 'If Jerry starts zeroing in on us as soon as the sailor boys lower the ramp, it'd be better to get off with that than your jeep. Jerry could puncture the sides of that thing with an air-rifle pellet!'

'Naturally – but I want to be off and directing the operation in double-quick time, Hawkins. The sooner we're off that beach and through our exit at the Periers Ridge, the better.'

Hawkins looked at Corrigan's hard face, hollowed out to a yellow death's head in the poor light. 'Something the matter, sir?'

'Oh, I don't know, Hawkins,' Corrigan said, as if irritated. 'You've done a tremendous job training the men. So have all the NCOs and officers who've been with the Iron Division since 1940 – especially in our Brigade. But right down from the Brig himself to the humblest lance corporal, there's far too much going by the book for my liking. The infantry are too ponderous. They've got no dash. And they dig in too soon.'

Hawkins took out his pipe, then remembered that smoking was forbidden and put it away again. 'I know what you mean, sir. The clodhoppers are a bit on the slow side. But how could they be otherwise, sir? The Brigadier – if you'll forgive me – is like that himself. After four years of exercise after exercise, the lads have got used to packing up at five o'clock and going home. It's just as if they were working in a factory, only they're wearing khaki instead of blue overalls.'

Corrigan looked glum. 'Exactly. And that's what's worrying me, Hawkins. Will they ever get off the bloody beach in the first place? And if they don't, what's going to happen to the Assault Troop, sitting out there on the naked beach in those bloody great half-tracks with nowhere to go?'

Now the bobbing invasion armada filled the Channel, steadily, relentlessly ploughing through the heaving grey waters. For four long years they had waited for this moment, the moment of revenge and retribution. On they came, rank after rank of them, ten lanes wide, each lane twenty miles across: five thousand ships, bearing a hundred and eighty thousand young men, British, Canadian, American, bound for the shores of Hitler's vaunted *Festung Europa.*

Out in front, destroyers and mine-sweepers sliced through the waves, eager to meet any enemy challenge, above or below the water.

Overhead, squadron after squadron of Spit-fires weaved and dived in the darkness, combing the night sky for attackers. Further out still, lumbering grey-painted battleships swung their mighty guns to port and star-board threateningly. Some of them had fought the King's enemies a quarter of a century before at Jutland; others had been raised from the bottom at Pearl Harbor, victims of the Japanese sneak attack three years before. Now they were ready and eager for action once again.

Slowly, ponderously, the great armada made its way across the Channel on this night of Monday, June 5th, 1944, keeping to the five buoy-marked, mine-swept lanes which would later split up into ten lanes off the coast, two for each of the five assault beaches. In the lead were the five attack transports, bristling with radar and radio antennae, which would be the nerve centres of the whole historic invasion.

A few of the young men slept – but they were the lucky ones. Some talked, joked, gambled; but their thoughts were elsewhere. Most, however, were being sick, retching miserably into the grease-proof vomit bags, or when these were full, into mess-tins, dixies, tin hats, fire-buckets – anything. Soon whole decks were awash with the nauseating filth, and the very air in the tightly packed, rolling holds stank of vomit.

In their misery and discomfort, these young men going to war sensed the helplessness of their position. They had been betrayed by the old men – the generals and the politicians. They had been sent into the unknown, to die violently – and soon.

Captain Corrigan prepared himself methodically for what lay ahead. This would be his fourth assault landing. He had his preparations down to a drill now. He had already changed and put on clean underwear. He knew he wouldn't be able to change again for days, perhaps weeks. Besides, if he were hit at the outset, he would stand a better chance of avoiding gas gangrene – often the result of dirty clothing being forced into an open wound.

Now he laid his cork life-jacket out beside him on the narrow bunk and hung his pistol, already attached to the harness, on a nail above, so that he could slip into both in seconds. Then he carefully put his compass into his helmet, followed by his extra clips of ammunition and his phial of morphia, which looked like a small toothpaste tube with a needle attached. Then he hung the helmet from another nail. Finally he stretched out fully clothed on the mattressless steel webbing bunk, with his field-dressing in one pocket and yellow emergency ration tin in the other.

This, he knew, was a historic moment, yet

curiously he felt nothing. All he felt was a bitterness at the way the war had gone all these long years since 1939, and anger at the waste of so many young English lives. What would happen in the next twenty-four hours, he could not tell. But he did know that he would not let his Assault Troop be sacrificed for nothing. In battle soldiers had to die, there was no avoiding that, but they had to die for *something*. His jaw hardened. His career was finished. There would be no place for him in the post-war British Army, he knew that. He knew, also, that he would not survive the war; his luck had almost run out. Now his only loyalty was to his men, those forty-odd young Englishmen whom Fate had placed under his command. This time they would not be wasted – not if he could help it.

Down below, the engines paused momentarily. Corrigan knew what that meant. They were entering 'Area Z', the assembly zone. When they throbbed again at the signal 'half-speed ahead', they would then start branching off into the swept channel that led to their beach.

Captain Corrigan looked at the dial of his leather-strapped Army-issue watch. It was exactly eleven o'clock. In one hour's time it would be Tuesday, June 6th, 1944. He closed his eyes to blot out the yellow light of the naked bulb swinging to and fro inches above his head. 'The sixth of June, nineteen forty-four,' Corrigan whispered to himself, savouring the sound of the words 'June, 'forty-four...'

Turning to his side, he settled himself more comfortably in the narrow bunk, conscious of the movement of the ship as she rocked in the swell, waiting for the order to proceed. He sighed. After tomorrow, the world would never be the same again. Slowly he drifted into a dreamless sleep.

At the open door, Sergeant Hawkins paused. In his hand was a mug of steaming cocoa for Captain Corrigan which he had cadged from one of the sweating Navy cooks.

The CO lay there in his narrow bunk, stretched out straight, absolutely motionless in the weak yellow light. He did not even seem to be breathing. Hawkins took one last look at him. As silently as he had come, he turned and went back down the long fetid corridor, already feeling the plates beneath his feet begin to tremble as the engines started up once more and the ship moved forward towards the beach.

# TWO: BEACH OF BLOOD

# ONE

As if some invisible hand had thrown a giant power switch, a tremendous flash of scarlet flame split the dawn greyness. With startling suddenness the great bombardment of the German coastal positions commenced. Huge naval guns roared, shipborne mortars belched, rocket batteries howled, sending their missiles racing into the sky trailing angry red sparks behind them. Red, white and green tracer zipped across the water, as the God of War drew his first, terrifying breath.

In their trenches, bunkers and fortified houses, now quaking and trembling like live things under the tremendous bombardment, the German infantry cowered, quivered – and waited.

Everything was ready for the Tommies. They had been four years at it, preparing the hottest reception they could for the men in khaki. Four years ago the British Expeditionary Force had been ignominiously chased out of Europe. Today, the German defenders were determined to deny the enemy so much as a toehold on the French coast.

They had grouped their defences around

the mouths of the valleys beyond the beach. Yet the beach itself was covered from all sides, and from their bunkers they could bring crossfire to bear on every square inch. But the real battle would not start there. For two hundred and fifty yards out to sea were planted rows of tall wooden stakes known as 'Rommel's asparagus', each one with a deadly mine secured to its top. Then came the barbed wire, minefields and murderous crossfire of the beach itself; and if that did not stop the Tommies in their flat piss-pot helmets, then the cliffs with their heavy gun emplacements and massed machine-guns would.

Now the first blunt-nosed barges were edging their way out of the thick grey smoke-screen. Soon the barrage would have to be lifted, in case the naval gunfire hit the first wave of the assault force.

*'Achtung! Sie kommen!'* German officers cried excitedly. *'Die Tommis kommen!'* NCOs blew their whistles. Corporals kicked the laggards angrily, yelling 'On your feet, you dogs! Do you want to live forever?' Artillery observers began to chatter rapidly into their phones.

Now the blunt-nosed barges were looming out of the smoke in increasing numbers, speeding to the shore, dragging their white wakes behind them.

*'Leg' an!'* the officers ordered.

Everywhere the gunners tensed, hands slippery with sweat, gun-layers pressed their eye against the rubber eye-piece of their cannon, watching the little black shapes fill the gleaming calibrated glass of the sight; riflemen thrust the stocks of their weapons harder against their shoulders. In a minute it would all begin.

Suddenly a landing craft struck one of the seaborne mines and went up in a vicious ball of red flame, scattering screaming men into the water. Flames spread as the escaping oil suddenly caught alight. Another craft ran into a mine – and another. Now there were assault craft sinking everywhere, or drifting around helplessly in circles, smoke pouring from their innards. Scores of men were struggling in the water, floundering and screaming, many dragged down by the weight of their heavy equipment.

But already there were others, running from the stricken craft, bent low as they doubled up the beach, like men running against heavy rain.

And suddenly the Allied barrage lifted.

The German defenders waited no longer. *This* was the vital moment – the moment they had been trained for. If they were going to stop the Tommies, it was now or never. Suddenly the same order rasped from half a dozen throats: *'Feuer!'*

All along the cliffs and from the sides of

the beaches a solid wall of fire erupted. The bullets scythed the length of the water. A whole line of khaki-clad figures went down instantly, spitting and gurgling, drowning where they sprawled. Another wave of men pushed through them, splashing crazily forward through the bodies, beginning their mad dash up the shingle. Then they too fell, as mines exploded on all sides, tossing their bodies high into the air, a mass of wildly flailing arms and legs.

A third wave rushed forward, urged on by their officers, blowing hunting horns, brandishing swords, screaming exhortations. They reached the first barrier of six-foot wire before they were mown down in their turn. Unable to advance or retreat, they waited almost like dumb animals for the inevitable slaughter. A fresh hail of machine-gun fire, and they were left hanging on the wire like so many bloodstained scarecrows, twitching weakly each time a stray bullet slammed into them.

A fourth wave made that terrible dash up the beach, charging forward over the brown carpet of corpses that stretched from the edge of the sea to the wire. But now the first of the bren carriers, tiny armoured vehicles, were splashing ashore in support of the infantry. Here and there the infantrymen grouped themselves behind the tracked carriers and advanced as if against pelting rain, slugs howling off the armoured plate inches away from their heads. From some parts of the beach there was now a steady chatter of bren gun fire as the Tommies took up the German challenge.

This time with a crash the carriers were through the wire and rolling forward. Then suddenly a fresh row of mines detonated. Several vehicles reeled to a crazy stop, smoke pouring from their ruptured engines, tracks falling behind them like severed limbs. Some of them, however, still miraculously clattered on.

Now ashen-faced men in a strange grey uniform came blundering out of the burning white smoke, hands raised in surrender. '*Kamerad*,' they called piteously, '*Nicht schiessen! Nicht schiessen!*'

But after the slaughter on the beaches, the infantry were in no mood for taking prisoners. The Germans were mown down mercilessly. As the khaki-clad survivors ran past them towards the cliffs, rifle butts slammed down, bayonets flashed and were withdrawn a gleaming scarlet. Today the only good Jerry was a dead Jerry...

Now the German machine-gunners and artillery men further back lifted their fire from the beach. The risk of hitting their own comrades was too great. Instead they concentrated on the barges, which were now nosing their way through the minefields, crazily intent on depositing their khaki-clad freight.

The shattered infantry already disembarked did not wait for a second chance. Without orders, they pulled out their entrenching tools and began to hack furiously at the wet sand. Already the attack had come to a standstill. The infantry, what was left of them, were digging in – and the cliffs remained uncaptured.

*'France!'* somebody called, as the assault troopers crowded the deck of the tank landing craft.

Corrigan pushed to the rail.

Away to the left, he could see the pale blue hills of the Le Havre peninsula and the vague mass of the port itself. Immediately ahead, the coast smoked heavily, streams of grey and black fumes from the shelling rising rapidly into the morning sky, broken by spurts of cherry-red.

Now the LCT began to slow down, edging its way towards the packed shipping off the coast, waiting their turn to run the gauntlet of fire from the shore batteries. Destroyers, cruisers, mine-sweepers, all crowded there on the choppy, sparkling sea, occasionally reeling to one side alarmingly as a German shell exploded close by, sending a huge, whirling spout of water high into the sky.

Next to Corrigan, Trooper Wolfers, a

gigantic sandwich in his paw as usual, said in awe, 'I didn't think there were so many ships in the whole world, sir. By gum, there's hundreds of 'em!' His words were drowned as a flight of Bostons hurtled in at four hundred miles an hour, machine-guns blazing, heading for the German batteries on the cliff.

Wolfers opened his mouth again, but his words were fated never to be heard. Behind them, the old *Warspite*, which had fought at the Battle of Jutland long before Wolfers had ever been born, opened fire with her 15-inch guns. Flames as long as towers spat from the huge cannon. With the noise of an express train going full out, the three one-ton shells hurtled towards France.

Corrigan grinned and shouted above the racket, 'Eat your sandwich, Wolfers, and save your breath. You're going to need it!'

Now the bemused troopers forgot their own danger and simply stared in amazement at the tremendous spectacle as the tank landing craft approached the embattled shore. A Spitfire fell out of the burning sky, turning and turning, as it hurtled earthwards in its last, fatal dive. A house on the shore was ripped apart by a direct hit, masonry and bricks flying hundreds of feet into the air. A crippled, blazing landing craft, its hold filled with dead and dying men, zigzagged madly through the great mass of shipping, a headless corpse slumped over the helm. And now the khaki-clad bodies were floating towards them on the tide, bobbing up and down in their life-jackets in the oil-scummed water  and all this set against a huge back-drop of flames and smoke. It was terrifying, exciting, appalling – and unforgettable.

A star shell exploded to port of the slow-moving landing craft. It hung there for an instant, bathing the up-turned, gawping faces of the assault troopers a glowing, unnatural silver.

'Jerries!' a look-out yelled in alarm. *'Soddin' Jerries!'*

Sergeant Hawkins gasped. Next to him, Slim Sanders, still stowing away the money he had taken from the sailors in the all-night-long Housey-Housey game, shouted: 'Cripes, now we're in for it!' and hurriedly grabbed his life-belt.

Three sharp-prowed white craft were hurtling towards the great convoy, bows high out of the waves and sending twin spurts of white, foaming water hissing upwards.

*'E-boats!'* yelled the look-out.

The landing craft's twin 20mm cannon opened up. A stream of white tracer shells, one thousand rounds a minute, spurted towards the three German marauders. On all sides the guns of the great armada joined in. A white wall fell between the tightly packed fleet and the bold attackers. But the

E-boats were not to be stopped. They were approaching at a tremendous speed.

Corrigan flung up his glasses. He caught a glimpse of white faces behind the protective screen of the tiny bridge on the first, racing craft. Then it gave a crazy lurch. Something black and sinister dropped from its bow. Next moment the E-boat was roaring round in a tremendous arc, its superstructure almost touching the boiling water. On all sides rose that dreadful cry, 'Torpedo!! *Torpedo!!*'

Corrigan held his breath, his eyes riveted to the flurry of bubbles as a ton of high explosive hissed towards the packed shipping. The tin fish could not miss. The torpedo *had* to hit something!

It did. There was a great hollow boom, drowning even the fire of the heavy naval guns, and suddenly the destroyer to their starboard side seemed to stop dead in her tracks, as if she had run into an invisible wall. She keeled over towards the waves, a great ragged hole torn in her side, and almost at once began to sink. Panic-stricken sailors could now be seen leaping overboard or throwing caley floats into the sea. Broken in two and in her death throes, the ship's bow and stern suddenly rose in the water, stuck on the bottom of the shallow sea, to remain wedged in a gigantic, ironic 'V for Victory'.

Now the E-boats came racing in again,

once more breaking through the protective smoke-screen concealing the fleet from the shore batteries. Immediately the Allied ships woke up to the mortal danger they were in. Machine-guns opened up, clacking like rusty typewriters. Tracer zipped furiously across the sea. Multiple pom-poms, great banks of massed guns known as 'Chicago pianos', rattled frantically; 20mm guns blasted. A wall of fire rose at once to the front of the Allied shipping.

But the E-boats seemed to bear a charmed life. They came through unscathed. Once more, torpedoes skimmed the water, rushing towards their targets.

'Oh, no!' Wolfers gasped, dropping his sandwich in his shock. A great clanging boom rang out as metal struck metal. A sheet of bright red flame rent the smoke. To their front another ship exploded, sending metal debris flying everywhere, flame spurting from every joint in the plates.

On and on came the three German E-boats, twisting and turning crazily at tremendous speed, wings of water rising high behind them in the shell-churned sea. Watching them, Wolfers dug his nails into the palms of his sweat-soaked hands. Next to him, Slim crouched, tensing himself for the shock of the next explosion.

Suddenly the first E-boat lurched violently, breaking to the right in a great wild curve and sending spray splashing twenty feet into the air. Another batch of torpedoes sped towards their target.

Wolfers groaned. Next to him, Slim cringed with the shock as the torpedoes struck home on the landing craft in front of them. A terrifying orange flame shot upwards. The landing craft's deck dissolved into a mass of molten, bubbling metal, wreathed in flames. Even at that distance the watchers could feel the searing heat. It struck them across the face, sucking the air out of their lungs, making them gasp and choke for breath like asthmatics in the throes of an attack.

Almost immediately the long, ugly ship started to heel over. The flames seared the length of the plates like a giant blowtorch. The buckled, ruined deck bubbled and writhed as if it had a life of its own. Crazed, burning men flung themselves overboard into the debris-littered water. A 30-ton Sherman tank began to roll towards the sea, pitched overboard, then slowly but surely began to sink beneath the red-glowing water. Explosion after explosion racked the doomed craft. Then with frightening suddenness, she slid below the surface with a great shriek of escaping steam.

'Oh, my God,' Wolfers cried, 'did you get a butcher's at that, Slim!' He stared in awe at the spot where the ship had disappeared, as the first trapped air bubbles came rushing to the surface to burst with an obscene plop. 'I wouldn't have believed it if I hadn't seen it with my own two–'

*'Here they come again!'* a frantic voice screamed hysterically.

'Bloody 'ell, sir,' Sergeant Hawkins cried, as all around them the big naval guns once more opened fire on the three small German vessels, 'they're brave buggers!'

'I could do without their bravery, thank you,' Corrigan said coldly, focusing his glasses once more. 'What the devil's wrong with our gunners? The whole bloody fleet's parked here and yet they can't finish off a couple of fifty-ton rowing–'

He stopped in mid-sentence. One of the E-boats had been hit. Suddenly its sharp, curved prow was low in the water and its speed diminishing by the second. Yet still the other two came on – even though it seemed that every gun in that great armada was trained on them.

Next instant, the number two E-boat lurched violently and Corrigan could see a burst of ugly yellow smoke as she launched her 'fish'. They were long and ungainly until they hit the water, but once in their element, they gathered speed by the second, heading remorselessly for their target.

This time it was a gas-carrying landing ship that was hit, the whole rear deck erupting in a searing sheet of flame. Burning fuel immediately spread down the tilting deck, engulfing a panic-stricken huddle of seamen. Sailor after sailor leaped overboard, screaming piteously and trailing purple flame behind him like a rocket. But even in the water there was no escape, for a hundred-foot-long blowtorch of flames now hissed across the sea, burning, devouring everything in its path.

Just as Wolfers clasped his hands over his ears to drown out those terrible cries, the last torpedo struck his own ship with a deafening crash. Hot air slapped him in the face. Instinctively he opened his mouth to prevent his eardrums being burst by the detonation; and then he was on his knees, his nostrils filled with the cloying stench of escaping petrol, ears assailed by cries, curses, pleas for help, realising with horror that the tragedy had struck even before they had reached the beach. *They were sinking!*

## TWO

'Make smoke... For God's sake, make smoke!' Corrigan cried desperately. The stricken vessel's speed was now slackening appreciably and her deck was sloping to one side at a crazy angle. Impatiently he pushed past a dazed young sub-lieutenant with blood trickling down one side of his ashen face, and ran to the smoke canisters, closely followed by Sergeant Hawkins.

From all sides came cries, shouts, and yells of agony. Bodies of men, soldiers and sailors, lay everywhere in the debris caused by the explosion. From below came a hiss of escaping steam, and already the first of the engine-room staff were stumbling out onto the deck, their faces blackened, eyes round and wild and gleaming white with terror. The ship's whistles were shrilling, and a petty officer was running up and down banging a gong; it was as if he were a steward, Corrigan couldn't help thinking, inviting them to bloody dinner.

'They'll zero their eighty-eights on us any moment now!' Corrigan gasped. 'The gunners always pick the easy targets. *We've got to have smoke...*'

'They'll have us by the short and curlies,' Hawkins agreed. 'We're bloody well crawling along...'

Next to him a white-faced corporal, trembling in every limb, cried, 'Look at that–'

The rest of his words were drowned as a shell exploded on their port side. A huge cliff of furious white water suddenly raced high into the sky and great fist-sized chunks of shrapnel howled through the air. The corporal screamed and went reeling backwards, clutching his shattered face with tightly pressed fingers, through which blood already seeped a bright scarlet.

Corrigan grabbed the trigger of the first launcher. He pulled hard. One of the long canisters sailed into the air.

Across the water, the German gunners were ruthlessly pouring fire on another of the lame ducks. They could hardly miss–The ship was already motionless and listing badly to port. Gouts of white flame spurted up all along its deck. Suddenly the whole vessel was on fire. Sailors and soldiers ran back and forth, trying in vain to beat out the flames that engulfed them: flames that ripped at them, tore into their flesh, turning them into black, bubbling pulp from which the blood oozed scarlet like the juice of an overripe fig. Now the tracer ammunition began to explode, leaving still more dead bodies strewn over the deck, their flesh charred and shrunken, their backs arched into taut bows, skeleton arms flung wide, to be devoured by the all-consuming flames.

Then, mercifully, the first smoke canister exploded, blotting out the terrible scene with a thick pall of black smoke. Another folowed, and another. Suddenly they were alone, limping along through the choking smoke, the roar and snarl of battle muted by the thick fog, heading blindly for the unseen shore.

The landing craft's bow was almost under water now. They were crawling along at a snail's pace, and the men lining the upper deck, all wearing lifebelts and many with their boots off and tied round their necks, watched glumly as the water level rose steadily higher and higher. From below came weird, eerie groans, as if from a monster in its death agonies.

Up on the bridge with the captain, a lieutenant who looked as if he could not have been long out of school, Corrigan watched anxiously, willing the stricken craft to make the shore – wherever that might be. He knew all too well that the vehicles below were not waterproofed. They could not plough through the sea, or even under it, as some of those of the invasion force could. Unless they reached the coast, then his vehicles would be lost and he would be unable to carry out his mission.

'What do you think, skipper?' he asked, as the smokescreen started to lift here and there. 'Will we make it?'

The young naval officer kept his eyes glued to the needles behind the shattered glass of the dials; the blood still dripped down his arm unheeded. 'Don't know, Captain. It depends on how far we are from the coast...' He broke off suddenly and stared ahead.

A slight breeze had torn a large hole in the

curtain of smoke and through it they could now see tall, white cliffs and a handful of red-brick houses above what looked like a small harbour and jetty. The place could not have been more than half a mile away.

The young skipper bit his bottom lip.

'What do you think?' Corrigan urged again.

'We might, possibly,' he answered at last. 'But where the hell are we? I don't recognise that place. It wasn't on any of the photos I saw. At all events, it's certainly not one of the designated beaches.'

'What does *that* matter?' Corrigan said happily, feeling a sense of new hope. 'Let's get to it first and then play it by–'

Corrigan's words trailed away to nothing. For ahead of him on the cliff-top, figures could be seen racing along towards a familiar long shape. He did not need to be told that the figures were Germans. The long shape, too, was unmistakable. It was a damned 88mm cannon! It would pulverise them, turn the already crippled ship into a mass of twisted steel and burning wood within seconds. He had to make a decision – and make it now.

'Captain,' he said urgently, 'those are Jerries up there, with an eighty-eight.'

'I know,' the other man said grimly, face set and tense. 'I was at Salerno. I've seen them before.'

'We haven't got a hope in hell.'

On deck, Sergeant Hawkins had already got a bren gun in action and was now squatting behind it, blazing away at the running men in short, controlled bursts. But Corrigan could see it was pointless. The range was too extreme for the bren and the white tracer was curving downwards, falling well clear of the cliff and the deadly cannon.

Corrigan hated to admit to failure before he had even had a chance to take his young assault troopers into action, but there was nothing for it. Clattering down the twisted steps from the bridge, he clapped his hands to his mouth and cried above the first, harsh crack of the 88mm: *'Sergeant Hawkins! Sergeant Hawkins! Get the men ready, personal weapons only... We're going to abandon ship...'*

'Crikey,' young Wolfers gasped. 'I can't swim!'

Slim Sanders gave him a crooked grin. 'Well, mate, this seems about as good a time as any to learn, eh?'

'Make a bloke feel well and truly welcome, sir, don't they?' Sergeant Hawkins gasped, pulling on his boots and trying to ignore the fact that the water now pouring from his hair was tinged the colour of tea. He looked up at the cliff, packed tight with barbed wire and with little mines balanced on the posts here and there.

Behind them, the landing craft had now

grounded in the shallows some two hundred yards out, her superstructure a shattered ruin. The German gunners on the cliff above them still continued to pound the vessel, although the skipper had at last agreed to abandon her, together with what remained of the crew. Now they, too, were swimming and wading ashore after the last of the assault troopers.

'At least, we've been trained for this sort of thing,' Corrigan yelled, eyeing the cliff above. 'All right, men,' he spun round and addressed his wet, bedraggled troopers, crouched in the damp sand, weapons at the ready. 'I won't kid you. It'll be a bugger. They must have seen us come ashore. If they've got infantry waiting for us up there, it's going to be – well – not nice!' He grinned suddenly.

They grinned too, even Slim Sanders.

They weren't a bad bunch of lads, thought Corrigan. So far they had done very well. There had been no panic under fire, and even when he had given the order for them to abandon ship they had remained cool-headed and disciplined. It was a bloody nuisance losing their bearings in all that smoke, but they could not be all that far from the main beach; he could hear infantry fire, mingled with the thunder of the big guns coming from the dense fog of war to his right.

'My guess is,' he continued, 'that if they have footsloggers, they'll send them down to block our progress up the beach over there, beyond the jetty. It's the ideal defensive site. I doubt if they'll send them down here, because somewhere or other this beach is undoubtedly mined. So we'll kill two birds with one stone. We'll go up the cliff. That way, we'll avoid the minefield *and* dodge their infantry. They won't expect that.' He grinned at them confidently. 'But then they don't know the Assault Troop. All right, let's get to it!'

He shifted his infantry rifle closer to the centre of his broad back and at the same time loosened his revolver in the webbing holster – just in case. Next moment, he reached up and grabbed the first strand of barbed wire, held by two rusting metal stakes driven deep into the cliff side.

Just in time he suppressed a gasp of pain as the prongs dug cruelly into his palm. The wire was perfectly taut and hardly sagged at all when he put his full weight on it. 'It's all right,' he said, turning to the others. 'We can use it like a ladder. Okay, Sergeant Hawkins, you bring up the rear. You, Sanders – after me! If any Jerry pops his head over the edge of the cliff, you know what to do?'

Slim Sanders nodded, cigarette dangling out of the side of his thin mouth; he knew exactly what to do.

'Captain!'

Corrigan turned. It was the captain of the landing craft, the young lieutenant, coming up with the rest of his weary sailors. 'Yes?'

'What do you want us to do, Captain?' he asked. 'You brown jobs have been trained for that kind of thing,' he indicated the cliff. 'I don't think my matelots are up to it.'

Corrigan thought quickly. 'Take the beach and try to link up with our people. Watch out for mines, though. Head for that jetty over there.'

'Thanks,' the naval officer said, obviously relieved not to have to scale the cliff. He turned to his men. 'Right, chaps, spread out in a line and keep your eyes peeled. There might be mines.'

In a long, careful row like a skirmish line advancing towards the enemy, the sailors began to move towards the jetty a half a mile away.

Hawkins flashed Corrigan a hard, questioning look.

Corrigan shrugged. 'They're expendable,' he said coldly. 'They'll give the Jerry infantry something to do if they're over there. My sole concern is the Assault Troop. Come on, Hawkins, let's get cracking.'

Hawkins opened his mouth as if to protest, but changed his mind. He took a last look at the doomed sailors. If the Jerry infantry didn't get them, the mines would.

Then, shaking his head sadly, he began to urge the men forward.

The climb up the cliff was hell. Time and time again they were stopped by the cunningly constructed wire constructions, specifically designed to repel invaders. Each time, they would manage to overcome the obstacles by sawing or hacking at the wire with their jack-knives, cursing and yelping with pain as the cruel prongs tore at their hands.

To Corrigan, leading the climb, it sounded as if a herd of ponderous elephants were making their way upwards. Surely every German for miles must have heard them? Yet maybe the thunder of the guns might have covered their approach a little. He hoped the sailors crossing the beach down below would serve to distract the enemy's attention, too.

Finally he managed to pull himself over the cliff edge and lie there full-length, heart thumping like a triphammer. His lungs were wheezing like a broken leather bellows, his hands ripped to ribbons.

He cursed. The 88mm cannon in its sandbagged emplacement was only a hundred yards away, with beyond it to the right, a low concrete bunker, its walls covered in zig-zag camouflage. From it, a steady stream of German riflemen were now running towards the ravine and down to the beach below, where the first angry shots were ringing out. Obviously the sailors had blundered right into the German positions.

'Wow, what a beaut!' hissed Slim Sanders, dropping next to the big officer, as he took in the gun and the bunker to their front. 'They really have got us by the short and curlies this time.'

Corrigan nodded grimly. How the devil were they going to cross that hundred yards to the battery without being spotted? There was no cover whatsoever. And there could still be troops in the bunker to the right. It would be sheer suicide to attempt to rush over open ground like that.

For a moment Corrigan lay there, unable to think, while more and more of his assault troopers came grunting and puffing over the cliff edge behind him, crouching down in the grass, weapons at the ready.

'That's the lot, sir,' Sergeant Hawkins whispered, hardly out of breath, it seemed, in spite of the gruelling climb. 'There are–'

That moment his words were cut off by the sudden roar of aircraft engines coming in from the sea. Immediately Corrigan swung round on his back. Three dark shapes were skidding across the surface of the water at a tremendous speed. To left and right from each side of the bay, enemy flak opened up. Glowing white anti-aircraft shells zipped through the sky. At three hundred miles an hour, the planes pressed home their attack, swooping in through the brown puffballs of smoke, miraculously unscathed.

'*Bostons, sir!*' Wolfers cried. He had been a plane-spotter in the Home Guards before volunteering for the Army; he knew his stuff.

Next instant the three two-engined dive-bombers were racing across the cliff top, dragging their huge black shadows behind them, machine-guns chattering, cannon thumping. Earth exploded everywhere around the gun. Madly the Germans dived for cover as the Bostons zoomed down at almost tree-top height before levelling out and then swooping high into the sky again, trailing white contrails through the hard blue behind them. In a flash they were mere black specks against the blue backdrop.

'Listen,' Corrigan said, privately uttering an urgent prayer, 'if they come back in again and start shooting up that Jerry battery, we're on. Got it? As soon as I give the word, up and at 'em!'

'You heard the officer,' Hawkins added his authority to Corrigan's, 'no messing. No hanging back. In there and give 'em the point. *Fix bayonets!*'

Here and there a man swallowed hard at that dread order, and Hawkins could see many a young face turn a sudden white. He knew the feeling. He had felt the same as a sixteen-year-old back in 1918 when he had gone over the top for the first time. But this time the men were obedient enough. Each one rolled over on his back and attached the small thumb-thick bayonet to the end of his rifle.

'Here they come, sir,' Slim snapped.

'Stand by!' Corrigan cried, rising to one knee and unslinging his rifle.

The Bostons seemed to fall from the sky. In they came, hurtling down at a hellish speed. Again the flak opened up. Everywhere the sky was suddenly spotted black. Still the Bostons pressed home their attack. Then, suddenly, one of them staggered. It lost speed immediately. Thick white smoke started to pour from its port engine.

Corrigan, watching, had no feelings for the crew. He just prayed the others wouldn't break off their attack. They did not. As the crippled Boston came lower and lower and the first parachute blossomed forth in a burst of white silk, the other two came swooping down, bomb bays open. This was it. Corrigan waited no longer.

'All right, Assault Troop… *Charge!*'

They were up as one, madly pelting across that hundred yards of open ground, rifles tucked tightly to their hips, following Corrigan's flying heels.

Overhead, the first deadly black eggs came tumbling out of the Bostons' pale-blue bellies. The ground to the rear of the flak gun seemed to erupt in a long, electric ripple. Bomb after bomb exploded. The air was ripped apart. Shrapnel flew. The blast whipped the uniforms around the skinny bodies of the charging men. Carried away by the crazed excitement of the charge, they whooped and screamed like drunken Red Indians, springing over the shattered sandbags and plunging their bayonets into the gunners crouched behind them. Over and over again they lunged and stabbed with their red-tipped bayonets, wild, obscene, guttural animal cries coming from their throats, until finally Sergeant Hawkins had to push in between them, using the butt of his rifle, kicking them, cursing them, yelling furiously, 'They're dead! For fuck's sake, can't you madmen see – *they're dead!'*

Suddenly the fight went out of them. Some stared down, horrified at the sight of the men they had murdered, sprawled among the sandbags, bodies coated with blood. Others simply slumped down, weapons falling from the fingers, gasping as if they had run a long hard race. A few stared into space, mouths open foolishly, seeing nothing, hearing nothing, already turned into unthinking zombies by their first taste of battle.

Sergeant Hawkins noted that look. He had seen it before. It was a protective device; a means of shutting out the horror of battle. He'd best keep an eye on them; they'd be the first ones to crack. Hastily he made his count and stumbled over the mutilated bodies of the German gunners, back to where Corrigan was staring at the bunker.

'No casualties, sir,' he reported.

'Excellent. The lads did well, Hawkins.'

The old sergeant nodded. 'Nothing less than I expected, sir,' he said, and jerked a thumb at the strangely silent bunker. 'What about yon thing?'

Corrigan sucked his front teeth thoughtfully. 'I don't know, Hawkins. I just don't know.'

Above them, the Bostons swooped in for one last time, then, recognising the khaki below, waggled their wings before zooming away across the green, gleaming sea to England.

Slim Sanders looked up from looting the dead bodies of the Germans and watched the Bostons' departure with a sneer. 'Look at 'em, bleeding Brylcreem boys! Off back to Blighty! Egg and bacon for breakfast and a bleedin' good feel of the WAAF cook's twat as well. Jammy buggers!' He pulled out a dark brown sausage sandwich from a little cloth bread-bag belonging to one of the corpses. 'Here, tuck into that, Wolfers. You're always hungry.'

Wolfers took the sandwich, but gasped when he saw the wet patch on it. It was the dead gunner's blood. Hunger fought with disgust. Hunger won. He started to chomp it down.

Meanwhile Corrigan was still gazing over to the bunker. Something about it was puzzling him.

'If it *was* occupied, sir,' Hawkins said, breaking the captain's brooding silence, 'then the sods should have opened up by now. Perhaps they all went down on to the beach to nobble the sailor boys?'

'Perhaps,' Corrigan echoed, though he did not sound very convinced. 'Anyway, there's only one way to find out. We've got to get past the bloody thing somehow, whatever we do.' He made his decision. 'You stay here and hold the fort. Sanders, Wolfers and you two troopers – follow me!'

'Cripes,' Slim Sanders cursed, neatly pocketing a bulging wallet, 'why pick on me? Yer poor ordinary squaddie never gets a bleedin' minute to himself.' But he followed obediently enough, muttering to Wolfers, who was still gulping down the last of the sandwich, 'And you remember to keep yer ugly head down, sonny. Come on...'

Obeying Corrigan's hasty hand signals, the group rapidly split into two, Sanders and Wolfers approaching from the left, Corrigan and the two troopers from the right. All five squirmed forward in the short grass, their khaki-clad rumps moving rhythmically from side to side.

Now Corrigan, slightly in the lead, could smell that old smell, the one that for him always meant Germans: a mixture of German field-grey serge and that hard ersatz wartime soap they used. They were there all right. He knew it. But why the devil didn't they open up?

Slowly, Corrigan rose to his feet. It was a pretty reckless thing to do, considering that inside that low concrete structure were armed men, desperate men, men who had been trained to kill anyone in khaki. But Corrigan did it just the same.

On the other flank, Wolfers stopped crawling and gasped, 'Hell's bells, Slim, look at that, will yer?'

Sanders stopped crawling, too, and spat drily into the parched yellow grass. 'He wants to be a bleedin' hero, he does,' he sneered contemptuously. 'A beautiful quick corpse, more like. Don't you take no crap from that bloke, Wolfers. He's bad news, I can tell yer from experience.'

Slowly, deliberately, Corrigan slung his rifle over his shoulder and raised his hands to show whoever might be watching that they were empty. Then he started to walk slowly to the silent bunker. When he was only fifty yards away from it, he halted once again. Speaking clearly and selecting his words with care, he called out: 'You are surrounded. Come out now. Throw your weapons out

113

first, then come out with your hands raised. Nothing will happen to you, you have my word...'

Nothing happened.

Behind Corrigan, Sergeant Hawkins raised the bren and aimed it at the nearest gunslit, finger curling warily around the trigger of the light machine-gun. Tensely he waited. If Corrigan had not been Corrigan, he would have been given a Victoria Cross for the kind of courage he was displaying now. But there would be no more good gongs for Corrigan, and Hawkins knew it; he had blotted his copy book too often.

Corrigan strode forward another twenty yards. Again he stopped and repeated his message.

Still nothing stirred. Now the air was electric with tension. Sergeant Hawkins could feel the sweat trickling down the small of his back. More than once he had to blink to clear his eyes of the beads of sweat that fell from his bushy eyebrows. What the hell were those Jerries playing at?

Then it happened. First there was the sound of heavy boots running on concrete. Then a crazed, helmetless figure came running out of the entrance of the bunker, screaming, *'Dreckschweine! Englische Dreckschweine!'*

The German's face was contorted with rage, and the machine pistol clutched to his hip was already spitting fire as he emerged into the daylight. Slugs ripped out the grass just in front of Corrigan's feet. Corrigan flung himself headlong to the ground. Next moment, Sergeant Hawkins pressed his trigger. The bren slammed hard against his shoulder. White tracer zipped across the field. The German screamed piteously, spun round by the impact. The machine pistol fell from his grasp and clattered to the ground. He slammed against the wall of the bunker and began to slide down it, trailing a smear of thick red gore from his shattered spine. Suddenly fire erupted from the slits.

Sergeant Hawkins pounded away at the bren, giving Corrigan and his party covering fire as they pelted back to the gun position. But inwardly his spirits sank. Now they were in for a real bloody stand-up slogging match.

## THREE

The boy was dying. Under Sergeant Hawkins' direction, a couple of the other assault troopers grabbed his arms to steady him as he writhed there on the floor of the gunpit in mortal agony. The rest simply stared down in disbelief at the ever-growing scarlet strain that spread across his blouse.

Hawkins took his bayonet, prised open the trooper's grating teeth and swiftly slid the blade in to prevent him from biting off his tongue. With his comrades watching, the dying trooper ground his teeth on the blade, his body twitching convulsively, his moans growing steadily weaker, his strength slowly ebbing away.

In his last moments, Hawkins cradled the boy's head in his arms, muttering softly to him, rocking him back and forth like a mother, until finally he was dead. Then he tugged down the boy's eyelids and cut off his identity disc with the bayonet blade. 'It was all over quick, lads,' he said, to the circle of pallid faces staring down at this, the first of the Assault Troop to be killed in action. 'Believe you me, it's better to go like that than have a leg off, or one of yer lungs destroyed – be a cripple for the rest of yer days and an army pension. No – better this way.' Nodding gravely he slipped the dead boy's plastic identification disc into his pocket: a whole lifetime condensed into a couple of letters and numbers impressed on cheap green plastic: *'Jones, A, Tpr ... 14444175 ... RC'*

Slim Sanders said, 'Put him in that hole there,' and pointed to one of the bomb-craters left by the Bostons. Grabbing an abandoned German rifle, he placed the dead man's tin hat on its butt and stuck it muzzle-first into the earth. For the time being that would serve as cross, priest, burial-service, until the ghouls of the Graves Registration came along to dig him up again for a proper burial.

Corrigan watched with no apparent emotion. He had seen it all before. This time, these young soldiers were understandably awed, moving slowly and solemnly, as if out of respect for the dead man. But soon they would be hard and callous. They would rifle the man's pockets for whatever they could find; his pack would be auctioned off to the highest bidder; and when they were too weary, they would not even bother to bury him. Give them a few more deaths in action and they would be as unfeeling and as brutalised as that little Australian crook, Sanders. And it was better so; otherwise they would go stark raving mad.

Corrigan soon forgot the dead man; there were the living to attend to. Again that damned pillbox was silent. Not a sound came from it. Not a breath of smoke drifted from the tin chimney at the back, although the Germans were great sticklers for timetables and now was the time they usually ate. If it had not been for the figure in field-grey sprawled in a pool of congealing black blood near its side, he could almost have believed that the place had been abandoned long ago.

He beckoned Hawkins towards him and

the sergeant scuttled across, head well down below the parapet. The little NCO was a brave man, but he was no fool. 'Got his AB 64, as well, sir.' He tapped his breast pocket to indicate that he had removed the dead man's paybook.

Corrigan grunted. 'What about that eight-eight?'

Hawkins shook his head. 'One of the buggers must have pulled the sodding firing-pin at the very last moment, just as we charged. We can't fire the sod without it.'

Corrigan nodded. So they would not be able to soften up the bunker with the big gun; it was as useless as a popgun against an elephant. 'The Piat?' he asked, indicating the primitive spring-loaded anti-tank rifle on the floor of the gunpit.

'Don't think so, sir,' Hawkins said with a frown. 'Of course, we could try, but I have my doubts.'

'Blast and damn!' Corrigan cursed in sudden fury. 'We could be stuck here with that damned bunker for the duration. There must be some way...'

'Sir.'

Corrigan spun round. It was Wolfers. In his huge paw the youngster with the ugly, acne-marked face was carrying a large, round pack with what appeared to be a nozzle attached. It looked for all the world like the sort of pack that market-gardeners used to spray their crops. But Corrigan, with a thrill of recognition, knew it was not. 'Where the devil did you find *that?*' he asked, while at his side, Hawkins, who had recognised it too, looked sombre and apprehensive.

'Me and Trooper Sanders, sir. We was rummaging around, sir, in the back there … I thought it would be the thing for over there. I learned how to use it when I was at the Recce Battle School at Reeth, beyond Catterick–'

Corrigan cut him short with a wave of his hand. 'Do you really mean you want to chance it?' he asked quickly. 'You know the risks? As soon as the Jerries see you and recognise that thing on your back, the shit's really going to fly. If it's the last thing they ever do, they're going to try to knock you out before you get close enough to use it.'

'I'll have a go, sir,' Wolfers said loyally, his ugly young face flushing a deep red.

'Are you sure, son?' Hawkins asked. Better even than Corrigan, he knew the risk the big Yorkshire lad was running; they had used the damned things often enough in the old war and he had seen the lengths old Jerry would go in order to keep the terrible weapon out of range.

'Yes, Sarge, I can cope.'

Corrigan waited no longer. 'All right, let's fix up a bodyguard for our young hero toot sweet.'

'But, sir–' Hawkins protested. But Corrigan was no longer listening. The big, ugly boy had offered him a chance to take the damned pillbox which was barring their way to the Iron Division's beach, and he was going to take it, cost what it may.

While the rest of the troopers gathered around the big youngster with the pack on his shoulders, Slim picked up the ugly-looking Piat anti-tank rifle and fitted a bomb into the muzzle. Hawkins looked at him. 'And where do you think you're going with that, Sanders?' he asked.

'For a bleeding walk – what do you think, Sarge? I'm gonna give the kid a chance. Somebody's got to help the silly young bastard.'

'What you gonna do?'

'I'm gonna try to blast the gun-slits with this.' He tapped the clumsy weapon, with its padded butt that looked like the bandaged foot of a gout-sufferer.

'Christ! Standing up, the kick from that thing'll knock yer on yer skinny Aussie arse – it's like a mule!' Hawkins snorted.

'I'll manage,' Slim said grimly.

Hawkins shook his head. 'Christ, as I live and breathe! Trooper Slim Sanders doing a good turn for somebody else! Wonders'll never cease!'

Next moment, Sanders had sneaked over

the top of the parapet and was running towards the bunker, the heavy Piat bouncing up and down on his shoulder.

'All right,' Corrigan cried, 'let's go – and keep young Wolfers covered!' He flashed a look at the big trooper, whose ugly face was now set in grim determination. 'Good luck, lad.'

Then they were up and streaming forward, heads bent low.

Suddenly the Germans inside that strangely silent bunker woke up to the danger they were in. They must have recognised the pack that Wolfers was carrying for what it was. The next moment, vicious red fire spat from every slit in the concrete walls.

Slim stumbled to a halt, the slugs kicking up a line of earth at his feet. Desperately he aimed as best he could. The Piat thundered at his side, the recoil knocking him clean off his feet. The bottle-shaped bomb hurtled forward and smacked into the concrete just above the nearest slit, exploding with a tremendous roar. The whole bunker seemed to shake. Lumps of concrete hurtled through the air. The rifle that a second earlier had been poking out of the slit, was now buckled as if it had been made of rubber.

Groggily Slim got to his knees again and started to fit another bomb, his ears ringing, red and silver stars exploding like shells in front of his eyes. Hawkins was right. The thing had a kick like a bleeding mule.

Now there was shouting and screaming on all sides. Covered by Corrigan and Sergeant Hawkins, Wolfers ran pell-mell for the bunker, firing his tommy-gun from the hip as he went. Everything was roaring and flashing. Tracer zipped back and forth. From somewhere there was the high, hysterical hiss of a Spandau. Mortars thunked and plonked. Then suddenly the air was filled with a thick whooshing sound. *'Down!'* Corrigan screamed and shoved Wolfers to the ground. It was as if someone were swinging a large, fiery broom around. The air was full of lethal razor-sharp splinters. Someone yelled shrilly. The pitiful cry went up: *'Stretcher-bearer!'*

But there was no time for the wounded man now. Corrigan dragged the heavily laden Wolfers to his feet. 'Nearly there now, lad!' he gasped.

Wolfers yelped, struck by something hard and hot. He looked down. His left hand was split. Thick red-purple blood was oozing out of the wound and dripping down his dirty fingers. 'Bloody hell,' he gasped in astonishment, 'I've been wounded!' For a fleeting moment he felt faint; then he was overcome by a kind of fear-anger. 'Bastards!' he cursed, and once more he began to run towards the bunker, its walls now a sea of fire and drifting smoke, the big pack bouncing up and down on his broad shoulders.

'Here!' Corrigan yelled, stumbling to a stop.

He and Hawkins flung themselves to left and right in front of Wolfers, ignoring the slugs cutting the air on all sides and continuing to blast away at the slits.

With fingers that felt like thick, clumsy sausages, Wolfers fumbled with the hose. Then he had it. 'Ready, sir!' he yelled, above the bitter snap-and-crackle of the battle.

Hastily Corrigan and Hawkins sprang out of the line of fire. 'Then do it!' the officers yelled, still firing.

Wolfers did not hesitate. He was alone and at his most vulnerable. If he was hit now, he would die the most horrible death imaginable. Already the German in the nearest slit was frantically turning his machine-gun round to deal with him before it was too late. He pressed the trigger.

A soft hiss. A *whoosh* like some primeval monster drawing its first fiery breath. Suddenly a long tongue of oil-tinged, vicious blue flame shot out of the muzzle of the flame-thrower and slapped against the concrete. Next moment it engulfed the whole bunker in its terrible fiery embrace. The firing stopped at once. For one brief moment, the walls glowed a dull, ugly purple; then Corrigan and Hawkins were pelting forward to left and right of the bunker to throw themselves into the dead ground, there to wait for the inevitable end.

Safe now, Wolfers took his time. He could imagine the men trapped inside, clawing and jostling each other in their panic to escape from the terrible, all-consuming flame, gasping and choking feverishly, screaming for air. He pressed the trigger again. One, two, three seconds...

Once more the awesome flame wreathed the bunker in a glowing, vicious circle of fire. The camouflage paint began to bubble and boil, as if the concrete beneath were alive. The air was full of the acrid stench of burnt paint.

Corrigan turned and shouted, 'Enough, Wolfers – enough! That'll do it.'

Carried away by that terrible spectacle, Wolfers had to force himself to take his finger off the trigger. Then the flame died down, and men the like of which he hoped never to see again as long as he lived came staggering, screaming, out of the narrow entrance to the bunker. Reeling into the open, they threw themselves on their knees, wringing their hands, pleading for mercy, their faces blackened, their hair singed, their uniforms charred and smoking, crying, crying, crying...

Wolfers fought back the hot, bitter vomit that threatened to choke him. Feverishly, trembling at every limb, he tore at the straps of the pack and with all his great strength, flung it away from him. *'I didn't mean it!'* he cried desperately, as the charred figure of what had once been a human being came staggering blindly past him. The man's face had been transformed into a blackened skull by that all-consuming flame; two scarlet suppurating pits were where his eyes had been, and he was groping his way with charred, stiffened claws through which the bones showed a brilliant gleaming white.

*'I DIDN'T MEAN IT!...'*

Ten minutes later they were on their way. In front shuffled their prisoners, shoulders bent and clutching at their trousers, for their captors had cut their belts and braces. Next came four Germans bearing the wounded assault trooper on a door taken from the captured bunker. Behind came the rest of the assault troop, with Wolfers standing head and shoulders above the others, still sobbing.

At the rear, Corrigan nodded to Hawkins. The sergeant was standing next to the blinded German whom they had pumped full of morphia and propped against the tree. Wordlessly, Corrigan handed him the pistol they had taken from the German officer.

Hawkins knew what to do. The German was dying anyway. 'Sorry, old mate,' he whispered softly, 'but it's the only way.'

He patted the unconscious man's skinny

shoulder and placed the muzzle of the captured pistol to the right rear portion of his blackened skull. The knuckles of his right hand whitened. He gulped slightly and pressed. The pistol cracked and jumped. The back of the German's skull exploded. Hawkins jumped back just in time to avoid the thick, red slurry that splashed up and covered the tree. Then he tossed the pistol away, and without another word he and Corrigan started to tramp after the column, heading for the beach and whatever perils lay in wait for them there.

Behind them, the corpses began to stiffen in the bitter evening breeze that blew in from the sombre green sea below, and at last silence fell over that place of death...

## FOUR

The Brigade's beach was still under shell-fire, and the scene was confused, smoke laden and congested. The assault infantry had dug in and no one was shifting them today, with the result that the traffic behind them simply piled higher and higher, the congestion increasing by the hour as more and more troops and vehicles landed.

'Balls-up!' Corrigan commented. He was

now leading his little column down a lane marked by large white tapes, which indicated that it had been cleared of mines, and through the slit-trench line. Here, unshaven, weary infantrymen crouched under their flat steel helmets, looking at the new arrivals impassively and without curiosity.

'Situation normal, all fucked up, as the Yanks say,' Sergeant Hawkins agreed. 'Can't they see they're sitting ducks just crouched there like that?'

'Don't blame them, Hawkins,' Corrigan said in disgust. 'Blame their officers – blame the brigadier. He should have never given them the chance to bog down like that.'

Now they started to file past a couple of hundred British dead, lying in long rows like so many wooden logs. They were stiff, holding their postures like statues, yet most of them seemed whole, with hardly a mark on them. Why didn't they get up and move on? But a closer look showed the grey-whiteness of the flesh, the traces of black congealed blood at ears or nostrils, the brown stain on the khaki. They were dead all right; dead, most of them, within the first five minutes; dead before they had even had a chance to fire a shot.

Now the assault troops came upon the wrecked ruined assault armour which had gone in with the first wave of infantry: half-tracks, tanks, armoured cars, tipped to one side, without tracks, blackened by smoke, tyres ripped, great silver holes skewered in their sides. That morning, Corrigan told himself, there had been a great killing on these two miles of sand; and there would be more slaughter on the morrow unless they got up and moved towards the Periers Ridge tonight. Time was of the essence.

Just as Corrigan reached this conclusion, an airborne wireless-controlled bomb came homing in on the fleet. Immediately the anti-aircraft guns took up the challenge. Cannons thumped nervously. The sky above the anchorage filled with red, hurrying tracer, fiery sparks trailing behind the bullets as they flew upwards, covering the whole darkening sky with glittering, bloodshot stars. Remorse-lessly, relentlessly, the flying bomb hurtled through the tracer and the black puffballs of smoke. It started to come down, streams of fire pouring from behind it like a meteor. The German observer had spotted a target: the helpless grey rump of a tank landing craft anchored close to shore and about to discharge its cargo, two hundred yards away from Corrigan's Assault Troop.

'*Hit the deck!*' he yelled above the din.

Just in time, the men and their prisoners flung themselves into the wet, littered sand. The bomb missed the ship by what seemed like inches, exploding with a crump that made earth shake. Corrigan felt the ground come up and slam him in the teeth. His mouth filled with the hot copper taste of blood. He looked around in a daze. The entire front of the tank landing craft had been ripped away as if by some giant tin-opener, to reveal the interior, filled with untouched half-tracks, armoured cars, and jeeps – and all bearing the green-and-yellow flash and number 49 which designated the Reconnaissance Corps. They belonged to their own regiment.

All around him, men clambered to their feet, dusting off the sand, shaking their heads to try to regain their hearing and cursing the Germans. Corrigan, however, was frowning thoughtfully. Over there was a beautiful collection of armoured vehicles ripe for the taking. As they slogged forward, searching for the Regimental HQ, he began to think hard.

'Tell 'em to dig in, Hawkins, then join me,' Corrigan commanded. They were now approaching the sandbagged trench which formed the Regiment's HQ, tall silver radio aerials whipping all around it in the evening breeze.

Corrigan strode forward. A line of German corpses lay to his right among boxes of abandoned enemy equipment, their faces green with strange blotches of yellow and grey. It seemed no one had bothered to close their eyes, for now they leered upwards with a grisly sheen, their mouths lolling open, lips drawn back to reveal yellow false teeth like animals snarling their last defiance. Next to them lay two crumpled shapes covered by a tarpaulin. Officers' brown boots poked out beneath it. British dead, thought Corrigan, as he flung back the flap of the sandbagged tent.

'Watch the bloody blackout – please!' said a weary voice.

It belonged to the adjutant, Captain Smythe-Smythe, known behind his back as the 'Eton SS', on account of his name and fruity upper-class, public school accent. He looked very pale at this moment, with dark circles under his eyes and he was sitting alone, drinking rum out of a chipped brown mug. 'Oh, it's you, Corrigan,' he said. 'Thought you'd gone for a Burton.'

Corrigan waited, but the young adjutant with the overlong blond hair and affected accent did not offer him a seat, so he sat down on the ration case opposite. For a moment or two he looked hard at the other officer in the hissing white incandescent light of the petrol lantern. 'Where's the CO?' he rasped. 'I want to talk to him urgently.'

''Fraid you can't, old boy.' The adjutant took a hasty sip of his rum.

'What do you mean, I can't?'

The adjutant gestured with the mug. Corrigan could see his hand was trembling badly. 'He's out there – with the others.'

'You mean he bought it?'

'Yes.'

Corrigan could see now that the adjutant was in deep shock. Once again, he felt the anger boil up inside him. Bloody marvellous! All that training – and yet not one of them had had the sense to realise what it would be like on the day!

'And the squadron commanders of "B" and "C" as well,' the adjutant went on. 'An eighty-eight bagged the lot of them, just as they were beginning an O group.'

The adjutant's lips started to tremble. For a moment Corrigan was afraid he might burst into tears. Right now he was not in the mood for acting nursemaid to sobbing officers.

'Who's in charge, then?' he demanded harshly. 'Where's the regiment? Who's running the bloody show now?'

The adjutant blanched, reeling back, as if he half expected the angry man in the torn uniform to hit him. 'Major Stirling of "A" Squadron – he's taken over, Corrigan, until the Brig appoints another CO... Oh, my God, Corrigan, it was horrible, absolutely horrible! I never thought–'

'Where's Stirling now?' Corrigan broke in.

'Over at Brigade HQ. But Corrigan, if you only knew what–'

Corrigan gave him no chance to finish. Angrily he swept back the flap of the tent and stepped outside, glad of the fresh air of the beach. Behind him, the 'Eton SS' began to sob.

Hawkins laid a restraining hand on Corrigan's arm. 'Don't be too hard on him, sir. After all, he's only a kid. Not more than twenty, if he's a day.'

'Oh, stop being a bloody old granny!' Corrigan snorted. Suddenly he was angry with everybody: the dead CO, the poor weak adjutant, the Brigadier – everyone who had got them into this stupid damned mess. 'Come on, let's find Brigade HQ...'

Some five hundred yards or so behind the infantry positions, red, white and grey telephone lines led into a cobbled courtyard set back from the road. Here among the old, gnarled trees an angry voice was calling, 'Hello, Sunray One ... Hello, Sunray One, do you read me? Over.'

An uncertain evening sunlight hung over the place, breaking through the darkening clouds. In the far corner, a cook in a dirty apron was hacking away at a pig hung up from one of the trees, monotonously singing the popular song of the year; *'You are my sunshine, my only sunshine... You make me happ-ee, when skies are grey...'*

Corrigan and Hawkins halted at a little wooden kitchen table at which squatted two cheerful-looking infantry officers, one of them with a blood-stained bandage around his head, both wolfing triangular link sausages and washing them down with mugs of tea from a tin pail at their feet.

'You looking for his bloody nibs?' asked the older of the two, before Corrigan could speak. He jerked a dirty thumb, running with grease, towards the red-brick house, its walls pocked with the shellfire and bullet-holes of the dawn bombardment. 'He's in there.' Next to him the other raised his hands to the sky and cried 'Salaam!', where-upon they both laughed like idiots.

Grimly Corrigan flashed them a hard smile. They were on their way back home; they were out of it. He had to remain here among this bloody awful mess.

He passed a tent. Inside, clean-shaven staff officers, washed and scrubbed-looking, were studying maps spread out on a table, which was adorned with a snowy-white looted tablecloth, a china tea service – and real scones. Hawkins swallowed hard, and even Corrigan looked grim. 'God Almighty, you'd think this was Aldershot, vintage 1938!'

Two well-turned out sentries, their boots polished and gleaming, clicked to attention as Corrigan approached the HQ, and slapped their hands down hard on their butts in salute. 'Temporary CO, Recce Regi-ment?' Corrigan requested a little helplessly, and was directed inside. He turned to

Hawkins before entering. 'See if you can get into the Brigade kitchen – I'll bet ten to one they'll have something better than compo rations there. I'll collect you after they've slung me out on my ear.'

Hawkins grinned and threw Corrigan a tremendous salute. 'I could do with a cup of char, sir – especially real old sergeant major's stuff with the spoon standing to attention in the dixie.'

Corrigan passed on inside. There were officers everywhere – infantry-engineers, pioneers, members of the beach parties, navy men, artillerymen. Indeed, it seemed the whole of the Brigade's officer strength was present in that rambling old house; and all of them had all the time in the world – drinking rum out of mugs, smoking, chatting, leafing through old copies of the *Tatler* and *London Illustrated News* which had come from God knows where. The scene could have come straight out of a peacetime mess.

Impatiently Corrigan pushed his way through the tight throng until he spotted Stirling, the new acting commander, a tall red-faced major who affected a dashing cavalryman's moustache, suede boots, foulard of parachute silk and a fly whisk. All in all, he looked as if he had just returned from the Western Desert; in fact, until two years ago he had been a pen pusher in a provincial solicitor's office.

Corrigan hailed him and the new CO turned. 'Oh, it's you, Corrigan,' he said without interest, lowering his mug of whisky. 'Thought you'd gone for a Burton.'

Corrigan bit his lip. That was the second time he had heard that bloody phrase in the last half hour. It was almost as if the damned regiment was sorry to find that he was still alive.

'No,' he answered, 'here I am, just like the proverbial bad penny. Jerry did his best, though, I can assure you.'

Irony was wasted on Stirling. 'What can I do for you, Corrigan?' he asked. 'I want a word with the Brig urgently.'

'It's more a question of what I can do for *you*, Stirling.'

'What do you mean?'

'When can we move out?'

'Move out!' Stirling said hotly. 'My dear chap, there can be no talk of that until – first light – at the earliest. Good grief! It's absolutely not on.'

'Why not?' Corrigan asked bluntly.

'Because, Captain Corrigan, I say so.'

This last came from the brigadier himself, mug in hand, looking at the tattered captain as if he had just landed from Mars.

Corrigan and Stirling stiffened to attention, then Corrigan said carefully, 'May I ask why, sir?'

'You may not,' snapped the brigadier, 'but

I shall tell you all the same. Got to tidy things up. The front's ragged. Mines, infantry not in the right place, artillery support all over the shop. Traffic jam to the rear. Ammo not getting up front. In other words, Corrigan, I want a tidy show before I do another damned thing. Got it?'

But before Corrigan had a chance to speak his mind, the brigadier passed on and was immediately engaged in hearty laughter with a couple of naval captains, both flushed with whisky.

'Well, Corrigan – you heard,' Stirling said sternly.

'Yes, I heard.' Corrigan managed to keep his voice cold, but inwardly he was raging. 'But do you seriously think that the Jerries are going to oblige us by *waiting* until the Brig has arranged his nice, tidy show?'

'For God's sake, man – he'll hear you!' Stirling hissed. 'He's only over there.'

'Let him hear. He won't last the week. I'll bet your month's pay against mine that he'll be out of the Brigade on his ear by the end of June. He's no bloody good.'

'Corrigan, you're going a bit too far. I know you're a hero, with a chestful of gongs and all the rest of it. But enough's enough! Now I'm going over to speak to the Brig, but before I go, this is what I'm going to do with you. I'm putting you in my "B" Echelon.'

'You're doing *what?*'

Stirling slapped his fly-swatter against his leg impatiently. 'Dammit! Don't I make myself clear? I'm putting you in "B" Echelon until we can re-equip your assault troop.'

'But – hell!' Corrigan exploded, so that the officers closest turned and stared at him curiously. 'I've just seen a whole boatload of our equipment back there on the beach. Tanks, flails – all there, just for the taking.'

Stirling was unimpressed. 'But not for *you*, Corrigan. You'd better get back to your chaps. I shall see you at HQ at eight hundred hours tomorrow morning. Now I must get hold of the Brig at once...'

And with that he was gone, pushing his way through the crowd, leaving Corrigan staring after him in furious impotence, his hands balled into hard fists.

Now an uneasy silence had fallen over the crowded beach, broken only by the occasional beat of a low-flying aircraft engine as the Spitfires patrolled in a wide circle. Out at sea, the ships' searchlights parted the clouds with silver fingers, scanning the sky for signs of enemy activity. But like the weary infantry, the German defenders had apparently stopped the war for the night.

Corrigan's assault troop, however, did not sleep. Fed, washed, shaved and one hundred percent alert, they now listened to Corrigan rap out his orders in short, hard, angry phrases.

'...I didn't bring you up that bloody cliff and through that business with the bunker to have us transferred to the "B" Echelon. We're not rear-echelon wallahs. We're fighting soldiers.'

There was a low rumble of agreement from his listeners.

'So Major bloody Stirling can go and take a running jump. We're going to do the job we came over here to do. Namely to get through the gaps and recce towards Caen. And I'll tell you this too, men: tomorrow morning all hell is going to break out on this beach. We either get off it or we *die* here!'

In the glowing darkness he could see Sergeant Hawkins nodding his head in agreement.

'So this is the drill. We know where we can get hold of the wheels that we need – they're in that beached tank landing craft. At the moment nobody wants them. So we'll just borrow them.'

'*Borrow* them?' a few of the men echoed, puzzled. 'How exactly, sir?'

By way of answer, Corrigan looked over at Sanders, who appeared to be counting looted silver coins. 'Trooper Sanders, how would you like a quick promotion?'

Sanders looked up, startled. 'What do you mean, sir?'

'Well, you've promoted yourself often

138

enough in the past, you little rogue. It was a "major in the engineers" when you were on the run in Cairo in '42, a "naval lieutenant commander" in Tripoli on leave in '43, and you even claimed to be a humble captain back in Blighty quite recently.'

Wolfers guffawed at this revelation and put his bandaged paw to his mouth. Slim Sanders felt himself blushing and was grateful for the darkness. So that hard-faced bastard Corrigan had had him taped all the bleedin' time! Still, you had to hand it to him...

'Well, I'm now going to give you a chance to outrank all your – er – roles,' Corrigan continued. 'How would you like to be an instant light-colonel?'

Slim gulped hard, and the others in the troop who knew of his little tricks, chuckled. 'But I don't know what you mean, sir...'

'This. If a light-colonel of the Recce Corps turns up at that tank landing craft with his drivers and demands those armoured vehicles to be driven off immediately under cover of darkness – well, I can't see some junior Navy type stopping him, can you?'

'No, sir,' Sanders stuttered. 'But where do I get a light-colonel's crown and pip, sir?'

'I'll tell you. Back at RHQ, you'll find our late colonel nicely tucked away beside one of his squadron commanders under a tarpaulin, sleeping the sleep of the just – for ever.'

Sergeant Hawkins frowned. Corrigan was

too hard. It was not done to talk about the dead like that.

'You're not averse to working over dead bodies, Sanders, are you?' Corrigan snapped. 'All right, then. Off you go and get those pips. Report back to me in five minutes. Don't stand there gaping, man – get going!'

Sanders doubled away into the darkness.

'The rest of you will fall in under Sergeant Hawkins until the – er – new CO gets back. He'll march you to the boat to collect our vehicles. Wolfers...'

'Sir.' The big trooper clambered to his feet.

'Do you think you could drive with that injured hand of yours?'

'I think so, sir,' Wolfers answered, always the willing horse, his hysteria overcome now.

'Good. Then you'll come with me.'

'To do what, sir?'

For the first time since they had arrived at that bloody beach, Captain Corrigan smiled. 'To do what?' he echoed. 'Why, my boy, to steal a ruddy tank...'

# FIVE

Dawn came slowly, turning the grey sky to the east a faint, hazy pink. This morning the sun seemed reluctant to rise above the horizon, as if hoping to avoid casting its warming rays on the stark war-torn landscape below.

Corrigan and Hawkins, lying flat in the damp grass, watched as the countryside around them was slowly illuminated in all its new horror: brown shellholes like the work of giant moles; poplars stripped of their foliage and looking like gaunt, outsized toothpicks; the mutilated, burned-out wrecks of sixty-ton Tiger tanks... And the bodies. They lay everywhere, exposed in all their terrible mutilations: the bloody stumps where feet had been blown off; the caved-in ribs revealing the dirty white pulp of lungs; the puckered, mangled limbs which appeared to have been worked over with a blunt can-opener; the ripped-open guts, the obscene, bloated grey contents strewn over the ground like ghastly squashed snakes. Dead men lay everywhere, German and British: the human cost of D-Day.

But Corrigan and Hawkins, hiding there

in the wet grass, were hardened fighting men; they avoided looking at the dead. Instead they stared at the landscape ahead, which seemed so gentle, so pastoral, so empty, but which they knew was packed with hard, young German fanatics, ready to turn this soft, rural scene into another bloody battlefield any moment.

'That's the Periers Ridge,' Corrigan whispered, 'up beyond the fields. You can see it's well wooded in places. Bloody bad place for armour, though; we'll have to skirt the woods and keep to the meadows.'

'Looks awfully exposed,' Hawkins commented softly.

'Speed and surprise, that's the only answer,' Corrigan said confidently. 'Once we're through the hard crust to our front, I think we can do it.'

'They've mined the bridge, by the look of it, sir,' Hawkins cautioned, pointing at the little stone bridge that led to the German-held hamlet of Periers-sur-le-Dan. 'You can see the lumps of tarmac where they've buried them. Teller mines, I expect.'

Corrigan was unmoved. 'You worry too much, Hawkins,' he said without rancour. 'Don't forget, we've got that little gift from the Royal Armoured Corps. Though of course, they won't realise that they've given it to us till later.' He smiled coldly, remembering how easy it had been to purloin the clumsy-looking device from the RAC's night laager. 'Wolfers, Sanders and me will go in with the flail and cross the bridge first. Of course, the racket's bound to wake every Jerry from here to Berlin, but no matter – we'll take the brunt of their fire. Then you'll sneak in with the rest of the troop over that ford at two o'clock, swing round the rear of the hamlet and pick us up there. Clear?'

'Clear, sir,' Hawkins snapped dutifully. It was a sound plan, but he could not help thinking that Corrigan was being a little over-optimistic. Supposing the flail got caught in one of the hamlet's narrow streets by a single young Jerry armed with a Panzerfaust. Corrigan's goose would be cooked then, and no mistake. 'But what if the ford's mined, too, sir?' Hawkins objected.

'It isn't,' Corrigan answered cheerfully. 'I did a personal recce two hours ago while you were still tucked up in your blankets, sawing wood ten to the dozen. Now let's circumcise our watches. I have exactly … zero six hundred hours.'

'Zero six hundred it is, sir!' Hawkins snapped promptly, pushing home the winding device.

'Give me five minutes after I start for the bridge, and then off you go.'

'Take care, sir,' Hawkins said, looking hard at Corrigan's tough, lean face.

'I will, don't worry. After all, I'll have to be

143

around when the CO has me court-martialled for that little bit of piracy...'

Next minute, Corrigan was doubling for the ugly-looking flail, parked silently in the shadows at the side of the cobbled country road.

'All right, Sanders?' Corrigan whispered, pressing the throat-mike.

'All right, sir!' Sanders' voice came from down below, in the thirty-ton monster's driving seat.

'All right, Wolfers?' Corrigan asked. The big Yorkshire boy was crouched over the 75mm cannon below in the turret, next to the device that operated the flail.

'All right, sir,' Wolfers answered, his voice a little hoarse with a mixture of adrenalin and nerves.

Corrigan took one last look at the silent, grey hamlet huddled around the slate-steepled church and glistening in the dew, then pulled down the turret hatch. 'Driver,' he called very formally. 'Advance!'

Suddenly the three-hundred-horsepower engine burst into mighty, pulsating life. Above, the rooks nesting in the ruined trees rose in hoarse, cawing protest. Blue streams of smoke shot from the flail tank's exhaust, filling the morning air with the stink of engine fumes. Down below, Sanders thrust home the first of the tank's thirty-odd gears;

there was a rusty metallic squeak, and it lurched forward, rattling towards the little stone bridge at twenty miles an hour. They were on their way!

They bumped up the ramp. Already on the other side of the river, men were pelting from the tumbledown grey houses, pulling on their tunics, hurriedly grabbing their weapons and racing to their positions. Corrigan, squinting through the periscope, cursed. The balloon had gone up already. He prayed they were not armed with Panzerfausts. Then, ignoring the Germans, he swung the periscope to left and right to cover the bridge. Hawkins was right: there they were – the large circles of freshly disturbed tarmac which hid the anti-tank mines.

'Operate the flail – *now!*'

Wolfers obeyed instantly. He knew the effect that one of the great round Teller mines would have on the base of the tank if they ran over one with their tracks. He pressed the button.

To their front, a drum suspended in advance of the tank by two arms slowly began to revolve, soon gathering speed. Now, great lengths of steel chain attached to the drum started to slap the tarmac like a gigantic cultivator. The racket was hellish, earsplitting – but to the men inside, comforting. On and on they crept, closer to the mines, the chains whirling and drumming, the mighty engine roaring, the first ineffectual German rifle fire pattering off their thick steel sides like heavy tropical rain off a tin roof.

*Crump!* The first mine exploded harmlessly, sending up a pall of smoke and a shower of flying tarmac and stone. The flail tank rocked violently as if struck by a sudden tempest. Slim Sanders cursed fluently, but kept her steady.

The flails hit another mine. Huge clods of earth and cobbles slapped against the turret. Through the periscope Corrigan saw them coming and ducked in the nick of time. But the worst was still to come.

Now they roared down the ramp at the other end of the bridge, leaving it smoking and ruined behind them. Slim braked hard on one track, and they slewed to the right. In front of them loomed the first line of tumbledown stone cottages. Each one, they could now see, was heavily defended, a little fortress in its own right. And from every window came scarlet slashes of flame.

'Stop flailing, Wolfers!' Corrigan yelled. 'They won't have mines in the street! Man the seventy-five!'

With surprising speed for such a big fellow, Wolfers squirmed into the gunner's seat behind the big breech of the 75mm cannon, pressed his eye against the rubber suction-pad of the sight and waited for Corrigan's orders. Below, Slim Sanders, sweating like a pig, pressed his foot down hard on the huge accelerator. The tank raced forward, rolling into the village street with an ear-splitting roar that echoed back and forth in the stone canyon.

A small anti-tank gun hurriedly set up in the middle of the street flashed into view. Wolfers responded instantly, opening fire with the 75mm. Smoke flooded the turret. One gleaming, smoking shell-case came clattering out of the breech. The anti-tank gun shot high into the air, engulfed in a ball of blinding yellow flame. Next moment the thirty-ton monster was rolling over the dying and wounded crew, crushing them to pulp under its whirling tracks.

'Panzerfaust!' Slim shrieked from below.

Corrigan flung the periscope round. A tall, skinny soldier was standing in an alley off the main road, a clumsy-looking rocket-launcher perched on his shoulder. He pressed the trigger. The bulbous rocket raced towards them, trailing fiery-red sparks. Slim hit the brakes. The tank shuddered to a stop. The bomb exploded harmlessly to their front in a thick blanket of white smoke, buffeting the tank from side to side and nearly catapulting Slim Sanders out of his seat with the impact.

Wolfers spun the co-axial machine-gun round, screamed exuberantly and pressed the trigger. Tracer spat forward viciously. It caught the German in his stomach, nearly cutting him in half. He staggered away, trying to catch up his escaping intestines in his arms like a housewife with a bundle of dirty washing. To no avail. Next moment he pitched face forward into his own steaming guts.

Now the fire coming at the tank from both sides was tremendous. They were struck time and time again, the tracer howling off their armour-plating like glowing golfballs. Slim Sanders smashed through a barn. A group of Germans clustered around a heavy machine-gun fled in panic. Too late. Wolfers' machine-gun chattered at close range. Bones splintered. Blood splattered the floor in great crimson gobs. In their abject terror, the Germans' bowels turned to water, their screams reaching a terrifying crescendo as the slugs slammed into them, whirling them around, turning them to and fro, tossing them to each side like leaves at the mercy of the wind.

They barrelled through a greenhouse, crunching over the shattered glass. A rough stone wall barred their way. Slim Sanders swung left, slugs howling off the back of the flail, and they roared on down a narrow lane. From upstairs windows, Germans tossed grenades down on them. Wolfers' machine-gun spun round to take up the challenge. A hail of bullets, and the men in the field-grey flopped lifelessly over the windowsills.

Sanders hit the brakes. The big tank screeched to a crazy stop, every rivet squeaking in protest. Corrigan was suddenly pitched against the turret and yelped with pain. *'What the hell–'* The angry protest died on his lips. Broadsides on, a great armoured shape barred their progress. 'Cor, luvaduck!' Sanders' hushed voice crackled across the intercom. 'A bleedin' Tiger!'

'They've spotted us!' Corrigan cried urgently.

Wolfers grabbed the firing bar.

There was a tremendous crack, followed an instant later by the stomach-jerking lurch of the recoil. Acrid yellow smoke filled the turret. The 75mm solid shot shell hurtled towards the German tank, a white, hurrying blur bringing death and destruction. A huge hollow boom. The Tiger rocked madly. The shell went howling off harmlessly in a spurt of white, leaving only a fleeting purple glow on the Tiger's turret.

'But I hit it, sir!' Wolfers yelled, *'I hit the bugger...'*

'Slim – ram the bugger!' Corrigan shrieked.

Already the Tiger's huge overhanging cannon was swinging round in their direction. One moment more and they would be reduced to a mess of charred, shattered limbs: something the Graves people would have to hose out with hot water.

Sanders pushed home first gear. *'Come on, you cow!'* he screamed, willing the tank to reach the German before the enemy could fire.

The flail shot forward. The German cannon was almost round. In seconds, that gloating Kraut gunner would be notching up another kill.

'Hold tight, gents!' the little Australian yelled, 'here we bloody well go...'

The next moment, the flail slammed into the side of the German tank with an awesome boom. The periscope in front of Corrigan's eye was suddenly reduced to a gleaming spider's web of broken glass. Almost immediately, a thick, white, choking cloud of smoke began to pour from the two shattered vehicles. Corrigan banged his ears to stop the mad ringing. Wolfers was slumped over his cannon, moaning, blood trickling from his nostrils and on to his chin.

'Sanders – all right?'

'Yes, but my soddin' head's fallen off.'

'Out ... at the double... Out!'

Corrigan drew back his hand and slapped Wolfers hard, across the face. 'Out... Get out! Quick!' he screamed.

Wolfers' eyes flickered open stupidly. 'What...?'

Corrigan hit him again. Outside, he could hear the sound of running feet getting louder. The infantry were coming. He could wait no longer. He grabbed the dazed trooper by the hair. Wolfers yelped in pain. 'For God's sake,' he cried through gritted teeth, 'let's get the hell out of here...'

Sergeant Hawkins had put out scouts. The green corn that covered the slope up to the ridge was too thick and high for comfort: it could easily conceal another fanatic of the kind they had encountered in Periers-sur-le-Dan; and besides, he didn't trust the woods to his right. How English those thick elms and oaks looked: blue, green and dense – and so peaceful. Yet he had no intention of letting his half-tracks run the risk of an ambush.

So the assault troopers waded through the breast-high corn, followed at a snail's pace by the 'V' of the armoured vehicles, slowly advancing ever closer to the Ridge which barred the exit from the beach and led down to the plain of the River Orne below.

Minutes ticked by leadenly. The air was hot and heavy. The blue waves of the heat-haze rippled over the corn. The men on foot dripped with sweat, their brick-red faces looking as if they had been greased with Vaseline. Slowly they waded through the tall stalks, rifles held at the high port, nerves tingling, bodies tensed for that first angry chatter of machine-gun fire.

Nonetheless, when it came, it came as a

shock. A ferocious tearing sound. A ripping, a whizzing, as something hurtled a furious rate through the still air. Then, over to the right, a bright light flared up.

'Eighty-eight!' somebody shouted.

With a great baleful scream the first shell exploded to the front of the men in the corn. Hawkins caught a blurred glimpse of one of his troopers falling, struck by a piece of shrapnel. The man was swinging round, his face looking as if someone had just thrown a handful of strawberry jam at it; for a moment he seemed to hang on to the air, his mouth open, a great black hole from which no noise came. Then, dramatically, he slapped the ground – and all hell broke loose.

'Blast and damn!' Corrigan cursed angrily, throwing himself down next to Hawkins in the crushed corn. 'For a moment I thought we were going to get away with it.'

Behind them the half-tracks and the other vehicles were scuttling away in reverse, making smoke, and frantically heading for cover. Meanwhile the 88mm cannon in the woods to the right of the troopers pounded the cornfield, sending up whirling fountains of earth all about them.

'No such luck, sir. But there's only one of the buggers, thank God. It's just to the left of that patch of oaks at–'

The rest of his words were drowned by another explosion, as the angry German gunners, cheated of the vehicles, turned their attention on the men hiding in the corn. A succession of ear-splitting blasts rent the air in an awesome, volcanic tumult of roaring heat. Over and over again, gigantic orange fireballs seethed and rolled upwards.

The bombardment seemed to Corrigan to go on for ever. He wished he could scream, relieve the unbearable tension. The air was furnace-like, scorching his hands and face. He choked and gasped for air… And then, at last, it was over and the din died away, leaving behind a reverberating silence.

Out in the field, the men were so stupefied that at first they could not answer when Sergeant Hawkins asked if there were any casualties. Finally, exasperated beyond all measure, he had to bellow at them: 'Fucking well answer, when I ask – *any casualties?*'

That seemed to bring them to their senses. There were various cries of *'All right here, Sarge'* and *'Okay, Sarge'*.

Hawkins sighed hard and turned to Corrigan. 'Well that's it, sir. One casualty. The poor sod who bought it right at the beginning.'

Corrigan nodded, raising himself to peer over the corn. His mind was racing. He knew they could not hang around here. The firing could well have alerted other German units, and there were still plenty of Jerries left alive down there in Periers-sur-le-Dan. By now they would have had ample time to recover from the shock of that mad dash through their positions. He had to act – and act soon.

'All right, Hawkins,' Corrigan said miserably, 'let's get to it.'

'Infantry attack?' Hawkins queried, equally miserably.

Corrigan nodded numbly.

Hawkins cursed under his breath. Then, rising to his knees, he called: 'All right, me lucky lads, let's be having yer... We're going to give them ruddy Jerries a taste of cold British steel... *Bash on, the Assault Troop!*'

But inwardly his heart sank at the thought of what lay ahead for his youngsters.

## SIX

They advanced at a crouch, each man wrapped up in his own thoughts. Some had to force their legs to move through the corn; others moved like zombies, though even they jumped nervously each time the faint noise of a shell exploding reached them from the beach.

Corrigan was in the lead, rifle in hand. He had taken the precaution of tearing his badges of rank off his epaulettes, just in case the Germans had snipers posted to protect the 88mm position. The snipers would automatically go for the officers. Behind, at the regulation five yards' distance, came Hawkins, dirt rubbed across his stripes, his old, wizened face set and grim.

Now they were almost out of the burning corn and into the trees. Corrigan strained hard, waiting for the first shot or shell, eyes here, there and everywhere, searching every feature of the landscape for danger. Why were the Germans so silent? They knew the men of the Assault Troop were out there. Why hadn't they opened up?

He held up his right hand. Behind him, Hawkins automatically did the same. The men froze in their stride, weapons at the ready, hands damp with sweat. Corrigan placed his hand, fingers outspread, on the top of his helmet – the infantry signal for 'rally on me'. Hurriedly Hawkins trotted forward and crouched next to a kneeling Corrigan, flies humming greedily around his red, sweating face.

'Spotted anything, sir?' he whispered.

'No, that's just it,' Corrigan answered, looking worried. 'Why the hell have they let us get this far?' He brushed away a midge angrily. 'They know we're coming.'

'Perhaps they've buggered off.'

'We would have heard the noise of the towing vehicle, Hawkins.'

'Maybe they've just abandoned the eighty-eight,' Hawkins said hopefully, and licked his parched lips. At this moment he would have given his right arm to be sitting bellied up to the bar of the sergeants' mess, sinking a pint of mild and bitter.

'Doubt it. Why should they? They've got all the aces at the moment. No – that's just wishful thinking, Hawkins. They're in there all right, waiting – but *waiting for bloody what?*'

'Well, sir,' Hawkins answered dutifully, 'there's only one way to find out, ain't there?'

'I know ... I know,' Corrigan said with a bitter sigh. 'All right, follow me.' They started to advance once more.

Now they were well into the wood, and the atmosphere was hot and brooding. The crouching men moved forward on the tips of their toes, apprehensive, afraid to make the smallest sound, placing their heavy nailed ammunition boots delicately, gingerly, almost like professional dancers. More than once, Hawkins caught himself holding his breath, as if the sound of breathing might give him away. 'Christ Almighty,' he cursed to himself, 'you're shit-sacred, Hawkins. Now get yer finger out. Yer can only die once.' But it was no good; next moment he found he was holding his breath again.

Up front, Corrigan peered to left and right in the green gloom. The battery could not be more than a hundred yards away now, somewhere up ahead in a clearing. Once he thought he heard a soft call in German, but eventually he managed to convince himself it was simply his over-active imagination playing tricks on him. All was silence. Not even the birds sang – if there were any in those tall, green oaks. Grimly Corrigan skirted another ancient oak and stepped forward into the thick ferns at its base. Suddenly he tripped, and felt himself falling, cursing as he landed on his knees among the ferns. 'What the devil–'

Then he saw the familiar, dread symbol on the wire which had tripped him, and swallowed hard.

Seeing him kneeling, motionless, as if frozen to the spot, Hawkins doubled over to see what the matter was. By way of answer, Corrigan pointed solemnly at the little tin sign attached to the wire.

'Oh, sod it!' Hawkins breathed, 'not *that!*'

Silently, ignoring the flies swarming all around them from the hot ferns, the two of them stared at the white plate with its black skull-and-crossbones sign and that terrifying legend beneath it: *'Achtung-Minen!'*

'So that's why they haven't bothered with protective infantry,' Hawkins muttered.

'Of course,' Corrigan agreed angrily. 'Why waste infantry when you can do a better job with mines? I'll bet they've sown a whole bloody minefield right round their position and they're sitting there on their fat German arses telling themselves they're as safe as bloody houses.'

'It might be a trick, sir. I remember back in '40, the Jerries often codded us with those signs – and no mines.'

Corrigan shook his head slowly. 'Wish you were right, Hawkins, but I doubt it. They've had two or three years to get this coast ready for us. They'll have sodding mines there, believe you me.'

'Well, what are we going to do, sir? The lads have no mine detectors, but they do know how to detect and lift with their bayonets.'

'We haven't got time for that,' Corrigan snapped, his mind already made up. 'We can't move forward without nobbling that bloody gun, and we can't go back either. So,' he shrugged, 'we'll have to go through it. I'll lead.'

'Sir–' Hawkins began, but Corrigan cut him off harshly, almost brutally.

'No buts, Sergeant! We do as I say ... I'll go first. You warn every man to follow exactly in my footsteps.' He slung his rifle with an air of finality. 'All right, let's go!'

Gingerly Corrigan lowered his left foot, feeling his way with his toecap, wriggling his toes inside the stiff boot, as if that could somehow make them more sensitive. Nothing – so far. He drew a deep breath and

158

forced his right foot after the left.

They had been going five minutes now and had covered perhaps twenty yards. All of them were soaked with sweat, their faces flushed an ugly brick-red, their eyes wide and wild with apprehension. And they were packed together in a tightly bunched single file – a sniper's dream.

The minutes passed leadenly. The only sounds were the maddening buzz of the hordes of flies and the harsh rasp of the troopers' breathing. In the lead, Corrigan forced himself by sheer naked willpower to continue, each step seeming to take an eternity of deliberation. His heart beat crazily, his breath was now coming in short, hectic gasps.

Then the inevitable happened. As Corrigan lowered his foot one more time, *he felt metal scrape against the hobnails of his right boot!*

Just in time he prevented himself from withdrawing his foot. Instead he kept it resting on what he knew was the plunger which activated the mine.

Behind him the line of sweating troopers shuffled to an awkward stop.

'Hawkins,' he called in a dry, cracked voice, trying to keep himself from panicking, the sweat trickling down his tense face in thick rivulets.

'Sir.'

'I'm standing on one.'

As he stood there rigidly, Corrigan could hear Hawkins gasp; but when the sergeant spoke, his voice was calm and measured: 'I'm coming up, sir.'

He felt Hawkins' arms encircle his waist; and then, with infinite slowness, the old sergeant bent and thrust his fingers into the earth. Gingerly, he probed, while Corrigan waited in an agony of apprehension.

'Schu-mine, sir,' Hawkins reported finally, in a breathless voice. 'No tricks so far.' He grunted again. 'Feeling underneath the sod – *now*... Keep perfectly still, please, sir.'

A moment's tense silence. Corrigan could feel a single cold bead of sweat trickling down his spine. His heart was thumping madly. If Hawkins found an attachment underneath, linking the mine to another, he would have to order him to move back and then lift his foot. If he was lucky, he would escape with his life. But his leg would go, there was no question of that. He would be a cripple for life...

'No matchbox detonator,' Hawkins grunted, digging deeper under the mine, '...and no wire attached.'

'*Whew!*' Corrigan breathed a sigh of heartfelt relief. 'Thank God for that.' For the first time he looked down at Hawkins, who was crouched at his feet, with his hands buried right under the mine. 'All right, you know the drill?'

'Yes, sir. I start to lift, you keep your foot on the plunger. When I say *now*, you lift yer foot off toot sweet and I throw the sod.'

'Exactly.'

'Shall I start?'

For once, Hawkins forgot the 'sir': and Corrigan knew why. One slip at this stage, one wrong move, and they would both get the full benefit of the exploding mine – and Hawkins would get it right in his face. Split-second timing was essential. For a moment Corrigan hesitated; then, in a voice that seemed to come from a thousand miles away and from someone else entirely, he said: 'Right.'

'Lifting, sir!'

'Yes.' Together with Hawkins, Corrigan lifted his foot with seemingly incredible slowness, keeping his foot on that terrible plunger which could mean the difference between life and death. Desperately he fought not to lose contact, feeling the sweat stream from every pore, straining his ears for that barely audible metallic scrape which would mean that his foot had slipped and that everything was over.

'Out,' Hawkins croaked, broken-voiced.

Corrigan fought to keep himself from shouting. 'Count up to three, Hawkins,' he commanded.

Hawkins swallowed hard and spat. '*One... Two... Threeee!*'

In the same instant that Corrigan ripped

his foot off the plunger, Hawkins slung the mine forward in a low, underarm lob.

Corrigan crouched. Hawkins bent his head, helmet facing outwards to take the blast.

To their front, the ground erupted in a bright scarlet flash. And another – and another. On all sides mines were exploding. Clods of earth and shrapnel flew everywhere. Corrigan felt himself struck hard on his helmet and almost blacked out, red and white stars exploding in front of his eyes. Beyond and to the left there was the sound of running feet and someone cursing harshly in German. A trooper suddenly screamed behind him. *'Christ, I've been hit!'*

Suddenly they were surging forward like thoroughbreds from the starting-gate, screaming, shrilling, zig-zagging past the steaming brown holes, blundering through the trees, heedless of the pliant branches whipping and ripping at their faces, intent on one thing only: to kill those who had made them suffer so terribly in those last few minutes.

Gasping for breath and drenched in sweat, Corrigan clung to a tree and let them stream past him. He could not hold them back any longer. He had seen it all before. In the end, they were all reduced to this, the ones who had to pay the bloody 'butcher's bill' of battle. Sensitive or stupid, war always

162

turned them into brutal, remorseless killers in the end.

Hawkins sighed. In spite of the distant sound of gunfire from the sea, the valley stretching before him seemed somehow green and peaceful. All the same, the hand of death lay heavily across that pastoral scene.

The crazed young assault troopers had now completed the brutal slaughter of the German gunners, most of whom had been shot down mercilessly in that first mad rush through the trees. Now the only sound was that familiar dry crack of a pistol at regular intervals, as they staggered from body to body, blowing the heads off any Germans who still showed signs of life. Many were flourishing, newly-looted German pistols and laughing crazily, eyes wild with excitement at this exhilarating new sport.

Corrigan, leaning against a tree, took a last, grateful pull of his cigarette, while Hawkins watched, tears in his faded old eyes. 'What did you expect?' he asked softly, amusement in his voice. 'That they would stay your nice, clean, tame soldier boys for ever?'

Hawkins shook his head and rubbed his knuckles in his eyes. 'No, sir,' he answered in weary resignation, 'I suppose you're right. They've been through a lot. It's understandable. They're a bit crazy now...' His voice trailed away helplessly.

'War makes men crazy, Hawkins.' Corrigan shrugged and flipped his cigarette away. In the background the shooting came to an end, and that crazy thirst for blood which had possessed the young men like a madness seemed to be satisfied at last. Suddenly they stood there limply, weapons hanging from nerveless hands, gasping for breath, staring at each other open-mouthed, eyes blank and bewildered.

'Did you notice their uniforms?' Corrigan asked, jerking his thumb at the bodies sprawled extravagantly in the dirt.

Hawkins stared, frowning, at the camouflaged overalls of the nearest German, a blond giant hardly a day over eighteen. 'Of course, sir,' he exclaimed, 'the SS!'

'Exactly. The brigadier's "Baby Division" has already arrived at the front... Some babies, eh?' He pulled on his helmet again and slung the rifle more comfortably across his broad back. 'Come on, Hawkins, let's get the hell out of here before the rest of the Babies arrive, eh? Somehow or other, I don't think they'll take to us – not after this...'

# THREE: THE GRENADIERS

# ONE

Caen was about to die.

All day long on June 6th, a thousand British bombers had pounded the French coastal city. Followed that night by five hundred American Flying Fortresses. On the second day the bombardment had started all over again. Now there were thousands of dying and wounded people trapped under the smoking ruins of the ancient cathedral city, and the Tommies were coming in yet again for another one-thousand-bomber raid.

As they raced to reach the city before the bombing started, the men in the swaying, camouflaged half-track were conscious of something sinister yet majestic about the scene. The sky was already an electric blue, for over Caen the sun had vanished. But the bombers stretching all the way back to England were still glinting in the sunlight, and the metal of their fuselages twinkling like fairy lights.

'Christmas trees!' Obersturmbannführer Bremer yelled above the roar of the half-track's engine, as Pavel, hunched over the wheel like a racing-driver, sent the big vehicle hurtling down the dead-straight road at Caen. 'The pathfinders are dropping *Christmas trees!*'

Everywhere the marker-flares were sinking down in slow cascades of golden rain, while here and there the first flak guns took up the challenge, spotting the blue sky with puffs of black smoke.

Pavel flashed his officer a broad smile that exposed his stainless steel false teeth. 'I shit on Tommies!' he cried in his thick Russian accent. 'I shit on them, Obersturm!'

Bremer rubbed his heavy unshaven jaw and then pulled his helmet down hard, ready for what was to come. 'You poor ignorant Popov swine, you don't know this of course, but a thousand years ago a Frog-eater named William set off from Caen to invade the Tommies' fogbound, miserable island. The Tommies have long memories. Now they're coming to Caen to pay the Frog-eaters back.'

Pavel lifted one buttock from the leather seat and let rip a tremendous fart. 'Arsehole up!' he yelled. 'Three cheers for England!'

Laughing uproariously, Bremer clapped his driver hard on his skinny hunched shoulder. 'That's the spirit, Pavel,' he cried, and then, as the first wave of bombers started to drone into the attack, 'Step on it, Pavel... *Davai, davai – here come the Tommies!*'

Vicious spurts of purple flame erupted from

the shattered buildings on all sides. Weakened houses collapsed in a slither of falling masonry. Men and women, screaming frantically, ran to and fro, vainly trying to escape from the merciless bombing. Everywhere the dead littered the streets. Blood bubbled down the gutters. Horses, eyes wide with panic, broke loose and clattered wildly up and down the cobbled streets, manes and tails a blazing fiery red. Shrapnel, red-hot and as big as a man's fist, smashed against the sides of the roaring half-tracked vehicle as it careened down the blazing streets of the dying city. Pavel swinging the 8-ton monster from side to side, missing bomb craters and exploding bombs by a hair's breadth.

At a hair-raising speed they swerved round the corner into the *Rue de l'Abbaye,* following the black and white signs to the HQ of the 716th Division. To their front, the burning houses swayed back and forth under the impact of the bombs like stage sets, showering the faces of the men with fiery-red sparks and grey ash. Bodies lay everywhere, some catapulted into the trees by the tremendous blast and hanging there like grotesque human fruit. A fire-engine was halted by the kerb, its engine still running; its crew had been suffocated by the heat and now sat naked and dead in their seats, helmets still perched on their yellow skulls. A one-legged man was whimpering in the gutter, dragging along another with no arms.

Bremer whistled softly through his front teeth. *'Himmel, Arsch und Wolkenbruch,* Pavel,' he cursed, 'I could castrate those Tommy bastards up there! Slowly – and with a blunt razorblade!'

Pavel nodded, unable to speak. He was staring ahead at a group of wounded from the military hospital who were hopping barefoot in the hissing embers, supporting themselves as best they could with crutches, spades, bars, and screaming, screaming, screaming...

'...My soldiers entered the battle in low spirits,' the general was saying in a shaky voice, as Obersturmbannführer Bremer forced himself into the crowded, swaying cellar, lit by a handful of flickering yellow candles. Pushing his way through the gloom, he finally spotted his chief, Colonel Kurt Meyer, otherwise known as 'Panzermeyer', and sat down beside him. Meanwhile at the other end of the cellar, the beaten general continued his tale of woe.

'...It was the enemy's enormous material superiority,' he went on. 'The men kept asking, where are our planes? Where are our tanks? Where are our heavy guns? They felt helpless. What could they do against this overwhelming superiority in machines and material?' The aged general dabbed at the corner of his wet eyes, while his weary, unshaven staff officers looked on in sympathy, nodding their agreement.

Bremer flashed Panzermeyer a quick look.

His chief nodded. He had realised it, too. Not only was the 716th Infantry Division defending the coast north of Caen just about at the end of its tether, but so was its Commanding Officer. As far as the coming battle was concerned, they could be written off.

Colonel Kurt Meyer of the Waffen SS touched his hand casually to his battered cap with its tarnished silver skull-and-crossbones, and stood up to speak.

'Meyer, 25th Panzergrenadier Regiment, 12th SS Panzer Division, sir – reporting,' he barked, deciding that the time had now come to end the general's painful catalogue of excuses and apologies.

The aged general blinked his watery eyes as if startled by the SS man's intervention, but Meyer gave him no chance to ask questions. He knew that every minute counted if the 716th's front was not to crumple altogether. 'Sir, may I pay you and your brave soldiers a compliment from the 12th SS? You have fought courageously and in the highest traditions of the Greater German Wehrmacht.'

Bremer smiled to himself. Panzermeyer was really laying it on with a trowel for the

171

old fool. Evidently he wanted rid of him and his senile staff as quickly as possible. Now he, too, rose and introduced himself. 'Obersturmbannführer Bremer, 25th Panzergrenadier,' he rapped out, then bowed respectfully to the general. 'My driver, an Ivan named Pavel and a well-known slit-ear of long standing, has liberated a case of finest Frog Champagne. I wonder if I could offer it to you and your staff as a token of the SS's admiration and gratitude for your spirited defence against overwhelming odds?'

It did the trick. The faces of the staff officers lit up, and the general positively beamed. 'I say, that is extremely decent of you, my dear Bremer – extremely!'

The big SS man with the Knight's Cross at his throat and decorations from five years of war emblazoned on his chest, wasted no further time. 'Pavel!' he cried, as the cellar swayed alarmingly under the impact of another Tommy thousand-pounder landing close by. 'Davai your Russki arse, and see that these high-born gentlemen receive their bubbly – at the double!'

*'Phew!'* Panzermeyer breathed out hard and pushed his battered cap to the back of his shaven skull. 'What a mess! What a shitting mess!'

Bremer grinned at the look on his chief's

dark saturnine face. 'Beware of strange women, shadowy doorways and quiet streets,' he intoned, reciting the old litany they both knew so well: 'Dark nights are dangerous, don't walk alone!'

Now it was Panzermeyer's turn to grin. 'The trees glow clubs – wear your helmet!'

'While there is a roof for a stone to fall from, watch your step!'

'Buy combs, children,' Bremer roared, 'there's–'

*'Lousy times ahead!'* Panzermeyer bellowed; and with that they fell into each other's arms, pounding one another on the back, each overcome with delight at seeing the other alive after the hellish journey to Caen and the new battle.

'All right,' Panzermeyer snapped a few moments later, as they crouched in the swaying cellar, studying the map spread out across the top of a ration crate. 'The 716th is washed out and the general has got his pants full, that's obvious.'

'So?'

'So, as always, the SS will have to pull the Army's chestnuts out of the fire. But this time, Gerd,' Panzermeyer added significantly, 'we won't be commanding our old hairy-arsed vets from the Russian front. This time we go into action with boys who've still got the eggshell behind their ears and have never heard a shot fired in anger. A bunch of greenbeaks, in other words.'

Another bomb landed close by and the candles flickered crazily, their enormously magnified shadows performing a wild dance on the quivering wall behind them.

'But they're good boys,' Bremer said stoutly.

'I know they are. I've the utmost confidence in them, Gerd, but until they're properly blooded, I'm not taking any risks with them. You see, we're fighting a new element here – something we never had to contend with in Popovland: enemy air superiority. The moment you stick your head up here in Normandy, the enemy *Jabos* are on to you in an instant, ready to saw your arse off in zero-comma-nothing-seconds.'

'You can say that again, Panzermeyer,' Bremer said ruefully, remembering his own nightmarish trip into Caen. 'Orders?'

'Orders?' Panzermeyer echoed, a hard gleam in his dark, determined eyes. 'As always in the SS, Gerd: march to the sound of the guns!'

'But where?'

'There are two spots. First, we've had an unconfirmed report that the Tommies have broken through somewhere along the Periers Ridge. Second, it's been confirmed that the Canadians 3rd Infantry Division has broken through the 716th's front in strength near here.' He stabbed the map with his forefinger. 'Do you see?'

Bremer nodded. 'They're nearly on to the Caen-Bayeux road.'

'Correct. Their objective is obviously the airfield at Carpiquet – which, conveniently enough for them, has been hurriedly vacated by the gallant gentlemen of the Greater German Luftwaffe.' The bitterness in Panzermeyer's voice was audible.

Bremer shrugged his broad shoulders. 'You know the flyboys, Panzermeyer. What would they be without their eau-de-cologne and field mattresses. You wouldn't have them dirtying their lily-white hands with anything so common as ground combat, would you?'

Panzermeyer forced a grin and looked up at the younger man. 'All right, arse with ears, what's it going to be – Tommies or Canadians?'

Bremer pretended to consider. 'I've already played one game against the Tommies back in '40 – and won. I think I'll try the Canadians this time. *Immer was Neues.* Maybe I'll improve my score this time.'

'As you wish, Gerd,' Panzermeyer snapped urgently, dark eyes now gleaming with that fanatical energy that would soon make him the youngest general in the Waffen SS. 'Then stop them, cost what it may, while I bring up the rest of the Division tonight. But watch those infernal enemy *Jabos*, Gerd.' His voice softened for an instant, 'and watch *yourself*, old horse. If you cop it, I won't have anyone left to drink with in the mess of an evening. These young officers only drink milk! *Nun los!*'

Bremer touched his big paw to his helmet and then had disappeared into the burning night. The 'Babies' of the 12th Hitler Youth SS Panzer Division were going into action for the first time.

## TWO

Like a timid metallic beetle, the Canadian armoured car emerged from the morning mist. Engine labouring under the strain, it mounted the embankment, clattering on to the silent, empty road, then stopped, its aerial whipping back and forth. The only sound now was the soft whisper of the morning breeze in the trees and the low rumble of the vehicle's engine.

'Stand fast, boys,' whispered Bremer, concealed a few hundred yards away across a field. 'The Canuck's trying us out.'

Carefully shading the top of his binoculars in case they glinted and gave away the positions of his men and vehicles dug in along the Bayeux-Caen highway, Bremer viewed the lone enemy armoured car. It was so exposed, so vulnerable – *and so awfully tempting, Gerd,* whispered the taunting inner voice that was always with him these days.

The lone Canadian gunned his engine loudly. Through his glasses, Bremer could see the clouds of thick, blue smoke against the grey of the mist. Still the armoured car did not move. It was a provocation, he knew, a deliberate one, a tempting of the Fates.

'Just keep cool, boys,' he said softly, 'he doesn't know we're here... He's trying it on.'

On both sides of him in the dry ditch, he could hear the controlled regular breathing of his 'Babies'. Once again he felt a glow of pride. The greenbeaks' fire discipline was tremendous, well worthy of their prede-cessors, dead these many years in the deep snows of Russia. 'Unblooded' they might be, and still wet behind the spoons, but they were behaving like hardened veterans.

Down the road the hatch-covers of that lone armoured car had been flung open and a figure in khaki now appeared in the turret. He was standing there bolt upright. Bremer shook his head in admiration. Whoever that Canadian was, he was a brave bastard. He deserved to survive what was soon to come. But of course, he would not. Nor would his comrades...

Apparently satisfied, the Canadian officer muttered something into his chest-mike, unaware that some eight hundred pairs of hard blue eyes were focused upon him, then, with a grunt, the Humber armoured car began rolling forward again along the road to Caen. Moments later, its twin breasted the rise, followed by a rattling half-track packed with infantry.

Bremer grinned happily. 'They've bought it, lads,' he whispered. 'Come on, my lucky Canadians: walk right into the trap... Mother spider's waiting to gobble you up.' Hurriedly, he hissed into his mike, *'Tiger One... Tiger Two... Tiger Three... Ready for my signal... Fire at will...'*

Now, Sherman after Sherman was emerging from the woods and clattering up on to the road, with a roaring of engines and squealing of tracks, blue petrol smoke pouring from their exhausts. It was an anti-tank gunners' dream: they were packed together on a narrow high-banked road without a patch of cover, moving unsuspectingly right across the front of Bremer's battalion, exposing a long, unprotected flank. Not even a blind, one-armed cripple with the shakes could have missed them. Gleefully, Bremer raised the pistol, ready to signal the start of the slaughter.

With a faint gasp, he pulled the trigger. There was a soft plop. A hiss. A flare went sailing into the grey morning. A crack. Then Bremer's upturned face was bathed a sickly, unnatural green.

In an instant all hell broke loose. The hysterical hiss of the Spandaus. The stomach-jerking spasm of recoiling anti-tank guns. The thick plop of the mortars. The sharp, dry, throaty crack of the Panzerfaust.

The Canadians packed on the road two hundred yards away were caught completely by surprise. A Canadian truck was hit just above the engine and exploded in a mad roar, the force of it ripping apart metal, canvas, human flesh. Men tumbled on to the road, picked themselves up and started to belt blindly down the road, dodging and weaving as shells exploded all around them. Bremer raised his machine pistol. He squeezed the trigger almost lovingly. The little Schmeisser slammed against his hip, leaping instantly into life.

A Canadian was hit in mid-stride; next instant he flopped down, his tortured body writhing in its death throes. Another went down – and another. A sergeant, three neat, white stripes on his sleeve, fell to his knees, hands clasped to the grey heavens as if pleading for mercy.

But no mercy came this morning. Sherman after Sherman shuddered to a violent, slewing stop as the shells slammed into them, bursting into flames and spilling their flame-wreathed crews out on to the road to be slaughtered by the machine-guns.

Suddenly a frenzied scream interrupted

Bremer as he mowed down the escaping Canadians with his Schmeisser.

*'Tommy Cooker at three o'clock!'*

Bremer swung round. A lone Sherman had broken away from the rest, smoke pouring from its ruptured engine, and was rumbling down the embankment, heading straight at them.

*'Pak!'* he yelled.

But already his young gunners, faces greased with sweat beneath their camouflaged helmets, were swinging their 57mm cannon round to meet the unexpected challenge.

At a tremendous rate the lone Canadian tank hurtled across the field towards them, flinging up huge clods of earth and grass from its flying tracks, its 75mm cannon coming round to bear on the ambushers.

But the young anti-tank gunners were quicker. The gun-layer pressed his eye to the rubber suction-pad. His cross-wires sliced the racing Sherman in half. He waited no longer. Madly he snatched the firing bar and the gun heaved up like a live thing. Yellow flame shot from the muzzle. For an instant Bremer closed his eyes and gasped for breath as he felt himself buffeted about the face by the blast. Then he looked up to see the Sherman reeling to a halt. Smoke – thick, white and blinding – was pouring upwards from its suddenly open turret,

180

ascending in a great white ring...

The death of that lone Sherman seemed to signal an end to further resistance on the part of the surprised Canadians. Everywhere the infantry broke, racing back into the woods from which they came, or throwing away their weapons and raising their hands in surrender. Several tanks smashed into each other in their panic-stricken attempts to get away. Others simply fell over the drop and lay there, tracks flailing uselessly, like inverted metallic beetles. Here and there tank commanders ordered their drivers to stop and raised their hands, faces suddenly grey and apprehensive.

*'Cease fire... Cease fire... Will you wet-tails stop firing this instant!'*

Barked commands were issued up and down the German firing line. Here and there a red-faced noncom lent urgency to his order with a swift kick in the ribs as some jubilant young grenadier continued to fire into the helpless, trapped Canadians. *'Can't you bloody well see they've had it? Cease fire!'*

Bremer, his broad face lit up with emotion, swung round on the little Russian who had once been his prisoner but was now his servant and confidant. 'Great God in Heaven, Pavel!' he cried, eyes gleaming madly, big hands outstretched to embrace the terrible scene before him. 'Could anything be more magnificent? Compared with war, surely all other forms of human endeavour shrink into total insignificance.'

Towering above the little Russian with his stainless steel smile, he screamed exultantly, *'God, how I love it!'*

'The fucking rotten bleeders!' cried one of the troopers, as the heavily camouflaged vehicles of the German grenadiers began to pull out from their ambush positions, leaving behind the Canadian dead and the wrecked smoking tanks. 'They didn't give them a chance,' he sobbed brokenly. 'It was a sodding massacre!'

'Oh, put a sock in it, will yer, mate,' said Wolfers.

Slim Sanders, crouched next to him in the woods overlooking the scene of the ambush, smiled approvingly. The kid was learning.

Sergeant Hawkins gazed interrogatively at Corrigan's face, but it revealed nothing. Hawkins willed him to make some comment, some angry outburst at the way the poor Canadians had been slaughtered down there on the road. But none came. Instead Corrigan said simply, 'All right, you can tell the men they can brew up now, Hawkins.'

Dutifully Hawkins repeated the order. Soon the assault troopers, fast becoming hardened to the horrors of war, forgot the slaughtered Canadians and attended to their stomachs. Several began to pull the little petrol 'Tommy Cookers' down from the half-tracks. Others started to lug down the wooden compo ration crates and pull out tins of bully, 'M and V' stew, fruit cocktail, ripping open the lids with their jack-knives. As always someone cracked the age-old joke: *'Which tin's got the cunt in, mates?'*

Corrigan watched their dirty young faces as they squatted around the hissing blue flames, frying slabs of corned beef on the ends of their bayonets, stirring the compo tea mix, greedily munching the hard tack biscuits; then he turned to Hawkins. 'Come on, your lads can look after themselves for the time being. We'll have a look-see at the Canucks.'

In silence they walked down the wooded hillside, no sound now evident, save the hum of the flies and the faint, dull rumble of guns from the beachhead. They might well have been two tourists taking a summer stroll.

They came to the road. The wrecked Shermans lay everywhere, huge gleaming steel gouges carved in their sides, broken tracks trailing behind them like severed limbs. 'Poor buggers,' Hawkins commented softly, staring at a group of Canadians caught in a desperate attempt to set up a machine-gun and now frozen like some hideous waxwork tableau at Madame Tussaud's.

'Fools – bloody innocent fools,' Corrigan grunted, taking his gaze from the dead Canadian machine-gunner, whose glassy eyes were already rimmed with buzzing bluebottles, and staring along the barrel of the Vickers. 'They walked right into it. Where was their flank guard?' He flung out his right hand angrily. 'Anyway, at least this business will take the pressure off us.'

'What do you mean, sir?' Hawkins asked, noting with distaste that that rotten little Aussie bastard Sanders was already at work further up the column, looting the dead. He stared up at Corrigan's hard, unshaven face, narrowing his eyes against the first rays of the sun which were now slanting obliquely through the dawn mist.

'Well, you know the Jerries. Now that they think they've blunted the point of our attack and brought it to a stop, they'll launch an immediate counter-attack while we're still off-balance. Though–' he paused, indicating the silver 'V' of a flight of Thunderbolts winging their way eastwards towards the German positions '–it might not be all *that* immediate while we've still got air supremacy.'

'But how will it affect us, sir?' Hawkins asked.

Up ahead, Sanders was now kneeling at the side of a dead Canadian officer and prising open his jaw with a bayonet; Hawkins knew why. The cruel little bugger had spotted the man's gold teeth; he was going to yank them out!

Corrigan paused, considering.

'Well, the Jerries know we're here somewhere; but as long as we don't worry them, they won't worry us. They'll be too busy with the big counter-attack. So let's assume that this is the line of our main positions at this moment.' With the toe of his boot, he drew a line in the dust of the road. 'And this is the River Orne.' He sketched in another line. 'I'd expect old Jerry to hit our main positions with the Orne here to his right, and try to roll them up. That way they can give us another splendid victory like the one we had at Dunkirk.' He gave a sly wink at the little sergeant, who, as Corrigan well knew, was a Dunkirk veteran himself.

Hawkins grinned. 'You're pulling my pisser, sir, ain't yer?'

Corrigan returned his grin. 'Sort of,' he admitted. Then he grew serious again. 'Well, while they're trying to throw us back into the sea, I plan to cross the Orne and link up with the paras of the Sixth Airborne – in other words, to complete the job that we were sent to France to do. Then, if the Sixth's commanding general so wishes, I recce the roads for the paras right into Caen itself. With the Jerries concentrating their strength elsewhere for the big counter-attack, it should be wide open. We *could* catch them with their knickers right down about their ankles. But we've got to do it *quick* – before Jerry can react to the new threat!'

Hawkins whistled his admiration. 'That really is something, sir. It'd make all this balls-up' – he indicated the Canadian corpses '–worthwhile. At least in a way they'll have achieved something–'

'*Sir!*' A loud cry from the hilltop suddenly broke into the sergeant's words. Both he and Corrigan looked up and saw Wolfers, standing silhouetted against the sun, hands cupped to his mouth.

'It's the CO, sir... He's on net... Wants to talk to you urgently!' Wolfers' voice boomed and re-echoed around the circle of wooded hills, while Corrigan and Hawkins stared at each other. Then Hawkins said, 'Christ Almighty, sir! I'd forgotten all about the Regiment.'

Corrigan nodded glumly. He realised that authority, slow, careful and ponderous, had caught up with him and the Assault Troop again; and he did not like the idea one bit.

Corrigan squatted in the baking-hot half-track, the sweat running down his face under the headphones, while the radio operator fiddled with his dials.

Not far away, just off the beaches, a furious tank battle was now raging, and the air was full of static and frantic calls: '*Dog Sunray here... For God's sake, spread out! You're bunching too much... Hello Roger Baker, I've been hit ... I repeat, hit... For Chrissake, where's hornet support... Hornet support... The fucking eighty-eights are pulverising us...'*

As he sat there, listening to the excited flurry of messages and counter-messages, Corrigan knew that everything was going wrong. It was just as he had feared all along. After all that waiting and all those years of training, the invasion forces simply had not had the push and drive to move out of the beachhead quickly enough before the Germans had recovered from the surprise of the landing. Now they were paying the price. The picture of those young blond giants slaughtering the Canadians on the road below flashed through his mind, and his frown deepened. Perhaps his joking reference to another 'Victory' at Dunkirk might not be so far-fetched after all. The Germans could still fling them out of Europe yet, unless they started moving soon.

'Hello, Sunray here... Sunray here.' Suddenly Major Stirling's fruity, affected voice cut into his reverie, he was coming over loud and clear, and undistorted by the static.

Hurriedly Corrigan acknowledged and reported his position.

As soon as Stirling had acknowledged back, his pent-up rage burst through. 'My God, man,' he cried, 'what in hell's name do you think you've been playing at, eh?'

At that moment Corrigan could visualise him at the other end; his silly solicitor's face crimson with fury, slashing down his fly-whisk on to the top of the khaki-covered radio set.

'What do you mean, Sunray?' he asked coolly.

He could hear Stirling gasp for air. 'You damned well know what I mean, Charlie One!' Stirling exploded. 'Disobeying an order, misappropriating WD property, abandoning a designated position... God Almighty – don't you know they could shoot you for that? It's classed as desertion while under fire!'

Corrigan remained unmoved. 'I've never yet heard of anyone being court-marshalled for "deserting" to the front, Sunray.'

Stirling spluttered with rage, lost for words. 'My God, Charlie One, you're an insolent bastard!' Then conscious that he might be overheard, perhaps by senior officers – he seemed to recover control. 'Now listen to me, Charlie One – and listen carefully. You will abandon your present position and return to map reference' Slowly and carefully, Stirling started to spell out the figures, obviously making a deter-mined effort to stay cool.

Corrigan sat there motionless, while the young tousle-haired radio operator stared at him in bewilderment; he knew that something was going on that might well change his life, but was unable to bring any influence to bear.

'Did you get that?' Stirling rasped.

Corrigan remained silent. As he sat there in the back of the littered half-track, his face was impassive, revealing nothing; but his mind was racing. He had had just about as much as he could take.

'Sunray speaking,' Stirling repeated. 'Did you hear me, Charlie One?'

Corrigan gulped, then went ahead. 'I heard you, Sunray,' he said quite calmly.

'Good. Then the password of the day is—'

'I don't need any password,' Corrigan interrupted. 'Besides, it wouldn't be too clever to give it over the air, Sunray. Jerry is listening in to this net, too, you know.'

'Why you arrogant—' Once more Stirling exploded, so overcome by rage now that he forgot all wireless procedure. 'What do you mean, you don't need a password?'

'Because, Sunray, I'm not coming back.'

*'Not coming back!* But you must be out of your mind... My God, man, I've given you a direct order. If you refuse, you're for the high jump... It's a court-martial offence...'

'Listen, Stirling, you pompous shit!' Corrigan hissed, suddenly overcome by a white-hot rage at the sheer, crass incompetence of the fool at the other end and

189

others like him who had been wasting men's lives for nothing. 'I'm going to do the job I was sent over here to do, and a whole bloody brigade-full of people like you won't stop me. *Now fuck off!*'

There was a strangled metallic squawk from Stirling as Corrigan ripped off the headphones and flung them to the floor of the half-track. 'Stand back, operator!' he cried at the bewildered boy, who immediately flew out of the way in alarm.

Corrigan did not hesitate. He grabbed the nearest sten and clicked off the safety catch. Mad with rage, he clasped the little machine pistol to his right hip and pressed the trigger. A stream of slugs slammed into the radio set, cutting off Stirling in mid-cry.

For one long moment Corrigan stood there, his face set in a wild lupine grimace, while on all sides the surprised troopers came running towards the half-track to see what the shooting was all about.

'All right, sir?' Hawkins gasped, staring up at Corrigan's contorted face in bewilderment.

Suddenly Corrigan relaxed. 'Never felt better,' he cried enthusiastically. He tossed the sten to the now ashen-faced radio operator cowering to one side. 'Here, take this. You'll need it now.'

He turned to Hawkins. 'All right, Hawkins, you've got yourself a new assault trooper. Now, what the devil are you standing there for like a fart in a trance? Let's get moving. I want to be across the Orne by this night... *Move it!'*

## THREE

'Roadblock!' Sanders hissed, parting the trees and peering down at the silver snake of the River Orne below.

'Bollocks!' Sergeant Hawkins cursed softly. This was the third roadblock or dug-in 88mm cannon which they had come across in the last two hours. It seemed as if every time they ventured out of the wooded banks overlooking the river, they had stumbled almost immediately into the German defences.

Hawkins settled down next to Sanders and Wolfers and peered through the foliage at the big cannon dug in at the side of the road. German infantry were clearly visible, squatting in their foxholes to the left and right, beneath the cover of the Bocage hedge. Beyond the ruined bridge which spanned the river was a shattered jeep, both of its front wheels gone, and in it were three dead paratroopers, sitting bolt upright, their faces black and swollen, looking like rotten cabbage stumps in an abandoned allotment.

'They were a bit slow on the uptake, Sarge,' said Wolfers, crunching on the ration biscuits with which his pockets always seemed to be filled. 'Thought them paras were supposed to be quicker off the mark than that.'

Hawkins did not answer. But again he was amazed at how quickly his boys had become hardened, brutalised by the war. Was this the same kid who had sobbed and moaned when he had seen the frightful casualties he had inflicted with the flame-thrower that first morning?

Hawkins surveyed the German positions along the little road leading to the river, set between thorn hedges, thick with white flowers, and dug in the rich, lush fields. From here they could cover not only the other bank, where the wrecked Sixth Airborne jeep stood, but also the ground to their rear. A Spandau machine-gun was dug in to the rear of the 88mm, and it covered nearly a hundred yards of open fields leading up to the fearsome cannon.

'We don't stand a cat's chance in hell of rushing that popgun,' Sanders said, seeming to read the old noncom's thoughts. 'Not in daylight, at least. The bleeders'd cut us to pieces.'

'We've got the half-tracks, Slim,' Wolfers objected, mouth full of crushed biscuits.

'So?' Slim sneered. 'As soon as the Jerries spot 'em, they'll have that bleeding gun round at the double. We'd be dead ducks before you could say Jack Robinson.'

'Shut up, will you?' Hawkins snapped in irritation. 'I can't hear myself bloody think with you two goin' on like a couple of bloody housewives.'

Wolfers shut up immediately. In spite of his new hardness, he still had a great deal of respect for Sergeant Hawkins; he knew just how much he cared for his men. Slim, however, muttered under his breath: 'Yes, sir, and a thousand arseholes bent and took the strain, for in them days the word of the king was law!'

Hawkins stared down at the river again. In another hour the sun would begin to set, and the CO had expressly ordered him and his patrol to report back before darkness, so that they could plan the crossing of the River Orne well in advance. For there were not only Germans to contend with, there were also – so Corrigan guessed – trigger-happy paras on the other side of the river who were liable to shoot first and ask questions afterwards. What was he going to do? Was it worth pushing on further in the hope of finding an unguarded crossing or ford?

'Sarge.' It was Sanders, and this time his voice was urgent.

'What is it?' Hawkins hissed, suddenly alarmed.

'There's somebody coming ... back on us.'

Hawkins acted instinctively. He drew back inside the bushes, and clicked the safety off his Tommy-gun. 'Freeze!' he urged, as the other two did the same.

A line of sweating, cursing men were struggling down the hillside, their rifles slung, camouflaged capes draped over their shoulders, twigs tucked into their helmets. Each man was loaded down with cans of gas or lugging heavy wooden boxes of what had to be small-arms ammunition.

Hawkins held his breath. Beside him, he could hear the big Yorkshire lad's knuckles creak as they tensed around the butt of his weapon. Then his nostrils picked up that characteristic stink of German black tobacco and human sweat.

*'Scheiss' Stoppelhopser,'* a voice grumbled, *'wat woollen die mit soviel Munition?'*

Hawkins could almost have reached out and touched the man who had complained, but he knew instinctively that these men posed no real threat: they were too exhausted, and too angry at the flies which buzzed around their crimson, sweat-lathered faces. Five minutes later, the last of them had staggered past, and the three troopers relaxed, watching them continue down to the gun, to be greeted with good-humoured catcalls from the bored gunners and riflemen dug in there.

Hawkins sat back on his heels and watched the Germans dump their loads. 'Blood cushy number, eh, Sanders,' he commented to the skinny little Australian. 'They're either very new to the front or they couldn't care less. Bringing up supplies at this time of the day in broad daylight! They soddin' well deserve to get a packet–' Just then he stopped short, noticing that Sanders was not listening. 'Well?' he grunted. 'A penny for them, yer cunning sod.'

'I was just thinking, Sarge, that's all,' the Australian said cautiously.

'Thinking what?'

'Jerry peasoup ain't bad, Sarge. And some-times they put a nice bit of belly pork in it – or one of them spicy garlic sausages…'

'What the hell are you talkin' about, Aussie? Has the bleeding sun gone to yer head or something? Trying to swing yer ticket, kidding me that yer dolalli? I wouldn't put it past yer, yer sly little bugger.'

'Ner, nothing like that, Sarge. I was just thinking aloud, that's all.'

'They can take yer away for that, yer knows – in a rubber wagon,' Hawkins said darkly.

'Go on, Sarge,' Wolfers said, his interest suddenly kindled by the mention of pea-soup and belly pork. 'Give him a chance,

195

Slim's a smart one, yer know.' He looked eagerly at his running mate.

Sanders took his time; he always liked being the centre of attention. 'Well, mates, I can tell yer, looking at the distance to that eighty-eight and all that space with no cover to hide yersen in, I felt like that proverbial whale off the coast of Aussie, that spends most of its time at the bottom of the ocean. Well, mates, I felt a bleedin' sight lower than that whale's arse – until I saw them blokes of the fatigue party. And then I had it.'

'Had what?' Hawkins snapped.

Slim looked at him, a smile on his cunning face. 'How we was goin' to get within sniffin' distance of that eighty-eight, Sarge.' He winked knowingly. 'That's all.'

A thin, cool mist was beginning to waft in from the river. Silently, it curled around the troopers as they lay among the trees, tense, expectant, straining their ears for the slightest sound. Down below, the Germans had 'stood down' before darkness fell, and were now chatting softly in little groups, smoking their last cigarettes before turning in for the night.

Corrigan looked at his watch once again. The German fatigue men bringing up the defenders' evening meal should be here soon – that is, assuming the men were going to be fed before nightfall. Already the dark shadows were beginning to sweep across the damp fields from the west. In another thirty minutes or so, it would be night.

The minutes ticked by, and the mist began to thicken, sneaking in between the trees like a silent grey cat. Soon it had all but covered the ground.

Hawkins nudged Corrigan.

Corrigan was caught off-guard. He jumped, startled. 'What is it?' he hissed angrily.

Hawkins jerked a thumb to the rear. 'Listen, sir.'

Muted by the mist, Corrigan could now hear the muffled snort of a tired horse. He stiffened and listened harder: yes, there it was again – *and* the faint jingle of a harness, the metal parts wrapped in sacking to deaden the noise.

'Stand by,' he hissed urgently, 'pass it on!'

In an excited whisper the order was passed from man to man. As they lay there in the damp bushes, their nerves were suddenly tingling with excitement. Soon it was going to happen – but it had to happen noiselessly. If the Germans were alerted, that fearsome 88mm cannon would pound them into little bits as they made their escape up the steep hill.

Now the first German fatigue-man came into view – and another. Behind them an ancient nag appeared, head bent wearily under the load of hayboxes perched on its skinny flanks.

Hurriedly Corrigan began to count. Surely they could hear the exited breathing of the men lying there, waiting to trap them? Six of them in all. Good. They could deal with that number – so long as nothing alerted them beforehand.

On and on they plodded unsuspectingly, like men who had done this job often enough before and expected to do it for a long time to come: born victims, the lot of them: shabby, middle-aged men, no good for the firing line, but cannonfodder for all that.

Now they were almost at the top of the rise, feet wreathed in mist as if they were wading through cottonwool. Twin streams of white spurted from the ancient nag's distended nostrils at each step.

Next to Slim, Wolfers raised his big, ugly head and sniffed the evening air. 'You was right, Slim,' he whispered joyously, saliva dripping down his chin in anticipation, 'it's peasoup!'

'Shut up!' the little Australian hissed tensely, knife gripped tightly in a wet hand. 'You and your bleedin' stomach!'

Now the leading man – a sergeant, judging by his collar insignia – was passing the lone poplar to the right of the track. It was the signal they had agreed upon. Hawkins whistled, once, twice, three times.

The sergeant's head slowly came up. He paused, puzzled by the sound, just as Corrigan had hoped he would be. Behind him, the others did the same, and one of them jerked cruelly at the nag's bridle to halt him as well. Immediately the skinny-ribbed horse began to crop the long grass. *'Was ist los, Dieter?'* someone called, but there was no alarm in the voice, just curiosity.

Corrigan took a deep breath and sprang to his feet. The fatigue-men turned, startled. The old nag reared up in alarm and one of the hayboxes fell to the ground. Its lid dropped off. Suddenly the air was full of the odour of thick peasoup. 'Bugger that for a tale!' Wolfers cried in alarm, and kicked the sergeant in the crotch. He went down without a sound, yellow false teeth bulging stupidly from his mouth as he lay sprawled full-length in the mist.

Slim Sanders sprang out, face set in a wolfish grimace. A heavy-set fatigue-man fumbled madly for his rifle. He never had a chance. Sanders pulled the German to him in an embrace of death, and viciously plunged his knife into the fat man's belly. With a gasp, heaving violently as that red blade went in and out, as if in throes of sexual ecstasy.

Hawkins stumbled and dropped his sten. The nag reared up again and lashed out with its hind legs. With a yelp of pain, Hawkins was hurled backwards with the force of the kick. Suddenly garlic-breath enveloped him. Ham-like fists wrapped themselves around his neck and his nostrils were assailed by the stink of the kitchen. Pressed up close to him, the big German grunted in triumph as he cruelly thrust his knee into Hawkins' back and exerted pressure.

Black and red stars exploded in front of the little sergeant's eyes as he writhed back and forth, desperately trying to break that vice-like grip, clawing vainly at the German's arm.

Now Hawkins was starting to sag, his knees beginning to give way. The German laughed triumphantly.

It was the last thing the German ever did. Dimly, Hawkins heard Wolfers' broad, angry Yorkshire voice behind him. Then there was the solid thud of a big fist slamming into the German's face. Next instant, Hawkins had fallen to his knees, sobbing for breath, while next to him, an enraged Wolfers systematically crushed in the German's face with his steel-shod heel.

A minute later it was all over, and Wolfers and the rest were digging their canteens into thick green soup. Sanders meanwhile set about looting the bodies, but he found little of value. 'Rotten thieving sods,' he muttered in disgust. 'Typical lousy cooks...'

Slowly the ration party plodded towards the waiting gunners at the German line, taking their pace from the nag, which seemed curiously frisky this particular evening. This, however, was not surprising, for its hayboxes were empty and the big soldier guiding it, his stomach pleasantly full of hot peasoup, kept breaking wind.

'*Na endlich*,' called the infantryman. '*Was gibt's heute abend?* Nigger sweat and giddi-up soup, eh? The usual shit! I'll bet you kitchen-bulls steal all the good stuff...'

'*Ja, Ja,*' mumbled the little man leading the fatigue party, head bent low as if searching for something on the ground.

Now most of the crew of the massive 88mm were leaving their camouflaged perches and unbuckling their canteens in preparation for the highpoint of their boring day: a taste of good hot food, and, if they were lucky, a stiff shot of Schnapps afterwards. The little man at the head of the column held up his hand. The big soldier behind him tugged at the old nag's rein and started to fiddle with the straps of the hayboxes. Meanwhile the other fatigue-men turned their backs on the hungry infantry and gunners, who were now approaching with canteens at the ready.

A German officer, still elegant in spite of the long, hot day, pushed his way through the soldiers. 'Get a move on, you!' he called out angrily. 'It'll be dark soon… I say, didn't you hear me, Sergeant?' he added, addressing the tall, lean man with the stars of an Oberfeldwebel on his epaulettes. '*Himmel, Arsch und–*'

The angry cry died on his lips as he saw what the Sergeant held in his hands. He staggered back, holding his hands up in front of his face in a vain bid to protect himself.

Corrigan pressed the trigger and the sten chattered crazily at his side. The officer caught the full burst in his face and slammed against the nearest tree, his features dripping down from his shattered face like molten red wax. Next moment, the fatigue party had spun round and were blasting the Germans with a murderous hail of fire. The startled gunners went down on all sides, writhing and screaming, bodies peppered with red holes stitched there by that terrible rain of slugs. Crazily, the survivors fell back, clawing and jostling each other in their panic to escape. A gunner pelted for the 88mm. Slim Sanders fired from the hip. He screamed and clawed the air, as if climbing the rungs of an invisible ladder. Another flung himself behind the Spandau guarding the rear of the gun position. Hawkins snapped off a quick burst, but missed.

Frantically, the German flung up the butt

of the machine-gun and clicked home the catch. In an instant he would be pouring one thousand rounds a minute into the invaders. But it was not to be.

The first half-track burst from the trees. Going all out, it hurtled across the field, throwing up a great wild lake of clods and earth behind it. At fifty miles an hour it crashed into the gunner, crumpling him and his weapon beneath its flailing tracks. A moment later it clattered on to the road, its tracks a bright, gory red. Behind it, the severed arm of the crushed gunner was flopping up and down, caught in the works, as if waving a grisly farewell.

## FOUR

A shadow darted from beyond the trees: a giant of a man in a familiar helmet, the whites of his eyes gleaming in the moonlight. For a moment he stood there in the middle of the track, legs spread like a Western gunfighter, sten gun clutched to his hip. 'Hold it there, tosher,' he yelled to the driver of the half-track which had braked so hurriedly. 'And if yer think I'm alone, look to left and right. We can blow yer from here to hell and back.'

Corrigan grinned wearily. They had found the paras of the Sixth Airborne.

'Can't yer see yer talkin' to a fuckin' officer?' Sanders snarled from behind the wheel.

'Yer speak the lingo, at least, tosher,' the big paratrooper said. Then raising his voice, he called to his comrades, 'All right, mockers... They're ours.'

Suddenly the little convoy of assault troopers found themselves surrounded by shouting, laughing rogues in camouflaged tunics and red berets, most of whom stank to high heaven. It was quite a welcome. The paras handed the newcomers looted German cigars and bottles of Norman Calvados and reached up to slap them on the back, all the time asking where they had been all this time and what had happened to the rest of the fuckin' Kate Karney: Or were they going to let the fuckin' Sixth win the fuckin' war all by itself?

Finally, when he had managed to silence the excited chatter, Corrigan asked where he could find the commanding general.

'Old Guts and Gaiters?' they roared. 'Why, sir, where the old bugger always is ... *right up front!*'

And they were right. Half an hour later, after a nightmare journey through the shattered countryside, where dead paras still hung from their shroudlines in the high oaks and wrecked gliders dotted the fields like broken butterflies, they found General Gale, the commanding general of the Sixth Airborne Division. He was right in the thick of a fierce fire-fight, defending a farm against a German mortar position dug in somewhere in the apple orchards to the right of it.

Corrigan's heart sank when he saw the ramrod-straight general with his white horse and bushy white moustache. He was directing his infantry from horseback with jerks of his cane and swift, barked commands that drowned even the *thump-thump* of the German mortar. To Corrigan he looked every inch the typical Poona-style Colonel Blimp, unable to make a decision before receiving orders in triplicate from the War Office. But this time, Captain Corrigan was to be proved wrong.

The battle seemed to have died down now. Stretcher-bearers were plodding slowly across the churned-up ground, bringing in their burdens of misery. A German self-propelled gun was burning merrily in the paddock just outside the farm. Half a hundred yards away from it, a tall, bareheaded para in a dirty white apron was poised over a steaming dixie of tea, crying, 'Come on, me lucky lads! Come and get it! Real old sarn't-major's char! Take the lining off yer stomach, this will... Come and get it!'

Bewildered and bemused, Corrigan tamely followed the general as he dismounted from his horse and joined the queue of thirsty paras waiting for their share of the precious beverage. The paras, it seemed, took their battles very casually. There were still German snipers in the apple orchards, and from behind the farm a machine-gun was still pouring a stream of red tracer into the trees. This was causing an avalanche of yellow-green apples to fall on the panic-stricken cows which lumbered wildly back and forth with fear, bulging udders swinging madly in the garish red light.

'Hold it steady, sir,' the para cook ordered the burly general as he held out his mug. 'Sorry we ain't got no rum to tickle it up like, but they say the headquarters wallahs have nobbled all the issue rum, like.' He winked, and the general winked back.

Corrigan took his tea and then followed Gale, who was accompanied by his body-guard-cum-radio operator, a bandy-legged Scot armed with a Tommy-gun and lugging a heavy radio on his back, to the corner of the farmhouse wall, which was now glowing red in the reflected light of the tracer.

'Now then, Captain, you say that the Iron Division is having difficulty in linking up with us?'

'Yes, sir.' Two hundred yards away, a burst

of flame suddenly welled up from the orchard and spewed into the burning sky like a splash of blood. General Gale seemed not to notice. Instead, he calmly took a sip of the scalding-hot tea. 'Nothing to beat a dish of tea at three o'clock of the morning, what?' he said heartily.

Corrigan knew that generals were supposed to make this sort of idle chit-chat while under fire. Their *sang froid* had a steadying effect on the men. But time was running out, and if the paras were going to move against Caen, they had to do so before first light. 'Sir,' he said, a little desperately, 'within the last twenty-four hours we've noted a thickening of the enemy resistance all along the Caen front. I personally saw an armoured regiment of the Third Canadian Division badly shot up and repulsed – by the SS of the 12th Hitler Youth.'

Gale looked up grimly, his broad face glowing in the flames, and brushed back his moustache which was wet with tea. 'So those brutes have put their oar in, have they?'

'Yes, sir, and more. It's my guess from what I've seen this last day that they're trying to hold your division, while the SS armour has a crack at the Iron Division. In other words they're planning a massive counter-attack on the beachhead.'

Gale nodded. 'Yes, it would be a typical Boche stroke. They're always exceedingly swift with their counter-attacks.'

Corrigan leaned forward excitedly, forgetting the tea. 'So, the way is wide open for your division.'

'Wide open to do what?'

'To attack towards Caen... We can recce the way for you, sir. Just say the word, and we'll be off in the next five minutes.'

Slowly, almost solemnly, General Gale lowered his canteen of tea. 'Captain Corrigan,' he said, 'that is absolutely out of the question.'

'Out of the question, sir?' Corrigan stuttered. 'But why – if I may ask?'

'Corrigan, come with me. I want to show you something.' The general put down his canteen, indicating to his signaller-bodyguard to bring his white horse. He then led Corrigan round the back of the farmhouse from which the tracer was coming. Here, Corrigan saw a big stone barn, typical of that area, with a sentry posted at the door, silhouetted a stark black in the lurid red light of the tracer.

The sentry clicked to attention and opened the door. A knife of yellow light slid into the night. The general kept his voice low. 'I can ill afford to lose the fighting power of that sentry. We need every man we can get in the line. But I don't want the others to see this. Take a look yourself, Corrigan.' He stood aside and let the puzzled captain peer in.

Corrigan gasped. Staring back at him in the faint yellow light of the single naked bulb high up under the beamed roof, was a dead man. Even in the poor light, Corrigan could see the line of bloody holes stitched across the front of his leather jerkin where he sat, upright in death, his gauntleted hands stretched stiffly in front of him, his eyes magnified and hideous behind his motor-cycling goggles.

But the dead dispatch rider, sitting there in that nightmarish posture, was not alone. There were dead paras everywhere, their battledress ripped open to reveal gashed flesh, pulpy and glistening red like fresh meat in a butcher's window. Their bodies were sack-like and yet stiff, their fists clenched, genitals protruding from burst-open flies like wax fruit, their eyes not quite shut, but leering with grizzly sheen, lips drawn back, teeth set in a last animal snarl. Some were minus heads, minus arms, legs – mere featureless packages of bloody meat. And there were scores of them, row after row, stretching to the furthest recess of that terrible charnel house. The whole place stank of death.

The big, red-faced general nodded to the sentry and he closed the door again, mercifully shutting in the terrible smell.

Gently General Gale laid his hand on Corrigan's shoulder and drew him away.

Behind them, the battle for the Sixth's perimeter was beginning to hot up again, and in the distance, somewhere beyond the orchards, there could be heard the rusty rumble of tank tracks.

'Nearly two hundred... There are nearly two hundred dead men in there, Corrigan,' the general said softly. 'And that's just from this one battalion. *All* my battalions have suffered similar casualties.'

'I see, sir,' Corrigan answered, his voice unusually subdued.

'I'm hanging on here by the skin of my teeth. The only offensive action I can take is of a local nature, such as the skirmish going on here. The best I can do is to hold this flank until the ground troops from the beach can reach me in strength.'

'But Caen, sir,' Corrigan protested half-heartedly. 'We were scheduled to take it on the first day!'

'A planner's mistake, my boy,' the general interrupted him gently. 'Battle never goes the way the planners back in Whitehall think it will. It's always been that way – always will be.'

Corrigan's shoulders slumped in defeat. Of course General Gale was right. What could his lightly-armed paratroopers do against enemy armour? As if to underline the point, the noise of the German tanks beyond the apple orchards suddenly became louder and even more menacing.

'Go back to your division, my boy. See what you can do to get them moving quicker to link up with my poor chaps. That bridge you captured across the Orne will come in very handy. I think I can rustle up a composite company of clerks and cooks to hold it until the Iron Division reaches us.'

'Yes, sir,' Corrigan said despondently.

'Oh, and one thing, Corrigan...' The general had to raise his voice, as the first 88mm shell thundered through the night air with a sound like that of a huge piece of stiff canvas being ripped apart. 'You're a fine officer, a bold and brave one, I can see that. But if you'll take a word of advice from a man much older than yourself, try not to be so ruthlessly independent. It's not a quality that's very highly regarded in the British Army.' And he gave Corrigan a bluff smile of encouragement, his face red in the glowing darkness.

Behind them, another 88mm shell tore through the air exploded with a thick *crump*, sending stones scurrying and tumbling from the walls of the farmhouse. Somewhere glass smashed and tinkled and a man yelped in sudden agony.

General Gale reached out his hand. 'Good luck, Corrigan – and thanks.'

In a daze, Corrigan took the proffered hand.

Next moment the general was striding away, yelling to his bodyguard to bring him his horse. Corrigan watched as he mounted his white charger and galloped off towards the sound of the tanks, whooping and crying 'Tallyho!', followed into battle by a handful of cheering paras and his bandy-legged signaller, his aerial lashing the air.

Suddenly Corrigan was left standing there alone, spent and miserable. So all the sacrifice, all the effort, all the lives had been for nothing. Now he would have to return to the beaches in defeat and disgrace.

# FOUR: MORTHOMME

# ONE

Soon it would be dawn.

In Normandy the summer nights were short and Panzermeyer knew he would have to have his young grenadiers in position for the great attack before those damned Tommy *Jabos* took to the air again. He deliberately kept his orders brief as he stood there with his battalion commanders on the moonlit cobbled road under the cover of the trees, the only sound the distant crackle of the small arms battle taking place on the other side of the River Orne.

'So this is it, comrades,' Panzermeyer began. 'The Tommies now have a bridgehead up to the Periers Ridge and beyond, to a depth of nine kilometres. We aim to strike at that bridgehead with a full-scale concerted attack of three Panzer divisions, the 21st, the *Panzerlehr* and our own 12th SS and throw the enemy back into the damned sea where he belongs.'

'*Panzerlehr* will attack the British Third Division, with its right flank on the River Orne. The 21st Panzer will hit the main body of the *Canadian* Third Division – apparently there are two enemy third divisions involved.'

He paused, and they waited for their assignment, their faces hollowed out to stark black-and-white death's-heads in the spectral light of the crescent moon.

'It will be the task of our – er – "Babies" to hit the seam between the two enemy divisions. In other words, comrades,' he stared around at the circle of earnest faces, '*we* will have the kudos. For as you all know, the seam between two formations is invariably the place where a real breakthrough can be achieved. Gentlemen, there will be tin, plenty of it, in this one for you to adorn your manly chests.'

Once again, his young battalion commanders murmured their enthusiastic agreement. All of them were veterans of the Russian front, their chests laden with decorations and awards. Yet without exception, all of them were eager for still more decorations.

Only Bremer laughed and growled in his deep bass, 'They'll have to invent a new piece of tin for me, Panzermeyer. I've got the whole set already.'

Panzermeyer's hard face relaxed into a brief, tight smile. Even in the tensest of situations, Gerd Bremer could joke, and as always he was glad of the younger man's ability to relax things. 'Don't worry, Gerd,' he quipped. 'If we succeed in throwing the Tommies back into the drink for their final

Dunkirk, I promise to sit down and design it for you personally.'

His battalion commanders laughed softly.

Panzermeyer was businesslike again. 'Now our role in the 25th Panzergrenadier Regiment is vital. We are to take the heights and then hold key road crossings for the armour to pass through. Comrades, I say this without boasting; on our "Babies" depends the whole success of the operation. All right, these are your objectives for today...'

His battalion commanders licked their stubs of indelible pencil and began to scribble down his orders on the backs of their hands. Any naked light might well attract the attention of Tommy night-fighter pilots. It was safer to make their notes this way.

Finally he came round to Gerd Bremer, his most experienced commander. Panzermeyer took a deep breath and said, 'Well, Gerd, as usual you've got a beaut, there's no doubt about that, *alter Freund.*'

Bremer shrugged his broad shoulders, which seemed about to burst from the tight confines of his camouflaged tunic. 'Panzermeyer, I've had my hooter in the shit for so long that the crap's beginning to smell like attar of roses to me.'

The others laughed softly. The spectral moon was beginning to disappear and the sky was flushing a faint dirty white. Somewhere on a farm a cock crowed. Soon it would be dawn and by then they had to be gone.

'*Los,*' Bremer urged. 'Break it to me gently, Panzermeyer.'

Panzermeyer's dark bold eyes glittered. 'It is reasonable to expect that once the balloon goes up, Gerd, the Tommies will attempt some sort of a counter-attack against our positions. My guess is that it would come from a height surmounted by a little hamlet called Morthomme.'

Bremer frowned at the mention of the name, but Panzermeyer did not give him time to comment upon it. Instead, he hurried on with his briefing. 'Morthomme dominates the Bayeux-Caen road which will be our armour's main lateral communications axis. If the Tommies could break through there and capture that height, they could attack all our traffic.'

He frowned. 'Unfortunately it was abandoned by that cowardly rabble of the 716th Infantry Division. According to our Intelligence, however, it has not *yet* been occupied by the Tommies. As usual, the Tommies have settled down somewhere or other to take tea!' He said the last words in English and his battalion commanders tittered knowingly.

'Now Gerd.' Suddenly there was iron in Panzermeyer's voice. 'Morthomme is yours

to capture and to hold … cost what it may!'
Bremer snapped to attention. *'Jawohl,'* he
barked formally, *'es wird gemacht!'* Then his
voice seemed to lose some of its confidence
and he said musingly. 'But Panzermeyer,
isn't Morthomme French for–'

'Yes, it is,' Panzermeyer said sourly, cutting him short, his eagerness for action and
glory abruptly dampened. 'But believe me,
Gerd, I don't believe in portents. *Los! Comrades, to action!'*

They saluted hurriedly, knowing that
there was no time to waste, and scurried
away to the vehicles sheltering beneath the
whispering oaks. Abruptly the pre-dawn
calm was shattered by the roar of motors.
The air was filled with the cloying stench of
gasoline fumes. And then they were gone,
leaving Panzermeyer staring, troubled and
suddenly uneasy, to the west where the
Tommies were. 'Would they pull it off?' the
little voice in the back of his mind whispered uncertainly. 'Could his green inexperienced "Babies" stop them … *could they?'*
Slowly, his shoulders slumped almost as if
in defeat, Panzermeyer walked back to his
waiting Volkswagen jeep. To the east the sky
started to flush a blood-red.

'Will you just cast your glassy orbs on them,
sir,' the young lieutenant groaned. 'What a
bunch of currant-crappers!'

Bremer lowered his glasses. He had seen enough. The stubble-hoppers of the 716th Infantry were hoofing it yet again. Now they were pulling back down the hillside in a ragged line, a bareheaded officer trying to stop them, but without any success. It was obvious they'd panicked. He certainly wouldn't be able to use them for the attack on Morthomme, which reared up to the west from the morning haze.

'Those current-crappers, as you are pleased to call them, Lieutenant Krause,' he said mockingly, 'are carrying out a man-oeuvre which is known in Army circles as correcting the front. The gentlemen of the *Wehrmacht* have been doing it for some years now. That's why they need us SS ruffians to pull their chestnuts out of the fire for them.'

Suddenly there was iron in his voice. 'Right, Krause, see what they're up to and what they know.' Bremer flashed a glance at his wristwatch. 'I shall move out with the main body at exactly seven hundred hours. We attack the village of Morthomme one hour later – and let us hope that the Tommies have not yet occupied it.' He bit his bottom lip and felt himself already beginning to sweat. It was going to be another hot day. 'Otherwise it's going to be a son-of-a-bitch to take!'

Young Krause, blond and blue-eyed in his

black leather jacket, devoid of any decoration save the black and white enamel of the Knight's Cross at his throat, smiled. 'When have the SS worried about such trivial matters, sir?'

He saluted hastily and sprang effortlessly into his waiting half-track, packed with white-faced, nervous grenadiers going into action for the first time. The driver gunned his engine impatiently. Krause pumped his right arm up and down rapidly. It was the signal for 'advance'.

One by one, Krause's half-tracks, all heavily camouflaged with branches and leaves, broke free of the forest and started to waddle forward through the cornfield, cutting wide swaths through the broad sea of yellow. Bremer muttered a quick prayer and seized his binoculars again. The next half-hour was going to be critical.

The flight of RAF fighters shrieked in at 500 kilometres an hour. Angry purple flames crackled the length of their wings. To Krause's front, the men of the 716th flung themselves to the ground.

Too late! The fighters were on them. Red and white tracer zipped everywhere viciously. Men screamed shrilly. Others flung up their arms and pitched face-forward without a word, dead before they hit the ground. A few flailed the air, as if physically trying to fight off these cruel silver birds which swooped and whined above their heads, spitting their murderous fire.

'Great crap on the Christmas Tree!' Krause moaned in despair. 'Those Tommy flyboys should roast in hell. To the left flank *at the double!*' he roared in red-faced fury as the three Spitfires spotted the little column of vehicles cutting through the corn and came in at tree-top height, cannon and machine-guns pounding away.

Desperately, his sweating driver wrenched the wheel round. The big eight-ton half-track swerved violently to the left, flinging up the earth in a wild brown wake behind it, and started to scuttle for the safety of the wood to the right of the cornfield. Madly the others did the same, the column breaking up immediately, while ahead of them the retreating infantry panicked and came on, clawing and clutching at each other in their overwhelming fear, stamping over the bodies of their dead and dying comrades, pressing them deeper into the soil, ignoring their fervent pleas in their frantic attempt to escape.

Behind him, Krause heard the thump-thump of metal striking metal. He swung a look to his rear as his half-track plunged into the safety of the undergrowth. His third half-track had come to an abrupt stop. Smoke was streaming in black fury from its ruptured engine. Greedy little blue flames were beginning to ripple the whole length of the suddenly crippled vehicle as the grenadiers flung themselves madly over its sides and ran headlong for the trees, the enemy slugs cutting the earth in vicious little spurts all about their flying feet.

Angrily he raised his Schmeisser and fired a crazy burst at the silver killers. Too late. The English Spitfires were already swooping high into the bright blue of the morning sky, twisting and turning exuberantly at the success of their sudden strike.

A moment later the half-track exploded. Krause ducked instinctively and felt the blast lash his face like a blow from a flabby wet fist. For a moment he choked for breath, eyes closed. When he opened them again, the half-track was blazing furiously, surrounded by half-a-dozen troopers sprawled out in the careless, extravagant posture of those done violently to death.

He cursed, sudden tears in his bright blue eyes. Bremer's 'Babies' were dying even before they fired a shot in anger.

Now the remnants of the beaten 716th Infantry Division began to stream towards the line of contemptuous SS troopers Bremer had set up to stop them. Perhaps he might be able to use the rabble in his own force. As he stood imperiously on his half-track watching them come, he doubted it.

Chest heaving, helmets gone, most of them without their rifles, too, the stubble-hoppers advancing on the SS obviously had only one thing on their minds – escape.

A boy drew level with Bremer. 'Halt!' he barked.

The boy never even heard him. He blundered on, arms out-stretched, wild eyes staring into nothing like a blind man.

A couple of older men came panting towards the big SS officer, breath coming in short, leaden-lunged gasps, both of them without weapons.

A noncom thrust out his foot and the taller of the two tumbled awkwardly to the ground. The noncom kicked him in the ribs and he moaned miserably.

*'Nicht schlagen!'* he cried and cowered there, hands raised to protect his bare head, *'bitte*. Please, don't hit me!'

Bremer indicated that the noncom should step back. Beyond, one of his 'Babies' had rammed his butt into the mouth of a grey-haired trooper, shouting angrily, 'Why you treacherous shit, running away like that!'

'But I'm a German just like you, son!' the stubble-hopper exclaimed, the blood pouring down his unshaven chin.

The SS trooper, beside himself with rage, slammed his nailed 'dice-breaker' into the man's crotch. He shot to the ground, his false teeth flying from his shocked mouth. Deliberately the SS trooper crunched his heel down on them.

Bremer aimed his machine pistol into the fire and pressed the trigger. Over a volley of 9mm slugs he bellowed, 'Enough of that!'... Come on, stop it, you young troopers ... and you men of the 716th, stand fast, or it will the worse for you!'

The shots and Bremer's angry bellow had the desired effect. The stubble-hoppers came to a ragged halt on all sides, blinking their eyes like men awakening from a heavy sleep, staring at the line of youthful SS men as if they had just become aware that they were there.

Easily, Bremer sprang down from the half-track. He had spotted an officer among the rabble. He grabbed the man by the tunic and dragged him close to his own massive chest, feeling the stubble-hopper's foetid breath assail his nostrils. 'Out with it, man, quick! What's up there on the height?'

The ashen-faced officer stared up at him, eyes blank, lips trembling violently, as if he were suffering from a fever. 'All day, they shelled us ... never seen shells of that calibre ... and the *Jabos* ... they were everywhere,' he wailed. 'Shooting and killing... We hadn't a chance. We hadn't a chance.'

'I said, are there any Tommies up there on that shitting height?' Bremer bellowed scarlet-faced, spittle flecking the other officer's face. 'Did you hear me... *Los jetzt, raus mit der Sprache!*'

But the other man continued to babble on about the shelling and the planes. In disgust, Bremer let go of him and he dropped to the damp grass, sobbing like a heartbroken child.

'They're useless,' he cried, 'absolutely useless! You noncoms take over. Get the whoresons out of my sight!'

'All right, you perverted banana-suckers ... you asparagus Tarzans ... you arses-with-ears,' Bremer's noncoms began their litany of contempt 'get into that ditch over there and keep yer shitting turnips down.'

Suddenly Bremer's radio operator popped his head over the side of the half-track. 'Sir ... sir,' he cried excitedly. 'A message from Lieutenant Krause, sir.'

'What is it?' Bremer bellowed, forgetting the disgusting sight of German soldiers who had run away in battle. 'Out with it, man! Quick!'

'He's made contact, sir.'

'Contact?'

'With the English, sir. At least he's spotted them. Infantry and armour by the look of it, he says.'

Bremer hesitated, as if he did not dare pose that overwhelming question. Then it was out. 'Where? On the heights at Morthomme?'

'Yes, sir,' the operator replied cheerfully, as if it were the most obvious thing in the world, his clear blue eyes sparkling. 'The Tommies are up there all right, sir.'

Bremer felt the energy drain out of him, as if someone had suddenly opened a tap. Now he had a fight, a damnable fight on his hands. His 'Babies' were going to have to pay the butcher bill after all.

Morthomme would live up to its dread name.

## TWO

'Morthomme?' said Slim Sanders wearily, braking the half-track, as the bullet-pocked road sign came into view. He rubbed his red-rimmed eyes. They had been driving back towards the beaches for three hours now through the blackout, and they ached like hell. 'Where the fuck's *that* when it's at home?'

Standing upright in the cab of the half-track, Corrigan surveyed the collection of tumbledown grey cottages clustered around the little Gothic church. At any moment he was ready to give the others, two hundred yards behind him, the signal to back off if the place turned out to be occupied by the

Germans. Next to him, Sergeant Hawkins gripped his Tommy-gun hard and slowly scanned the scene.

There had been fighting at the little hill-top village – he could see that; or at least an artillery duel. The church steeple had been holed in several places, and here and there the roofs were missing from the cottages. But there was no sign of life.

'Shall I go and have a look-see, sir?' he volunteered.

Corrigan forced a grin in spite of his depressed mood. 'Never give up, do you, Hawkins? Still fussing over your chicks, even now that they've grown up to be bloody great roosters. All right – take Wolfers. I'll stay here with the rest. If the place is clean, we'll break and brew up. After all, we're in no hurry to get back, are we?'

Inwardly, Hawkins dreaded to think what was in store for them once they reached Brigade, but he tried not to show it. 'Righto, sir. All right, Wolfers, you heard the officer. Hands off the cock and on with yer socks. Take Sanders' sten.'

Together the big trooper and the under-sized NCO dropped over the side of the half-track and began to walk purposefully to the hamlet through the dawn gloom, the only sound the *clump-clump* of their nailed boots on the damp *pavé* and the cawing of the rooks in the tall trees.

Carefully, the two of them circled the little hill-top settlement, weapons held at the ready, noting the dead cows in the fields, bloated like barrage balloons, their legs sticking stiffly upwards.

'Looks empty to me, Sarge,' Wolfers ventured. His stomach was rumbling again, but unfortunately he had already eaten all the hard-tack biscuits the paras had given him. Maybe he would find a bite to eat in one of the cottages.

'Famous last words,' Sergeant Hawkins said grumpily. 'Come on, let's take a look inside.' He started forward, stepping over a pile of debris, following a line of telegraph wires cut down during the recent artillery bombardment.

But Wolfers was right: the place was empty – though there was ample evidence that the Germans had been there not so long before; their abandoned equipment lay everywhere in the empty houses.

'Shall we whistle up the others, Sarge?' Wolfers asked, in between chewing on a piece of hard garlic German Army issue sausage he had just found.

'Fer Chrissake, yes,' Hawkins said testily. 'And can't you sodding well stop eating? You certainly live up to yer bloody name, don't yer? And by the way, what kind of name is that anyhow? "Wolfers" – that ain't English, is it?'

'No, Sarge,' Wolfers replied, in no way put out. 'My grandpa was a Jerry. Came over in the last century to work in the mills. A lot o' Jerries did in them days. Oh, and by the way, Sarge–'

'Yes?' said Hawkins, without interest.

'Do you know what the name of this place means in our lingo?'

'No.'

'I did a bit of French at school. "Mort-homme", it means "dead man". Funny name to give a village, ain't it, Sarge – *Dead Man?*'

But Sergeant Hawkins had no comment to make.

Now they relaxed, their stomachs full of compo tea, fried soya links and bully beef. Corrigan, too, took his time over his mug of tea laced with issue rum. He could see no reason to hurry. The battle for the beach-head would be won or lost with or without the Assault Troop. Some of the men explored the deserted houses; others simply stretched full out on the pavement, feet resting on their packs, and slept. For the first time in days they were able to unwind – all, save the sentry on the approach road and the look-out perched high above the village in the wrecked steeple.

'What do you reckon, sir?' said Hawkins as he and Corrigan lolled in the cab of the half-track, feeling its steel plating grow warmer as the sun rose up above the horizon, flushing the morning sky a deep, glowing pink. It was going to be another hot day.

'Think about what, Hawkins?'

'The general situation, sir.'

Corrigan shrugged. 'Don't know much, don't care much. Suppose we'll win in the end, we always do. But *when* ... well, that's a different question.'

Hawkins studied the captain out of the corner of his eyes. Corrigan looked exhausted and despondent; in fact, Hawkins had never seen him look so low in all the time they had been together. 'You were right, sir,' he said encouragingly, 'and you did the right thing back there on the beach. We had trained too long and got too set in our ways. A couple of times in the last three days, I half-expected the umpires to blow a whistle, like they used to do back in Blighty, and stop the exercise – cos it was goin' on too long, gettin' too hard.' He laughed ruefully. 'Yer know the sort of thing: when do we stop for tea, like, sir?'

Corrigan forced a weary smile. 'I'll call you as a witness at my court-martial.'

Hawkins looked glum. 'Yer reckon it'll come to that, sir? Honestly?'

'I should think so. The Brig's a stickler for strict discipline, and Major Stirling is, after all, a product of the legal profession.'

Hawkins opened his mouth to make an angry retort, but thought better of it. He lapsed into silence again, half-listening to Wolfers up above them in the shattered tower. The big Yorkshire lad was munching happily on a sausage and singing between bites, *'Ain't it a pity she's only one titty to feed the baby... Poor little bugger's got only one udder...'*

Slim Sanders shook his head as he prised up the floorboards of the little bedroom only fifty yards away. That young Wolfers – it was time he grew up. Tougher and harder he might be, but he was still a kid – a stupid kid – at heart. Anyone with a bit of sense would be nosing around like he was, seeing what he could find, instead of carrying on like that. He couldn't bloody well sing anyway.

Sanders grunted and tore up another floorboard beneath the old brass bedstead. Soon he would have a hole big enough to feel around in. He might well strike lucky. He had heard that these Frog peasants always hid their dough under their beds because they didn't trust their banks. That was wise of them. Because if Frog banks were anything like the ones they had in the Outback, he, personally, wouldn't trust them as far as he could sling them. The fat, cunning Pommie buggers who ran the

Aussie banks would rob you blind.

He ripped up another plank, to the reproving look of the bearded worthies in black who peered down at him from the yellowing photo on the wall – its sole decoration, save for a crucifix and a framed poster of the liner *Normandie* sailing through a perfect sea. Suddenly he gasped. Something silver gleamed in the smelly darkness between the floor and the ceiling below. Quickly he reached in a hand and brought out a silver twenty-franc piece bearing the long-nosed, bearded silhouette of Napoleon the Third. 'Strewth,' he said, 'I've hit the jackpot! The ball-and-chain bastards really *have* hidden their dough here!'

Hands trembling slightly, he reached in again and brought out a handful of the dull silver coins. Blimey! – he hadn't been this lucky since he took up with that Sidney whore in '40 who had kept him very nicely until he had been fool enough to get as tight as a tick and volunteer for the Army. 'Christ, it's a small fortune!' he whispered. 'As soon as we get to Paree, I'm off. Them Frenchie whores better watch their step!' Laughing crazily, he reached into the hole once more.

But Slim Sanders' dreams of deserting to Paris with his newly-found fortune were fated to remain unfulfilled. For suddenly came that familiar clarion call, that blast of ferocious sound, that terrible, awesome, elemental keening...

In an instant the house began to tremble crazily. It was as if a giant hand had punched the place. There was a terrible cracking noise. Stones went tumbling down. Glass splintered. Above his bent head, the timbers creaked and snapped like matchwood. Plaster-dust rained down like thick snow. Below him, the old floor heaved and quaked like a live thing, sending the hoard of coins scurrying, rolling, fleeing in all directions.

Sanders was slammed against the shaking wall, choking and coughing helplessly as dust filled his lungs. Groggily he shook his head to clear away the red wave that threatened to swamp him.

For some reason a huge hole had appeared to his immediate front, and through it he could see flurries of steel, bushes, bricks, tearing across the village square, driven by a tremendous wind that swept all before it. Then it was gone, and he could once more see the steep hill which led up to Morthomme from the east...

For one long moment, he was unable to comprehend the evidence of his own eyes and just lay there gasping with shock, trembling all over, bathed in a cold sweat.

Down below, three lines of infantry, well spread out, were plodding up towards him, rifles held at the port, advancing with slow, stubborn, thoughtful purpose. In front of them, scuttling back and forth like metallic beetles, were half-tracks camouflaged with ferns and branches.

'Christ's blood,' he gasped, finally understanding what he was seeing, *'Jerries!'*

Colonel Bremer's Panzergrenadiers had arrived to do battle at Morthomme!

*Crump… Crump… Crump!* Once again a tremendous salvo rocked the hill-top village. Bushes and trees were lashed almost level with the ground as the hot wind of the blast hit them. A dead cow came flying through the air to slam into the horse-trough in the littered square. Behind the village, the apple orchard started to blaze fiercely. Leaves came tumbling down like green rain. Each fresh detonation was stupefying, pulverising, horrific.

Corrigan hugged the wall of the old post office, feeling the blast rip at his clothes and hearing the ping of the rebounding shrapnel. For a moment he was bewildered. This was completely unexpected. He could not make sense of it. What was *happening* at this remote village?

Then he had it – and his heart leapt with joy. He realised now that the Assault Troop had a function to perform after all. This was the great German counter-attack to the beaches which he had been expecting for the last two days – ever since he had seen the ambush and massacre of the Canadians. And he and his men were directly in its path!!

Suddenly his initial stupefaction left him. He felt completely unafraid and absolutely clear-headed. Just then, another salvo of shells came screaming in, like an express train hurtling through a deserted station. Corrigan waited no longer. He ran into the centre of the square, crying, *'Stand to! Stand to!'* Before him, a sudden, yawning gap of smoking chaos opened up. The blast buffeted him about the face, but he kept on running through the howling shrapnel. In seconds he was among his cowering, ashen-faced troopers, kicking them, grabbing them, cursing them, propelling them into a defensive position, while above him in the ruined steeple, an excited, half-crazed Wolfers tolled the bells like a madman.

Corrigan clambered up a pile of steaming masonry, blinking his eyes in the blinding white dust and stared down at the incredible scene. The scuttling half-tracks were now clattering upwards in a straight line, tearing yellow wakes behind them in the corn. The lines of infantry had broken up, too. They were now stumbling and running in crouched groups as best they could, clinging to the protection that the armoured vehicles provided. Suddenly there came a hoarse cry from a thousand young German throats.

'*Stand by!*' Corrigan yelled desperately and flung himself behind the abandoned bren gun. He flung it up on its little tripod and smacked the butt into his shoulder.

'*Prepare to fire!*' Hawkins voice screamed behind him, rallying the firing line.

Up above, the mad bell-ringer continued to toll his ancient bells. Corrigan clicked off the safety.

'*Alles für Deutschland,*' screeched the fanatical young men in their camouflaged uniforms. '*SIEG HEIL!*'

'*Fire!*' bellowed Corrigan.

The bren erupted furiously, and Corrigan felt the sudden, hard kick in his right shoulder. The stink of burnt cordite filled his nostrils. Madly, he swung the automatic to left and right, firing lower, watching the tracer zip across the hillside towards the advancing infantry.

Behind him and to his sides, his assault troopers opened up in a frenzy of fear. How could they hope to stop so many? But they *had* to. The wild men of the SS would take no prisoners today: it was kill or be killed.

The packed front ranks of the SS had become a chaotic mess of flailing arms and legs. Young SS men were bowled over by the score and ripped apart by that terrible volume of fire at short range. But already more young blond giants, eager for glory and sudden death, were stumbling over the writhing bodies to take their place.

Corrigan slapped another curved magazine into the bren, whose steel barrel was already beginning to glow a dull purple. 'Piat, Sergeant Hawkins – use the Piat!'

Hawkins slung his smoking Tommy-gun and, bent low, doubled to the nearest half-track, already half-buried in masonry from the initial shelling. Frantically he burrowed in the rubble, ignoring the bleeding fingers occasioned by the rough bricks, until at last he found the awkward-looking anti-tank rifle. He rummaged a little more and, dragging out a case of the bottle-shaped Piat bombs, doubled back to the firing line and flung himself flat next to Corrigan, gasping for breath. 'Orders, sir?'

'Knock out those half-tracks!' Corrigan yelled above the rattle of his bren, as he swung it from left to right, hosing the advancing German infantry with shot.

Hawkins flung a desperate look to his front. The Jerries were only a hundred and fifty yards away now. Behind them, the slope was littered with the bodies of their comrades, yet still the rest came on like automatons, as if nothing would ever stop them. With trembling fingers, he fitted a bomb into the muzzle of the clumsy-looking weapon and flung himself behind the padded rest.

All around him, his lads were working their rifles frantically, ejecting spent cartridges, pumping their bolts, pressing their triggers, eyes fixed hypnotically on the ever-approaching Germans, faces greased with sweat, as if they had been smeared with Vaseline. Hawkins hesitated no longer. He pressed the trigger. The awesome kick sent him reeling back, but by then the bomb was wobbling forward, streaking towards its target; the leading half-track.

The hollow charge exploded with a tremendous *boom!* The half-track lurched to a sudden halt, thick, white smoke streaming from its ruptured engine. Next instant it was blazing fiercely, and the infantry who moments before had been crouched behind it were forced to scatter wildly to left and right – straight into the deadly hail directed at them by the cheering assault troopers.

'Another, Hawkins! For Chrissake!' Corrigan screamed, suddenly ripping open his flies and pouring a stream of hot, steaming urine over the glowing barrel of the bren.

With fingers that felt like pork sausages, Hawkins thrust home another bomb.

A bareheaded SS officer, his white-blond hair gleaming in the sun, bounded past the burning half-track, waving his Schmeisser. Half a dozen young SS men ran after him. Now Corrigan could see his features quite clearly, down to the trickle of blood running down his pale, grim face from a wound in his temple. In a few moments he and his group would be inside the ruins – and then they would never flush them out.

*'They're charging!'* Wolfers screamed from the tower.

Corrigan raised his bren and took aim. He pressed the trigger. Nothing happened. *The damned thing had jammed!*

The young SS officer seemed to sense that something had gone wrong. He raced even quicker for the first building, the men pelting after him, arms going like pistons, heads bent low between their shoulders like men running through pouring rain.

Hawkins saw the danger. While Corrigan cursed and fumbled with the blockage in the bren, he fired. The bomb went wobbling towards the building to which the SS were racing. Metal hit stone with a tremendous *crash!* Bricks hurtled through the air. For a moment the whole scene was obscured by great clouds of flying dust and rubble.

Then it cleared.

The SS had vanished, buried beneath the rubble of the demolished building – all save for that lone, severed head rolling down the slope towards the retreating SS, like a football abandoned by a child...

# THREE

The sickle moon cast a cold, spectral light on the shell-shattered trees. An owl hooted far off. Otherwise all was silent, tense expectation. Up on the height yet another flare hissed into the silver night. Instantly everything was bathed in the eerie red light. Nothing moved. It fell slowly, to expire like a hissing, writhing snake in the damp night grass. Again the heavy silence descended upon the hillside littered with the bodies of those who had died the previous day.

A long way off, down on the beaches, there was the hoarse, angry chatter of a quick-firing cannon. For a few moments the horizon was flushed a faint pink, flickering on and off like silent summer lightning. Then once again, the sombre night silence fell on the hillside. The whole world might well have been dead at this moment.

Time passed. Now it was nearly one o'clock in the morning. Back home in the Reich, it was *Polizeistunde,* the hour when the guesthouses and inns closed. Now the happy drunk would be looking for the pavement-pounders who congregated out-side such places to hurry home with them to dance a mattress polka. The lucky bastards, Lieutenant Krause told himself enviously as he crouched there.

He and the sniper team, plus the mortar group which Bremer had sent him as reinforcements to make up the terrible gaps in his recce group, had been crouched in the shallow ditch at the base of the hill for nearly four hours now.

They had infiltrated the position as soon as the light had failed, while the Tommies above them on the shattered heights had been still wide awake. Now, Krause calculated, they would be lulled into that false lazy confidence that comes to soldiers in the middle of the night. Who, they always reasoned, who in his right mind would want to attack at this godforsaken hour? Surprise attacks always came in just before dawn. That was why both armies stood their troops to at dawn. Well, Krause told himself, trying to take his mind off the naked thighs and the juicy secret place of his last Berlin whore, Frau Krause's handsome hero of a son doesn't play those games.

He looked at the green-glowing dial of his wristwatch. It was now zero one hundred hours precisely. Time to go. 'The volunteers,' he whispered.

Next to him half a dozen men rose silently from the ditch like ghosts from the grave. All were veterans, his noncoms who had come with him from the *Adolf Hitler Body-guard Division* in 1943 to form the 12th SS. He smiled at them in the silver darkness. 'Buy combs, lads,' he whispered the old ritual. ''Cos there's lousy times to come,' they answered.

He grinned. They were good boys. They knew how to take care of themselves. He couldn't afford to lose a single one of them: Bremer's 'Babies' needed all the experienced men they could find to back them up.

'*Schön,*' he hissed, staring at their blackened faces, their eyes glistening in contrast, startlingly white, 'you all know the drill.'

'Done it a dozen times,' grunted Goetz, the fattest man in the whole division. 'Easy as falling off a log.'

'Shit,' Krause whispered, 'if you fell off a log, you'd cause an earthquake!'

The others laughed softly, the tension broken.

'Don't take any risks. Just draw their fire so we can pinpoint their positions. Leave the rest to us.' There was a murmur of understanding and Krause added, 'There'll be a case of champers and a French pavement-pounder for the lot of you if you pull this one off, even if I pay the whores myself.'

'You couldn't throw in a nice half litre of green-fart soup and a chunk of roof-hare as well, sir, could you?' Goetz asked.

'Anything. Peasoup and roast moggie it is.

Now off with you – and the best of luck.'

The little band of volunteers stole away into the glowing darkness. Silently, rushing from shellhole to shellhole, their boots wrapped in rags, they advanced steadily up the slope to carry out their deadly task.

Krause stared after them for a few moments, then they were gone. He checked his watch again. 'Five minutes,' he announced, 'in five minutes we follow – and hear this. I'll have the eggs off any one of you wet-tails who makes the slightest noise, do you hear? With a blunt razor blade!'

'The only thing that makes life worth living for your ordinary squaddie, cobber, is gash,' Sanders pontificated, as he and Wolfers squatted in a slit trench on sentry-go. 'If the brass didn't allow us to go and get a bit of gash every now and again, do you think they'd ever get us to do this sodding carry-on? Not on your nelly! It's juicy, ripe female gash that keeps us in the line.'

'Well, you get your share of it, mate,' Wolfers said without interest. His stomach was rumbling again – he hadn't eaten for at least two hours – and he wondered if he could nick a tin of bully beef without Hawkins's eagle-eye seeing him. It'd keep him going till morning at least.

'Well, you're right there, Wolfers,' Slim conceded reflectively. 'I've had my moments with the Sheils, I must admit. Did I ever tell you about the Sheila who picked me up in Cairo in '42 when I was done on leave from up the Blue?'

'Yes, many a time … but I know you're gonna tell me again. So wake me up when you're finished, Slim.'

The little Australian ignored the comment. 'Well, up she comes – French, she was – all silk and satin. I thought straight away she was on the razzle. But no sir, she was a real swell, right out of the top drawer, with one of those Pommy cut-glass accents, although she was a Frog–'

He stopped short. Next to him Wolfers tensed, and the face he glimpsed in the silver light was suddenly wide-awake and very alert. 'What is it, cobber?' he asked.

Wolfers swallowed hard, his prominent adam's apple rising up and down as if on a lift. 'I swear I just saw somebody out there. At three o'clock, near that big shellhole.'

He raised his rifle cautiously, clicking off the safety catch.

'Go on,' Slim sneered. 'You're seeing things, young Wolfers.' Yet the little Australian's voice was suddenly cast in a hushed whisper too.

'I'm not. Look!'

Slim strained his eyes. Tall, dark figures suddenly darted from the shattered skeletal trees to their right. Bending almost double they rushed forward a few yards and flung themselves into a shellhole. He swallowed hard. Even to a battle-hardened veteran like himself, there was something ghostly and eerie about the shadowy figures in the middle of the night.

Excited and fearful, the two of them waited, hearts beating like crazed trip-hammers, nerves jingling, their breath abruptly harsh and shallow.

An age seemed to pass. The two of them began to relax a little. Perhaps their eyes had played tricks on them. Slim swung his gaze from left to right, keeping it low in the fashion of the combat veteran so that he could see anything silhouetted a darker black against the horizon. Nothing. The lunar landscape to their front was deserted, save for the dead.

'You know, Slim, I don't know whether I can trust me own peepers. Was there something out there or wasn't–'

The words died on his lips. In a little patch of moonlight to their immediate front, a German soldier was standing. He stood there completely upright, as still as a statue. Wolfers could see the shapeless folds of his camouflage tunic, the glint of his bayoneted rifle, the tangle of twigs in his helmet cover. The man was deliberately courting death, but why? Slowly Wolfers began to take aim.

Slim acted just in time. His hand lashed

out and knocked the Englishman's rifle down. 'What the hell–'

'An old trick. They're trying to draw our fire. Check out our positions, the brave bastard! Look, he's gone again.'

Slim gasped and wiped his sleeve across his suddenly sweat-lathered brow. 'Christ, it's enough to make a bloke shit! Here, Wolfers, crawl out of this nice hole and gentle like so that they don't hear you and go and wake the CO. Tell him Trooper Slim Sanders begs to report that enemy troops are attempting to infiltrate our positions.'

'Should I really tell him that?' Wolfers asked, in wonder at Sanders' sudden formality.

'Of course not, you silly sod. Tell him the Jerries are probing. Now hop it smartish!'

Wolfers hopped it.

For the next hour the Germans, lurking outside their perimeter like grey ghosts, tried to draw the fire of the hard-pressed defenders. They were recklessly brave in their attempts to do so. More than once they exposed themselves, standing boldly and bolt upright in full view of the riflemen. At other times they chattered and shouted to each other arrogantly, groaning, screaming, some of them even breaking sticks for some reason. It was almost as if they wanted to make as much noise as possible. 'I can't figure it out, sir,' Hawkins complained, as not more than fifty yards away a heavily accented voice called, 'Help me, comrades ... help me ... I am wounded. Help me!'

'I'd help you with the point of my ruddy bayonet up your Jerry arse!' somebody called back.

'I mean,' Hawkins continued after hissing for the trooper who had replied to shut his mouth, 'they know the rough layout of our perimeter by now. What are they larking at? It's almost as if they're trying to make as much bloody noise as possible.'

'You're right,' Corrigan agreed, peering into the darkness and telling himself his boys were doing very well. Not one of them had been tempted to fire at the taunting Germans flitting about like wild animals out there.

There was a sudden scream, as blood-chilling as the cry of an epileptic suffering an attack. 'I don't know, Hawkins. Are they trying a war of nerves, trying to wear us out or something?'

'Search me, sir,' Hawkins grunted angrily. 'But they're getting on my bloody nerves all right, that's for sodding sure.'

Suddenly it happened. One of the young troopers' nerves broke at last. There was a rattle of a bren. White and red tracers zipped through the darkness. 'Take that, you rotten bastards,' an angry voice screamed.

'Now bloody well knock it off, do you hear me... *Knock it off.*'

In the darkness somebody chuckled and yelled, as Hawkins shouted angrily at the enraged trooper to cease firing. 'Thank you Tommy. We'll be back. *Auf wiedersehen...*'

Suddenly all was as quiet as the grave.

## FOUR

The hard dry crack of a high velocity rifle firing broke the silence dramatically. In the next slit-trench to Wolfers', a red-haired trooper who had just taken off his helmet to ease the weight for a moment screamed shrilly and reeled back against the rear wall. A neat purple hole had been drilled in the centre of his forehead. As he slid to the floor, Wolfers saw that the back of his head had been torn apart. There was a jagged, gory hole there, big enough to put a fist into.

'*Sniper!*' he screamed frantically, '*Sniper got Johnson!*' Then the hot sickening bile flooded his throat and he retched violently, the vomit pouring down his chin.

Johnson was the first. Now a reign of terror commenced on the Assault Troop's perimeter, as Krause's snipers took up the challenge from their well-camouflaged positions all along the front of Morthomme, deliberately provoking the Tommies into doing what Krause hoped they would: come out into the open to be slaughtered by his waiting mortar crews.

All that morning, the SS snipers with their high velocity rifles took their toll. The least slip and the careless trooper would be reeling back, gurgling and choking in his own blood, a bullet through the lungs. Or dead where he stood on guard, face blasted away or hole drilled through his head. At the range the Germans were using, their steel-tipped bullets could penetrate even a helmet.

By mid-morning, Corrigan had already lost five precious young men, and the rest were badly shaken, hardly daring to move in their trenches. Now they carried out their bodily functions in their own holes and rations were distributed by throwing the tins from one slit trench to the other. All activity on the perimeter had ceased.

Higher up, in the shattered church tower, an increasingly frustrated Corrigan and a worried Hawkins, who had been near to tears when Johnson was killed– 'He were only seventeen and a half, sir, the youngest lad in the Troop', he had wailed – had surveyed the shattered shell-holed terrain outside the perimeter all morning with their glasses. To no avail.

Wearily Corrigan let his binoculars fall to his chest and rubbed his red-rimmed eyes. 'It's no bloody use, Hawkins. They're using the best quality ammo. Not even a wisp of smoke, and they're cunning buggers, too. Nary a single glint from a telescopic sight to give away their positions.'

'But we've got to do something, sir. There'll be nowt left of the Troop if they keep going at this rate. The lads are scared even to fart,' Hawkins was so exasperated that he forgot he was talking to Corrigan. Hastily he added, 'If you'll excuse my French, sir?'

Corrigan nodded absently while he mulled the problem over in his mind. For some reason which he couldn't make out, the Germans were making an all-out effort to sweep the Assault Troop off the heights at Morthomme and they were using their best troops, the SS, to do so.

Now, it appeared that they were using attrition to wear them down. But was that correct? After the bloody and costly attack of the previous day, could they afford to wait till their snipers had finally killed off the last defender? He shook his head. He didn't think so. They wanted Morthomme – and they wanted it quick. So they were drawing them out, that was it. They had something nasty, very nasty indeed, waiting for the Assault Troop out there in no-man's-land.

'We could try the old triangulate scheme,' Hawkins suggested as Corrigan's mind raced. 'One man draws the sniper's fire – perhaps poking an empty helmet over the top of his slit while another chap is watching to pop off the German immediately he's given away his position.'

Corrigan shook his head doubtfully. 'I don't think it would work – not with that lot. They're experts. You know, I've checked everywhere on the slope just now with my glasses and there are bags of places for the buggers to hide. *Nothing!* Not even their crap. I bet they hide it like a cat does. No, Hawkins, we've got to come up with something better than triangulation to fool these laddies.' He bit his bottom lip, face creased in a worried frown.

Down below a sniper's rifle cracked. There was a muffled, abruptly cut-off howl of pain. A moment later an angry voice bellowed from the perimeter. 'Priest has bought it ... old Taffy Priest, right in the throat, *the bastards!*' Hawkins closed his eyes quickly and pressed the bridge of his nose hard, as if to fight off tears. 'Poor young devil,' he said thickly. 'And what a lovely voice.'

'Listen,' Corrigan snapped, cutting him short. 'This is what we'll do. Mass what's left of the half-tracks. We're going down there to bring in the lads under the cover of their guns. We pull back up here to the houses.'

'But sir,' Hawkins protested, his tears forgotten. 'You can't do that, reduce the perimeter to the village alone. Once it's dark, they'll infiltrate into the houses and then we'll never get them out. We ain't got the strength. It'll be all up with the Assault Troop by this time tomorrow morning.'

Suddenly Corrigan smiled. 'But, my dear old Granny Hawkins,' he said easily, 'we aren't *all* going to leave the perimeter. We're going to leave a little welcoming committee for Mr Jerry. Now away with you and get those half-track drivers rounded up... And you, Corporal.' He turned to his waiting signaller, heavy radio set strapped to his back as he crouched in the rubble of the belfry.

'Sir!'

'See if you can raise the beach. Tell them what our position is and about the Germans and ask them if they could tell us for God's sake what is so damned important about the village of Morthomme.'

Krause raised his head cautiously as the first half-track began to clatter out of the shattered village, its machine-gun, mounted on the cab next to the driver, already spitting fire. Almost immediately it was followed by another, and another. *'Grosser Gott!'* he cursed. They were a perfect target, and *he* had forgotten to have the *Panzerfausts* brought up. He ducked hastily as a volley of slugs came his way. He could feel the soil shower the back of his head and rattle off his camouflage helmet. What in three devils' names were the Tommies up to? Were they going to make a break for it? Surely not, right into the German positions!

The first half-track slithered to a stop right in front of the nearest group of British foxholes and cut them off from the snipers Bremer had sent him, its gunner still hosing the slope from left and right, the driver gunning the engine as if he were scared it might die on him.

'They're shitting well running away,' Fat Goetz cried above the crazy racket. 'The Tommies are hoofing it!' Carried away by excitement, the veteran noncom rose to his feet, Schmeisser in one hand, piece of half-eaten salami in the other, about to fire.

The Tommy gunner beat him to it in the very same instant that Krause shrieked, 'Get your damned carcase down, man! *Down! Volle Deckung!'*

Too late. Goetz fell, chest ripped apart, mouth still filled with uneaten sausage.

Krause thought fast. His trick with the snipers hadn't worked. Instead of streaming out to the attack, right into a carefully planned mortar barrage, they were drawing back.

He cursed again and then suddenly, as the

first half-track rattled back the way it had come leaving empty trenches behind it, he realised that this was as good. If the Tommies fell back to Morthomme he had them. There were too few of them to defend all the houses, and Bremer's 'Babies' were past masters at infiltration and house-to-house fighting. They had trained in little else for months before the Invasion had started. He raised his voice, 'Radioman, signal to Colonel Bremer, we're moving on ... Tommies pulling back to the village... Mortar commander!'

'*Zu Befehl, Untersturm!*'

'Fire at will ... own targets... *Los*, off you go!'

The young, hard-faced mortar squad leader needed no urging. Hastily he rapped out a series of orders, ignoring the slugs flying everywhere. Frantically his crews grouped around the gleaming steel tubes, whirled their wheels and made their adjustments to the tripods. Another Tommy half-track had come and gone, leaving empty slit trenches behind it. But there was another one on its way.

The squad leader raised his right arm, the forefinger of his left hand struck in his left ear to counter-attack the effect of the blast on his eardrums. He let it drop and bellowed, '*Feuer!*'

A thick thumping sound. An obscene

howl. The first fat-bellied bomb hurtled from the tube, became a hasty black blur and went screeching into the sky, trailing smoke behind. Rapidly, bomb after bomb chased it.

For a moment they disappeared. Abruptly, with a baleful howl, a stomach-churning roar, they came hurrying down once more. The ground erupted on both sides of the half-track. It shook violently, threatening to go over at any moment. Soil and smoke engulfed it.

Krause held his breath. Had they hit it? No, there it was again, reversing hastily, its whole structure shaking, sides lacerated with gleaming silver shrapnel scars.

'Down ten!' the squad leader yelled above the hiss of the Tommy machine-guns.

He waited tensely. *'Fertig!'* the aimers cried.

*'Feuer!'* he bellowed.

Another flurry of deadly birds sailed into the sky. Now however, the Tommies were making smoke and firing phosphorus grenades. Smoke, white, thick and impenetrable, rose rapidly, while the grenades sailed straight towards the mortar positions, trailing furious white sparks behind them. The next moment they exploded in a cloudburst of blazing cream flame.

In an instant the ground beyond the perimeter was turned into a foaming furnace of fire. White pellets of deadly phosphorus sprayed everywhere. Once such a pellet embedded itself in a man's skin, he could only save himself from being consumed by fire by immersing himself in water. Air set the stuff burning again.

Goetz's body was struck. In a flash it was burning furiously, turning black and shrivelling before the horrified eyes of the spectators. Within seconds Fat Goetz had become a shrunken, skinny pygmy.

Krause knew they could not fight that kind of opposition. Ignoring the danger, he rose to his feet. 'Cease firing,' he screamed. 'Take cover everywhere! Let them go, boys, we'll have their skinny Tommy guts this night for supper, believe you me. TAKE COVER!'

Hastily the young SS men flung themselves to the safety of their pits, the phosphorus grenades sailing harmlessly over their crouched bodies, as further up the slope, the half-tracks completed their evacuation of the perimeter to scuttle back to the safety of Morthomme under cover of smoke.

The first stage of Corrigan's risky plan had been completed successfully.

# FIVE

General Montgomery, the Supreme Land
Commander of the quarter of a million
Americans, Canadians and Britons now
fighting across the Channel, put down his
little wooden pen, the kind one might find
in any rural post office.

Outside, over the Solent, dark clouds were
beginning to race over the choppy water
where the grey-painted destroyers and the
troopers, filled with reinforcements for the
beaches, bobbed up and down busily. There
was a storm brewing. He didn't envy the
soldiers packed like sardines in the troop-
ships. They would have a rough night of it,
once the convoy sailed under cover of darkness.

Colonel Ewart, Montgomery's Chief-of-
Forward-Intelligence, waited, knowing what
great strain the bird-like little general
opposite him was under. The next twenty-
four hours might well decide the whole fate
of the great invasion. What was the latest
piece of malicious gossip going the round of
London's clubland? 'Monty is unbearable in
defeat and insufferable in victory'. Well, they
had seen him in victory often enough in

these last two years, that was for certain. Now they might well see, God forbid, the other side of the victor of El Alamein.

Montgomery sighed softly and said, 'Well, Ewart, what is it?' Ewart handed him the buff-coloured Army form and said, 'It took six hours to get here from Normandy, sir. But that was the situation on the Morthomme Height as of fourteen hundred hours today.'

Montgomery read the message quickly and as he did so, sudden animation flashed into his bright blue eyes. His cheeks tinged a faint red. 'Excellent,' he barked, 'but why did this message take so long to reach my HQ, Ewart? Why?'

Momentarily Ewart was hesitant, almost as if he were a little embarrassed. 'I gather this chap Corrigan who is commanding up there is something of a bolshy. Apparently he took the law into his own hands to get off the beaches. There's talk of an enquiry.'

'Come on, Ewart, out with it. Who delayed it?'

'His brigadier, sir, that is, Corrigan's,' Ewart answered uneasily. 'I managed to get him on the radio. Said he wanted a nice tidy show on the beach, before he moved his brigade off.'

Montgomery groaned. 'My God, Ewart, it's the same old nine-to-five mentality that all these chaps have who've spent the war in the UK. This isn't the time for tidy shows and teabreaks. This is the time for audacity and dash. No matter.' He dismissed the unknown Brigadier. 'I have the terrain in my mind's eye. If I'm not mistaken that hill at Morthomme dominates the main Bayeux-Caen road.'

'It does, sir.'

'You know what that means?'

Outside, one of the many barrage balloons guarding the shipping in the Solent had broken its cable and was now sailing off over Southsea like a fat grey slug. The wind was increasing in fury by the minute. The windows started to rattle.

'Yes, sir. It will be the axis the Hun will use once he starts sending in his armour for the counter-attack. I'm surprised they haven't done so already.'

'Hitler's behind it, Ewart. I am sure he thinks, thanks to your various dodges and wheezes, that Normandy is not the main attack and is keeping his armour for the main landings. But I doubt if it'll take him more than another twenty-four hours to wake up to the fact that Intelligence has fooled him. Then he'll throw in his armour.'

Montgomery sighed as if suddenly for the first time he was becoming aware of the full enormity of his problems. 'When he does, Ewart, that highway will become the most important piece of road in the whole world.'

Ewart nodded his agreement.

'All right, Ewart, this is to be done – most immediate. This insubordinate chap – what's his name?'

'Corrigan.'

'Yes, Corrigan. He is to be reinforced immediately. At least a battalion of infantry, and oh yes, anti-tank guns, seventeen pounders. Corrigan's going to need them if the Hun put in his Tigers...' His voice trailed away to nothing.

He flung a hard glance at Ewart. 'Come on, spit it out. Let's have no bellyaching. What's the matter?'

'Corrigan is cut off, sir. The Huns have infiltrated infantry behind Morthomme. The Iron Division is prepared to winkle them out, but I doubt if they can do it for twenty-four hours.'

'Twenty-four hours!' Montgomery exploded.

'Yes, sir,' the colonel answered miserably.

'Then put in the TAC Air Force. Give the chap the protection of an aerial umbrella at least, and don't forget the Tiffy tank-busters.'

Ewart indicated the black rolling clouds outside and the white-flecked heavy green sea. 'Met forecasts a storm, sir. It could ground the TAC Air Force. But of course, things could be better on the other side of the drink.'

Montgomery rose to his full five foot seven, eyes blazing, wilful face set and hard. 'I've had enough, Ewart. There's been too much pussy-footing around over there. Signal Ike I'm off.' He grabbed for his black beret, covered with half a dozen regimental badges in a highly irregular manner. But Bernard Law Montgomery had long ceased caring about King's Regulations.

'Off where, sir?' Ewart gasped.

'To Normandy, Ewart, that's where! Now give me my gamp.' He indicated his battered old green umbrella. 'I'll need it, won't I.' He flashed the astonished staff officer a wintry smile. 'After all, it is going to rain, isn't it?'

Numbly Colonel Ewart handed him the umbrella. The 'Master', as he liked to be called, was going to war once more.

With the darkness came the cold and the wind, straight from Siberia, it seemed, icy and bone-chilling.

Huddled like his men in the bottom of a supposedly abandoned slit-trench, Corrigan had a hard job to prevent his teeth from chattering. It was more like January, he cursed to himself, than June. For a while he tried to doze, knowing that the Germans would not attempt to infiltrate the silent ruins above them until they felt the British had been lulled into a false sense of confidence; that nothing was going to happen

262

this night. But it was impossible. The night cold was like a poisonous snake, wriggling in through the gaps in his uniform, biting at his toes and fingers, creeping insidiously up his back and arms, turning his big body into a trembling, shaking hulk.

At about ten, he heard the first stirrings some hundred yards below. Hastily, with fingers that felt like thick sausages, he tossed the pebbles into the next trench which housed Wolfers and Slim. In their turn they did the same. All along the 'deserted' perimeter, the concealed soldiers prepared, waiting tensely for what was to come, feeling the adrenalin beginning to pump into their bodies, chasing away the numbing cold.

Five minutes later, he heard Wolfers tear off the blue paper from his iron ration chocolate. The big hungry Yorkshire boy was stoking himself up for the battle in the darkness. Corrigan grinned. If they could eat, they could fight. He cocked his head to the wind and waited. It wouldn't be long now.

Time passed with leaden slowness. Time and time again, Corrigan fought off the temptation to raise his head above the parapet and see where they were. They were there, he knew that all right.

He could already hear the faint noises they made: the soft jingle of metal, the slithering of a crawling body through the mud, the muffled curse when something went wrong.

Corrigan took the risk. Cautiously, very cautiously, he raised his head just above the parapet. There they were! Dark figures advancing towards them, bent under the weight of their equipment so that they appeared hunchbacked, weapons held across their young chests at the port. In front there was a tall young man unburdened by equipment machine pistols gripped in both hands, his head clicking from side to side as he searched the night like a spectator at a tennis match. He would be the commander, Corrigan decided. Noiselessly, he slipped off his safety catch and took aim, seeing the officer walk ever closer into the trap, growing larger by the minute in the circle of the rifle's sight.

Slowly, Corrigan's damp finger curled around the trigger. He began to take first pressure. It wouldn't be long now.

Colonel Bremer clapped his thigh hard with his big hand. *'Grossartig!'* he cried with delight. 'Absolutely first class!' He beamed at the dispatch rider, his ankle-length leather coat splashed with mud, his face black save where his goggles had been. Then, there were two white circles so that he looked like a white man painted up to look like a darky, Bremer couldn't help thinking. 'The Met people are completely sure?'

'*Jawohl, Obersturm,*' the DR replied, staring at Bremer's tough, happy face in the flickering light of the candle which was the bunker's sole illumination.

'*Gut.* All right, go and get yourself a half a litre of fart soup ... and there's some nigger sweat, too. Tell the kitchen bulls I said you should have a shot of Calvados for your efforts.'

The dispatch rider saluted awkwardly in his heavy gear and waddled out, beaming all over his face at the promise of soup, coffee, and above all, drink.

Bremer smiled around at his staff. 'Well, there we have it, gentlemen. The Met people forecast heavy rains, storms and low cloud ceiling for the next forty-eight hours. Ideal for our counter-attack. It'll keep those damned Tommy *jabos* off our backs and for once we'll be able to move our armour by daylight.'

He indicated that the waiting orderly should break out the apple brandy, the famed Calvados of Normandy, and waited until every one of his officers had a glass filled.

'Let me give you a toast, *meine Herren*. Once young Krause has infiltrated Morthomme, we push forward with the divisional tanks, take the place and kick the Tommies arses back to that funny little island of theirs!'

He raised his glass. 'Kick the Tommies'

arses!' he bellowed happily, knowing that victory was within grasping distance.

'Kick the Tommies' arses!' they yelled in unison, raising their glasses to the third button of their tunics, elbows set at a forty-five degree angle as regulations prescribed, and downed the fiery apple brandy.

Then their glasses flew against the wall of the bunker to shatter there in a rain of glass. At that moment, the first muted cracks of rifle fire from up above indicated that Lieutenant Krause's raiding party had run into trouble. Something had gone wrong.

## SIX

After that first rifle shot had sounded like the knell of doom, there was a nerve-racking silence. The men in the holes could hear their own hearts thumping wildly. In spite of the cold they broke out into an instant sweat.

Opposite them, the Germans crouched as if they were preparing to run out into a heavy storm of rain, watching in horrified fascination as Lieutenant Krause's knees began to give beneath him like those of a newly-born foal, the Schmeisser slowly falling from nerveless fingers.

With a soft moan he sank to his knees, head bent, supporting himself on the ground with one hand while he beat the earth with the other, as if in rage at the dirty trick fate had played on him. Unintelligible grunts came from his lips. His shoulders heaved as if he were sobbing. For what seemed an age, he knelt. Then with startling finality, he gave one last moan that set the hairs erect on the necks of the men watching, and pitched forward. Dead.

Both sides awoke to their danger at the same moment. *'Vorwaerts!'* an urgent voice called in German.

'Fire at will ... targets of opportunity,' Corrigan ordered, and began pumping his bolt. *'Fire!'*

Suddenly the perimeter line erupted in violent fire. The young SS men scurrying forward, springing over the shellholes, dodging from tree to tree, went down on all sides, screaming in naked unashamed agony as they went rolling down the hillsides or pitched into the churned-up earth of the craters to choke in the mud at the bottom.

Now it was every man for himself, both English and German. Corrigan, carried away by the mad excitement of it all, stood completely exposed, crouched like a Western gunslinger, firing from the hip to left and right, unable to miss – the enemy were so close.

To his right came that old familiar frightening whoosh and the air was suddenly burningly hot.

*Flame-thrower!* He didn't hesitate one moment. He swung round. Yes, there he was, a young SS man flanked by his bodyguards, both armed with machine pistols, the heavy fuel pack bouncing up and down on his back, nozzle belching flame in his hands.

Corrigan fired. The first bodyguard swung round, holding his shoulder. Corrigan fired again – and missed.

The second bodyguard fired a burst. Corrigan could feel the heat of the slugs whizzing by him. Behind him one of the Assault Troop men screamed shrilly with pain.

Corrigan's old rifle blasted flame. The second bodyguard was lifted clean off his feet by the burst. He rose right into the air and slammed into one of the skeletal trees to remain hanging there from a branch like a grotesque human fruit.

The flame-thrower operator pressed his trigger. Like some primeval monster breathing fire, the stream of blue hissing flame shot forward, searing and scorching all before it. Corrigan dropped just in time. Before his horrified gaze, the ground began to burn in a long scorched track.

'*Flame-throwers!* ... *they're using flame-*

*throwers!'* someone cried in absolute terror. In a minute, Corrigan knew they would panic and run. Even veterans were absolutely terrified of that ultimate weapon. He had to do something.

He tugged out his last grenade. He flung it. It had the desired effect. The flame-thrower operator was put off his stroke. Blinded by the huge burst of exploding earth, shrapnel zinging and winging through the air lethally all around him, he dropped to one knee.

Corrigan didn't give him another chance. Darting forward, clipping a new magazine into his rifle as he ran, zigzagging from side to side like an American footballer making a touchdown, he fired on the run, just as the operator staggered to his feet again.

He screamed shrilly. Finger pressed on his trigger in his death-throes, he swung round, blasting his comrades pressing on behind him.

The night air was rent by terrible cries as they were fried by that searing horrific flame, turned to black shrivelled human wrecks before Corrigan's horrified gaze, frozen into charred scarecrows as they stood there, limbs oddly contorted, teeth gleaming a brilliant white in skull-like faces.

The rest halted as their nostrils were assailed by the stench of human flesh fried to a charred mess.

The men of the Assault Troop did not give

them a chance to recover. As one they surged forward. Scrambling and wading through a gory morass of rent, torn human bodies, their ammunition boots slipping on the jellied bloody flesh of the dead, they came in for the kill. Carried away by an all-consuming, fervent blood-lust, screaming like savage animals, eyes wide and glittering hypnotically, the two lines clashed.

Man to man, they swayed back and forth, fighting to the death. No quarter was given or expected. When a man went down, he never rose again. In hand-to-hand combat, they slashed, gouged, hacked, chopped, sliced, tore, ripped. Rifles were useless now. They resorted to their bayonets, knives, boots, shovels, bare hands. The battle for Morthomme was entering its final and most desperate phrase.

Dawn threw its ugly grey light on that terrible lunar landscape. Everywhere there were wrecked tanks, cars, half-tracks, mixed up with corpses piled three deep.

German and British intermingled haphazardly, great chunks of unidentifiable dripping human flesh.

But still the Germans came, rushing in out of the grey light, while the wind which heralded the storm to come raced across the battlefield. They tramped over the mottled carpet of their own dead, yelling their desperate hysterical cries, following their bold young lieutenants to their death.

From Morthomme, to which Corrigan had now been forced to fall back, the machine-guns opened up yet once again. White glowing tracer zipped down on to the bold young men. It scythed away the first rank, leaving them screaming and writhing in the churned up mud, pressed down ever deeper by the ranks following.

*'Alles für Deutschland'... 'Unsere Ehre heisst Treue,'* the second man screamed the motto of the *Waffen SS* as they ran into the maelstrom of lead. *'Our honour is our loyalty!'* A moment later they paid the price of that blind, fanatical loyalty. They went down on all sides as those cruel machine-guns smacked into them, clawing the air, eyes looking beseechingly to the wild tossing heavens in the moment of death, as if pleading for mercy.

This day there was no mercy. As the wind grey in fury and the dark rainclouds scudded across a sinister threatening sky, the SS were massacred on that hill outside Morthomme.

Up in the ruins the assault troopers fired their brens until the barrels glowed a dull red, with the gunners ripping open their flies to cool them with their own urine.

Still the SS came on. Closer and closer that wild tide crept to the top of the hill.

*Fifty yards... Forty yards...* Their young

boys lay everywhere, dead before they had started to live. Still they came on. Would anything be able to stop them now?

*Thirty yards...* Now they were lobbing their clumsy stick grenades into the houses held by other desperate fanatical young men in khaki.

*Twenty-five yards...* Squatting on the cartridge-covered stone floor, sweat streaming down his face, helmet gone, blood trickling the length of his sleeve, Corrigan fitted another clip and shouted above the murderous racket, the thump of the mortars, the crump of the grenades, the vicious crackle of the machine-guns. 'Get ready for it, lads! They're getting prepared for the final rush now.'

'Remember you're British!' someone called and for once there were no raucous comments. Grimly, the handful of defenders waited for the inevitable.

*Fifteen yards!* 'Here they come!' Corrigan yelled.

To his immediate front, he saw him. An SS officer. He had seen them often enough before in Italy. Cocky, arrogant, fanatically brave, the epitome of the *Waffen SS,* standing there with his peaked cap, with that silver death's head at a rakish angle, stump of cigar in the corner of his mouth, belt full of stick grenades. He squinted the length of his rifle and pressed the trigger.

The old Lee-Enfield thumped back hard. Routinely he ejected the cartridge and pumped back the bolt.

To his front, the skull of that lone SS officer seemed to erupt. It flew apart, gore and bone flying everywhere, his face cracking and disintegrating as if glimpsed in a breaking mirror.

That single shot seemed somehow to signal the end of the frenzied attack. One moment the SS were advancing fanatically, full of wild determination, crazy energy; the next they had broken and were running back down the way they came, the wind buffeting them, whipping their uniforms about their skinny frames as if it wished to speed them on their way.

Again the attack of Bremer's 'Babies' had failed, but as the handful of begrimed defenders among the smoking ruins watched them go, hollow-eyed, shoulders bent, chest heaving as if they had just run a great race, their ears still loud with the echoes of that dreadful battle, they knew they'd be back soon.

'She was some sort of wog,' Slim was saying slowly, as if he had to concentrate hard to get the words out. 'Big, fat, lovely pair o' pearly gates. You sank into her like a silk cushion.'

Wolfers was not even listening. Mournfully

he chewed on a dry cracker, too worn, too emotionally drained even to enjoy his food. He was not alone. All of them were exhausted, as they squatted there in the ruins. Hardly moving, eyes set and apathetic, not even aware of the rumble of the guns coming ever closer, they waited numbly like dumb animals for the slaughter.

Crouched in the ruined belfry, Corrigan and Hawkins, the only two men in the whole Assault Troop now capable of standing guard, watched the body-littered hillside, speaking little, conserving what energy they had left. Stiffly Corrigan relaxed his arm from the bell-rope with which he would sound the alarm if – when, a cynical voice at the back of his mind hissed gleefully – the SS came. 'How are we fixed for ammo, Hawkins?' he asked in a dry voice.

Slowly, Hawkins removed his pipe from his lips, taking his time as if the movement demanded considerable effort. 'Two mags a piece for the brens, sir,' he answered, 'and a bandolier and a half of ball for the riflemen.'

'The point-fives?'

'More there, sir, but I doubt if any of the lads could get to the half-tracks in time without being hit. They're too knackered to run now.'

Corrigan nodded his thanks and the two men relapsed into silence again, staring across that lunar landscape, heavy and brooding, as if the dead who lay there whipped by the wind were projecting their own sombre thoughts from it.

Wearily, Corrigan raised his head and stared at the sky. The cloud was as low as ever and it would not be long now before it started to rain.

'No go, sir,' Hawkins said hoarsely, following the direction of his gaze, 'the Brylcreem Boys,' he meant the pilots of the Royal Air Force, 'won't fly in this kind of weather … might spoil their hairdos.'

Corrigan forced a tight smile. Hawkins was a great old stick. Without him, he wouldn't be able to keep what was left of the Assault Troop together.

'Perhaps you might be wrong, Hawkins. I can imagine that even those stick-in-the-muds back at the beach must be getting their fingers out by now, if they ever want to capture Caen. They've got to come soon,' he said almost desperately.

'Famous last words, sir,' Hawkins answered glumly, 'though I hope you're right.'

Slowly the first big drops of rain started to patter down on the stone. Numbly the two of them stared at the first star-shaped explosions of wetness, as if they could not comprehend what they were. The storm had begun.

# SEVEN

The rain began to fall about ten in the morning. By ten-thirty it had become a steady downpour, cold, grey and constant. Everywhere the young SS soldiers sheltered in the ditches and the Bocage, while the orderlies bearing the steady stream of immobile or moaning casualties to the waiting box-like meat-wagons, covered their heads with potato sacks to keep themselves dry. At the bottom of the hill the ground had turned into a sodden, churned-up morass.

Bremer was sitting crouched in a barn that stank of human sweat and animal urine, feeling not altogether unhappy at the sudden downpour. Behind him in the further recesses of the rambling outbuilding, the wounded moaned and whimpered, mumbling the odd incoherent word, grinding their teeth in agony.

'Now God's pissing on us,' said one of his young officers, speaking in the crude fashion affected by junior lieutenants in the SS. 'What next?'

Bremer shook his head in mock severity. 'Kurt ... Kurt,' he chided, 'how will you ever get to Heaven when you utter such

*Schweinerei?*'Then he seemed to snap out of his bantering mood. 'Well, comrades, the rain might make it difficult for our armour, but it has its advantages for poor old stubble-hoppers like ourselves.' He pinched his nostrils against the sudden stench, as one of the nearby wounded evacuated his bowels in his agony. 'At least those damned Tommies up there won't be able to whistle up those shitting *Jabos* of theirs! Today it's going to be man against man – a straight infantryman's war.'

'What's the drill?' asked the officer named Kurt.

Now the others also began to crowd closer, for again their artillery was starting to plaster the enemy positions.

'The same as before,' replied Bremer, over the thump of the mortars just outside. 'We old hares of the Popov front don't learn new tricks so easily, Kurt. One, two, three,' he smacked his big fist against the palm of his hand to emphasise his points. 'First artillery, then half-tracks and armoured cars in the lead, then the stubble-hoppers. Sooner or later,' he concluded, 'we'll wear the Tommies down. We always do. *Ponemyu?*' He grinned at the listening officers.

'*Ponemyu, Obersturmbannführer,*' echoed the old hares of the Russian front, for they had long grown accustomed to salting their talk with oddments borrowed from that accursed tongue.

Bremer turned to his waiting servant. 'My helmet, Pavel,' he requested with un-characteristic formality.

Gravely Pavel handed him it and bowed low.

'Thank you, my dear fellow,' Bremer said, and then his natural good humour and sense of rough fun burst through. He slapped Pavel hard on the back, causing his stainless-steel teeth to protrude grotesquely from his gaping mouth. *'Come on, you dogs, do you want to live for ever, eh?'*

And with that dread appeal to sudden death and mayhem, the eager young officers with their bright, fanatical blue eyes went streaming out into the pouring rain for yet another attack on Morthomme.

Corrigan stared. Half-tracks rumbled across the fields below. Behind them came the infantry, slow and thoughtful as before. Ahead, shells exploded, flinging up dark pillars of smoke into the lowering, rain-swept sky. He gulped, feeling the rain drip off his rimless Tank Corps helmet and trickle down the small of his back. He had to hand it to the SS; they did not give up easily!

'Can't they take some stick, sir?' Hawkins said grudgingly, as the men reached for their weapons yet again. 'Any other lot of Jerries would have scarpered by this time.

Not this SS shower o' shit, though.' He shook his head, half in anger, half in awe.

Corrigan wiped the drops of rain from his face and nodded grimly. 'They expect to die. They know how to die ... and we'll help them to die, Hawkins. Has Sanders got the half-inches in position up there?' He indicated the ruined church steeple.

Hawkins nodded. 'Yeah – him and Wolfers are right in position. By gum, that Wolfers is strong! He carried three of the buggers up them steps in one go. It's true, what they say about Yorkshiremen  big in t' body, weak in t' head. Anybody else would have been knackered.'

*We'll all be knackered by the end of today, if you ask me,* said a cynical little voice somewhere in Corrigan's head; but to the little NCO, he said, 'Wolfers is a good lad... They're all good lads, Hawkins. You should be proud of them.'

'I am, sir. I am that! They've turned out trumps, every one of them.' With a fond look at his unwashed, stinking assault troopers crouched over their weapons in the smoking ruins, Hawkins turned his attention to the task in hand.

Slowly the German infantry were drawing closer, plodding steadily on amid the din, the spurts of scarlet flame, the ribbons of white smoke. But now, in addition to their human enemies, it seemed they fought

279

against nature, too: the rain that dripped from their helmets, the slippery slope, the mud that caked their boots so that whenever they lifted them it felt as if they were soled with lead.

Up above, in the smoking rubble the weary defenders waited, ducking every now and again when a shell or mortar bomb landed too close. Like their enemies, they too were miserable and sodden, angry with the rain, the enemy, the war – the whole bloody world. Their only prayer was that the Germans would come closer – quickly – so that they could vent their burning rage on them.

Up in the tower, Wolfers and Sanders crouched behind the massive half-inch machine-guns taken from the cabs of the half-tracks. They were surrounded by heaped boxes of ammunition, and Wolfers as usual was chewing routinely on a hard-tack biscuit, while Sanders fulminated on his loss.

'I'm tellin' yer, cobber, I could have had a dozen fancy Frog whores for that kind of dough – frilly knickers, black garters, the whole bleedin' lot! It ain't bleedin' fair. It's allus the little bloke who gets kicked in the arse.'

'You'll have to stick to knee-tremblers like me then, Slim, won't you?' Wolfers said unfeelingly, keeping his eyes riveted on the half-tracks which would be their target once the balloon went up. He was pleased to see that their decks were wide-open. That meant that with a bit of luck they would manage to do what the CO had ordered them to do...

Now the half-tracks and the leading Germans were moving through the shell-shattered orchard that flanked Morthomme to the right, the regular lines of trees forcing them to split up into little groups.

Wolfers swallowed the rest of his biscuit and jerked back the cocking handle of the machine-gun. 'Better forget yer fancy Frog whores in frilly knickers and black garters, Slim,' he warned. 'They're almost here.'

'Fuck 'em. It ain't my fight. I'm an Aussie.'

Wolfers was unmoved. 'Why don't yer see the padre, then? Or the MO? He might give you a chit to say you're excused fighting.'

'Fuck you!' Sanders said, picking up his machine-gun.

'And you ... and your mother too,' Wolfers said without animosity.

Slim Sanders grinned wolfishly, then laughed in admiration. 'You're learning, kid, you really are.'

The Germans continued to advance. Like sleep-walkers, compelled by some primeval urge to seek our their fate, however dreadful, the young soldiers in their dripping camouflaged tunics filtered through the apple trees. Ahead, the half-tracks blundered on as best they could, weaving and winding in and out of the lines of trees, gouging out huge, glistening furrows, splattering those behind with mud and earth.

Now all was tense silence in the waiting British line. It seemed as if the men lying there in the soaked rubble might well be dead, the raindrops pelting down on their helmets unheeded. They made no movement. They hardly seemed to be breathing. When were they going to react?

Now the grenadiers began to feel again a wild, unreasoning hope that this time they might do it; that it would be a walk-over; that the Tommies might have fled, unable to withstand the terrible bombardment raining down on them from the sky. Here and there a young grenadier called out confidently to a comrade. Someone started singing the *Horst Wessel Lied.* Another took it up – and another. Soon the whole slope echoed and re-echoed to the bold Nazi marching-song: *'Heute gehört uns Deutschland ... und morgen die ganze Welt...'* Surely *nothing* could stop them now?

Bremer grinned. He was right up front now, machine pistol clasped in his hand as if it were a child's toy gun. Raising his free hand, he pumped it up and down three times  the infantry signal for at the double. *'To the attack!'* he cried above the rattle of the tracks and the rumble of the artillery pounding the Tommy positions on the top of the hill. *'To the attack... Follow me!'*

And with a great triumphant roar, he plunged forward into the billowing smoke, laughing like a madman...

'Lead 'em in!' Sergeant Hawkins yelled, above that same triumphant roar as the SS streamed forward through the pelting rain. 'Don't waste any ammo now... Make every shot count, lads.' He cupped his hands about his mouth. 'You up there in the steeple – get onto them half-tracks ... *now!'*

'Yes, Sarge!' Wolfers cried back.

'Up yours, Hawkins!' sneered Sanders, and pressed the trigger of the 50-inch machine-gun.

Tracer started up, leaping forward in an urgent curve, then falling, gathering speed every second, towards the half-tracks below.

Suddenly fire erupted all along the British front, sending the young SS men plunging down to their deaths on all sides. Immediately great gaping holes were torn in their ranks and each man found himself alone in the noise and the smoke, lurching forward blindly to gamble with Fate. A rain of big 50-inch bullets descended upon a half-track, pattering down like vicious tropical hailstorms. The driver screamed piteously as his back was ripped open. He slumped over the wheel and went smashing full-tilt into a hedge. Behind it, another driver, unable to stop, slammed into its rear, the wheel splintering and the spoke cleaving the driver in two.

Suddenly all was chaos and confusion in the German line. As the Tommies kept up the murderous hail of bullets, the SS toppled forward, hands clawing the air, faces upturned to the streaming rain. Others sprinted after them. Without another glance at the men writhing and dying in the mud, they pressed forward, only to meet death in their turn. Perhaps a dozen men reached the outskirts of the village, only to be mown down there without mercy. With a howl of pain, Bremer looked down suddenly and saw that one of his fingers was hanging by a bloody sinew. Having survived five years of war without a scratch, he had been hit at last. Numbed and bewildered, he sat there in the streaming rain beneath the bullet-pocked sign that read 'Morthomme', staring at his hand in disbelief. All around him the rest of the first wave were dying, and already the surviving half-tracks were beginning to churn round in the flying squelching mud and rumble back the way they had come. The second attack on the hillside village had failed. Slowly Bremer staggered to his feet, oblivious of the enemy slugs cutting the air all around, and holding his shattered hand high above his head like a bloody flag, limped back across a multi-coloured carpet of his own dead.

'Witt's dead,' Panzermeyer's harsh voice, bitter and yet sad at the same time, came through clearly over Bremer's radio, in spite of the static and the drumming of the rain on the tarpaulin stretched across the top of the half-track. 'Naval gunfire, I think. And he's not the only one. The Tommies are stopping us. It's vital you capture your objective – vital!'

Bremer winced as the orderly pulled the bandage tighter around his wounded hand and nodded to the radio operator to hold up the mike for him to speak. 'Understood. But the Tommies are dug in well and are putting up fierce resistance.'

Panzermeyer was unrelenting. 'Don't let me down, Gerd. I'm taking over command of the division now. I'm going to suggest to the Corps Commander that we change the whole divisional attack axis, switching it to your objective.'

Panzermeyer could not be any more explicit over the radio in case the enemy was listening, but Bremer understood well enough what he meant. By late afternoon two whole regiments of grenadiers and a tank regiment, perhaps some fifteen thousand men and a couple of hundred tanks, plus hundreds of other vehicles, would be crowding together on the road network around Morthomme, waiting for him to capture it before they could drive to the west. Suddenly the success of the whole damned operation depended upon him and his battalion. It was a terrifying thought. 'When?' he rapped. 'When do you expect to turn the whole division this way?'

'With luck by fifteen hundred hours at the latest. This rain won't last for ever. I don't want to be caught in the open once those damned *Jabos* start flying again, Gerd...' Suddenly it seemed to Bremer that Panzermeyer's usual harshness had vanished, yielding to a note of pleading. 'Let's give those babies of ours a chance, eh? Take that objective for them, will you?'

Bremer's eyes suddenly flooded with tears. He was not an emotional man – Russia had hardened, even brutalised him, as it had done all the SS veterans. But he felt at that moment, just as Panzermeyer did, that the sacrifice of the Baby Division should not be in vain. The memory of those boys already dead *had* to be honoured with victory...

'Kurt,' he replied thickly, 'I shall give you Morthomme by fifteen hundred hours.'

'Thank you, Gerd,' Panzermeyer said. 'Thank you on behalf of the whole division. Good luck. *Ende.*'

'*Ende,*' Bremer echoed, nodding to the

operator to take away the dead mike. With a jerk of his head he beckoned to the orderly to finish bandaging his hand quickly. There was little time to lose. He had to take that damned hillside village – and soon. The question was, how?

He stumbled outside into the ankle-deep mud. Everywhere his babies lay in the mud with the rain drumming down on their helmets, staring up at the ruined village as if almost hypnotised.

The German artillery was pounding it yet again. In fact for over an hour since the failure of the last attack, the guns had been hammering the damned place so hard, it seemed impossible that anyone could still be alive up there. But a frustrated Bremer knew that there *were* men up there – men who were waiting patiently for his babies to come again: men as hard and as fanatical as his own.

With his good hand, he wiped the rain from his face and stared past the crumpled bodies that covered the slope, searching for a weakness in the defences: dead ground, *anything* that would enable him to get his babies up to within striking distance. If they could only cover that last hundred metres or so once the barrage had been lifted, without suffering the same fate as their dead comrades...

Suddenly he had it.

'*Himmel, Arsch und Wolkenbruch!*' he cursed. 'Why in three devils' name didn't I think of it before?'

So saying, Obersturmbannführer Bremer started to run through the mud, crying as he did so, '*Funker! Funker!...* Get those lazy bastard engineers! I want the Goliaths... Do you hear me? *I want the Goliaths – at once!*'

# EIGHT

'They're bringing in the CO... They're bringing in the CO!' The awed whisper ran the length of the company as they crouched in the rain, their capes glistening, the raindrops pelting off their helmets in wild fury.

To the left and right of the road, Churchill tanks rumbled across the fields throwing up great clouds of mud and wet soil. Behind them the infantry moved in cautious, soaked groups. Here and there sappers searched for mines, rooting them out with their bayonets like potatoes. Beyond them, exploding shells flung up brown pillars of smoke to the black, low-bellied rain clouds. Now and then a Churchill was hit and would explode, flinging out bright white ribbons of smoke as its ammunition began

288

to go off.

But for the waiting company, crouched at the side of the shell-pitted road, these things were only incidentals. What oppressed them was the rain. It trickled down their collars from the rims of their helmets, soaked their uniforms and turned the ground into a morass, making the muck cling to their boots in great clotted masses as if they were soled with lead. But now they rested, leaning on their rifles, whispering that dread chant from one to the other in tune to the steady drumming of the rain. *'They're bringing in the CO... They're bringing in the CO ... now!'*

Slowly the four riflemen, rifles linked to form a crude stretcher, carried him to the waiting officers. His men did not salute, as military courtesy demanded, but their young eyes told all. The CO was dead and the battalion he had created would never be the same again. The very youth seemed to vanish from their wet unshaven faces and they looked old.

Montgomery saluted. Behind him his little staff did the same. The second-in-command stifled a moan. Slowly the procession passed the little group standing there on the soaked Norman road, the *pavé* glistening, as if the cobbles had been polished.

For a fleeting moment Montgomery's eyes rested on the dead colonel's face. It seemed vaguely familiar, and the sand-coloured ribbon of the Africa Star on his chest told the little general he had been one of his veterans. Perhaps he had known him once in Africa, Sicily, Italy, somewhere. Now he was dead. It was always the best, the bold, the brave who went first.

He lowered his hand and turned to the young major who had now taken over the battalion of infantry. 'He was a brave man,' he said gently, noting automatically the flickering unsteady look in the major's eyes; he was afraid. 'I'll see his courage is rewarded.'

'He shouldn't have led that last attack himself, sir,' the major said, his voice barely under control. 'It's hell up there, sir.'

'No it isn't,' Montgomery chided him gently. 'You just think it is. When I was even younger than you, Major, I lay in the rain severely wounded, not fifty miles from here, and I thought it was all finished. Fourteen hours in the rain in no-man's-land.

'When the MO found me, he ordered me to be put with the dead. He thought I was a goner, you see.' He gave the major his crooked smile. 'But I wasn't. Thirty years later, I'm still around – and a general to boot.'

The pale-faced major forced a weak smile. 'Yes, sir,' he answered, only half comprehending the little general in civilian corduroy bags and a naval duffle coat that was far too big for him.

In the ditch to their right, the medics worked on the latest batch of casualties from the failed attack towards Morthomme. Men groaned, ground their teeth. The lung cases gave off bubble-popping sounds as the doctors worked frantically, ripping, cutting, sawing, injecting, bandaging, painting in morphine dosages on pale foreheads, attaching the precious red tags to blood-stained uniforms which meant 'immediate evacuation to the UK' – the Blighty ticket. The whole ditch stank of ether, dirty wet feet, urine and human faeces.

Montgomery frowned. It was bad tactics to allow your troops to see their own wounded, but it was too late for that now.

He was going to have to get these chaps moving again if they were ever to break through to Morthomme. Air was out completely. He'd gone right to the top, but they simply wouldn't fly and their damned air marshals back in London were backing them up. Sometimes he wondered whether the Air Ministry was actually part of the British Armed Forces. Now it was going to become a down-to-earth infantry-armour slogging match. There was no other way.

'Now this is the way you are going to do it, Major,' Montgomery commenced, telling himself that it wasn't every day that a full general laid down tactics to a battalion commander. 'You'll go straight down that road with your battalion, leap-frogging companies as soon as things get sticky for individual companies. To your left and right flank, I shall ensure that you are supported by at least a squadron of tanks.' He indicated the Churchills lumbering forward.

'All the time you will be covered by the concentrated fire of our naval forces off the coast, and the brigade's twenty-five pounders will give you marching fire. As soon as you hit the main line of Boche resistance, put in your reserve company with the bayonet. Take and hold a gap in the line so that my armour can pass to make the link-up with the chaps on Morthomme and there's a gong in it for you, a good gong.'

Purposely, Montgomery made his voice brisk, confident and businesslike. There was no other way to do it. The young major and his chaps were decidedly rattled by two failed attacks and the death of their CO. He had to get them moving again before they bogged down for good, and the light was running out. In two hours it would be dark again. 'All right, old chap, I'll let you get on with it.'

'Thank you, sir... Yes, sir,' the Major said in a fluster and gave the little general in the soaked duffle coat a hasty salute. In an instant he would doubling down the road towards his men. The third attempt to break through to Corrigan's trapped men was about to commence.

Now they were moving out to the attack. The rain battered at them, lashing their young faces cruelly, soaking their battle-dress immediately. Montgomery watched them go and was moved by their youth. His veterans back in Africa had been mature men. These were boys.

Above, the first of the naval shells started to scream in with an elemental banshee howl. To the front, black pillars of smoke and flame rose immediately to the sky in awesome profusion. To left and right, the tanks lumbered forward, slithering and sliding on the muddy banks and fields. Abruptly all was noise, confusion, danger.

The riflemen advancing down the road towards the enemy did not seem to notice. Bowed under their loads, lashed by the rain, they moved like automatons, each man's gaze on the boots of the man in front of him.

Now the two radios in the little command post began to crackle urgently. Messages came flooding in. The Germans were waiting. To the front green, red and white signal flares began to sail into the sodden dark sky. It was the enemy signalling for reinforcements. Somewhere to the left there came the familiar high-pitched, hysterical shriek of the German MG42 machine-gun, firing a thousand rounds a minute. An instant later there was slower fire of the British bren sounding like an irate woodpecker. Battle had been joined.

Sodden and miserable, the first company of infantry deployed on both sides of the road. The Germans were waiting for them. They were due in on both sides, strapped to the trees, concealed by the high hedges of the *bocage*, burrowed deep in the drainage ditches.

The British infantry spread out rapidly as the first slugs came whining in. Men went down, writhing with pain. Tree-trunks splintered. Slugs howled off stone walls.

In a flash, the infantry's sodden weariness had vanished. Abruptly they were tremendously alert, the adrenalin spurting into their bloodstreams, knowing that one second's hesitation would mean death. They plunged forward, shouting their heads off.

Now the Germans began to pop out of their holes, hands raised. *'Kamerad!'* they called piteously, *'nicht schiessen... Kameraden!'* But the infantrymen were too worked up. The rain, the fatigue, the bloodshed had been too much; they had to vent their anger somehow. Bayonets flashed. Butts slammed into faces. The lucky ones were hauled out of their holes brutally, kicked in the buttocks and sent stumbling to the rear, eyes wild with terror, hands stretched high in the air.

The first line had been broken. But there was more to come. These were ordinary German infantrymen, not the elite of the SS, but they fought on as if they were. Hadn't their officers posted machine-guns five hundred metres to their rear to prevent them from breaking and running? They'd fight and die. There was no other choice.

The lead company flopped down in the soaked grass and mud, gasping for breath like asthmatics in the throes of some terrible attack. The second company passed through them and the men of the first, the survivors, had not even strength to jeer them on their way to death.

For a while there was a strange uneasy lull in the fighting, as the second company marched down the road under the wet, dripping, shell-shattered trees, the men assailed by a sense of muddy sodden misery, the feeling that they were alone and very vulnerable, while the artillery roared and the tanks trundled on to left and right.

To the rear, the radios chattered as the messages flooded in giving details of the features reached, the times, the nature of the opposition, as the shattered battalion was driven on by its own momentum. Montgomery listened tensely in the pouring rain, not seeming to notice it, smiling automatically, routinely exclaiming, 'Oh, good show, well done,' as if he were watching a particularly exciting game of cricket.

He made cheerful little remarks to the wounded straggling back, eyes wide with shock and faces indignant at the outrage done to their very own flesh before they were snatched by the medics and bundled into the ditch.

The first armour-piercing shell came zipping flatly over the soaked fields like a glowing white golf ball. There was the hollow boom of metal striking metal. The lead Churchill came to an abrupt halt as if it had just run into a brick wall. One second later it was a sea of blue flame and its crew, blazing themselves, were running for cover, trailing fire behind them.

Automatically the infantry broke into a heavy run. Some shouted. Others cursed terrible obscenities. A burst of high-pitched fire ripped the first platoon apart. The men went skidding across the gleaming *pavé*, as if on ice. The ones following sprang over their writhing bodies.

Dark helmets rose from the folds in the ground in front of them. Thin-barrelled machine-guns blasted fire at them. Their pent-up fury and bitterness exploded. Careless of their losses, they rushed forward in awkward little bunches, firing, halting and running on again. 'That's the stuff, chaps!' their major cried, waving his ash-plant, his only weapon. 'Show the Boche what we can do. *Bash on!*'

Now the bayonets flashed as they raced towards the chattering guns, men going down everywhere, goaded on by mad freaks of the imagination, telling themselves even as they were hit that it wouldn't happen to them. On and on, they fought their way forward, stumbling into that withering fire to topple over, faces upturned in agony, clawing the wet air. But always there were others, pushing over the dead and dying with scarcely a glance for those who had once been their comrades until they, too, fell writhing among the littered dead.

Half-mad with despair and fear, eyes burning, the major ran with them, waving his silly stick, mouthing his public school platitudes, too afraid to be afraid.

The men started to bog down. He raged at them, beat them with his stick. But now the energy had drained from them as if a tap had been suddenly opened. For a while he couldn't move them. They clung to a knoll of trees stripped bare of their branches by the concentrated enemy fire, like ship-wrecked sailors hanging on to masts. Each fresh burst of fire swept away yet more of them. Then the tanks came rumbling up, splattering them with mud and stones, and they were moving again.

'Bash on!' he cried hoarsely, his voice broken. 'Bash on, you're going to do it this time, lads!' Ahead of him, he could see the wet wavering outline of Morthomme, glimpsed through the pelting rain. 'We're nearly there!... Just one more go, please ... just one more go...'

The young major swayed crazily. He waved his arms around and swung into the opposite direction. He attempted to walk on, swinging his arms as if he were on parade, making a strange wooden shuffling step, shoulders thrown back, blood spurting in a scarlet arch from his severed throat. His body slapped right into the ditch, dead before he hit the ground.

The steam went out of the attack. Not all at once. Here and there an officer or NCO managed to keep them going. But not for long. Men stopped to attend to wounded comrades, suddenly aware of them for the first time. Others seemed to feel an urgent desire to dig in. A few simply fell into the drainage ditches, burying themselves in their sodden depths and refusing to come out.

Within ten minutes it was all over. The survivors had gone to ground everywhere and Morthomme vanished again into the smoke and rain like an ocean liner glimpsed momentarily in its full majesty at sea before disappearing into the fog.

The drive to link up with Captain Corrigan's battered Assault Troop had failed again. Now it was Colonel Bremer's turn.

## NINE

The whole valley quaked and trembled under the tremendous bombardment. From end to end, the angry red lights blinked like the mouths of enormous blast-furnaces. The din was awesome. There seemed to be no end to the shells. They came over in an constant stream, filling the air with one continuous scream of fury, broken only by the ear-splitting din as they burst.

Now the village of Morthomme was nothing more than a collection of smoking ruins, heaps of broken masonry from which charred timbers and grotesquely twisted girders protruded, still glowing a dull purple from the fires started by the shelling.

The survivors cowered in their pits. They screamed like crazy men. Soaked by the pelting rain, they soiled themselves in their own waste. They trembled and shook at each fresh shell-boom, choking and gasping, their wide, staring eyes covered with a hot, wet sheen. Some wept and sobbed uncontrollably. And all the while it rained and rained, the raindrops lashed the ruined, churned-up earth, slashing the skinny backs of the men, swamping their squalid dug-outs, as if God on high were determined to wash these miserable creatures off the face of His earth for good.

'If only the rain would stop,' Hawkins moaned. 'The planes would come and that would be that.'

From another pit, a dying corporal whose legs had been blown off an hour before, dragged himself over to Corrigan and cried, 'For Chrissakes, sir, use yer pistol on me... For Chriss–' The rest of his desperate plea was cut short as he collapsed in the mud.

Corrigan looked at Hawkins' ashen, pinched face with its blood-scummed, quavering lips. Even *he* was at the end of this tether.

Hawkins wiped away the black hair-dye that was trickling down the side of his face and swallowed with horror as he saw the corporal fighting his way out of the mud to renew his plea. 'Sir,' he gasped, 'you've got to make a decision ... soon.' He swallowed again, wizened head held to one side, choking for breath. 'Please...'

Corrigan pushed back his helmet and wiped away the rain with a sleeve, wincing with pain as he brushed against the gash across his cheek. 'Decision,' he croaked, 'what decision?'

'Surrender, sir.'

Somehow, the dying corporal had managed to raise himself to his stumps again. 'Shoot me, sir,' he was calling piteously. 'Can't stand the pain... It's terrible. Please, sir, shoot me...' Again his cries were muffled as he slipped and fell in the mud.

For a moment Corrigan longed to drown out that terrible plea in the way that children do, by pressing his hands to his ears. 'Surrender!... I can't surrender the Assault Troop, Hawkins!' he gasped in horror.

'Soon there'll be none of them left *to* surrender, sir,' Hawkins croaked doggedly, as yet another shell exploded nearby, showering their pit with gravel and wet soil. Around him, the men started whimpering again like trapped animals. 'The lads have had it... There's no fight left in 'em; and anyway, how can yer fight against *this?*' He shook his old head sadly, the hair-dye running down his wizened sad face like black tears. 'It's the end of the road for the poor old Assault Troop.'

'Rubbish, man!' Corrigan tried desperately to inject certainty, confidence into his voice, but failed miserably. 'We've just got to hang on a little longer. The shelling'll stop soon... The rain, too... Then Air will spot us and come to...'

His voice trailed away to nothing, for Sergeant Hawkins, he saw, was no longer listening. Behind them in the other pit, the corporal without the legs gave one last, despairing moan and fell dead into the mud.

The shelling stopped with shocking suddenness. For what seemed like an age, the young troopers were motionless, unable to take it in. Then gradually the echoes of the shelling faded and finally died away altogether in the surrounding hills, to be replaced by the steady, persistent hiss and beat of the rain.

Slowly, very slowly, it dawned on them that the murderous bombardment was over at last. Here and there a dirty white face with shocked eyes poked itself above the edge of the holes, to peer questioningly out at that smoking lunar landscape.

Corrigan did so, too. Down below, he could see the SS in their green camouflage tunics, massing; but as yet the shell-cratered slope was empty save for the dead. He shook his head in a vain attempt to rid his ears of the ringing.

Hawkins wiped his face and looked at him in bewilderment. 'What do you make of it, sir?' He, too, could hardly believe that the man-made storm of steel and sudden death had passed at last.

Corrigan shook his head. 'Don't know, Hawkins,' he croaked. 'I mean – why stop *now?'* He stared over to where a dead German lay sprawled on the slope, his body sliced in half by his own shellfire. From the massive wound in his abdomen there stretched an endless length of intestine like a ghastly marker rope. 'They're not attack–'

*'Sir!'* It was Wolfers' voice, calling from somewhere over to the left flank near the shattered church, now a pile of smoking rubble. *'There's something funny over here, sir.'*

Wearily Corrigan staggered to his feet. 'You're in charge here, Hawkins,' he ordered, and stumbled away.

Wolfers lay stretched full-length among the rubble of the church. Next to him, Sanders sprawled unconscious, felled by a heavy wooden crucifix that had fallen from the wall. It looked as if the crudely carved, Gothic Christ-like figure was protecting the Aussie with his own body.

'Sanders?'

Wolfers shook his head. His face was blackened by explosive and most of his blouse was in tatters. 'No, sir – just out. He'll come to in a half a mo.' He, too, spoke slowly, with considerable effort, as if he were very tired. 'There's a funny sound down there.' He pointed a dirty, bloody hand down the slope.

'Funny sound?' Corrigan echoed. After the numbing bombardment, it seemed to take a long time for things to register on his brain. 'What kind of funny sound?'

'Like the trams back home, sir.'

'Trams?'

Cautiously, the two of them peered down to where that strange, whirring sound was coming from. Wolfers was right: it *did* remind Corrigan of the electric trams of his boyhood.

For a few moments, Corrigan could not see anything in that jumbled landscape other than wrecked vehicles, smashed equipment and dead bodies. Then he spotted it. Emerging from the drifting smoke came a small object like a squat, metallic slug, crawling upwards at a snail's pace.

Wolfers saw it, too, as it advanced purposefully towards them with its soft, electric, whirring sound.

'What the hell *is* it, sir?' he asked, suddenly shaken out of the strange lethargy that had stolen over him.

For a few moments Corrigan was silent. He was remembering that time at Anzio when they had come crawling down from the hills towards the beaches, looking for all the world like kids' toy tanks. That was until the first one had hit the bunker held by the Yorks and Lancs… Later they had not been able to find a single whole body in the half a company which had held it.

'Goliath,' he hissed. 'It's a Goliath!'

'A what, sir?'

'That little bastard has got two hundred pounds of high explosive packed inside it,' Sanders snarled from behind them, pushing aside the cross which had pinned him down. 'You should have left me buried here. When those fuckers–'

But Corrigan did not wait to hear any more. 'Come on, Wolfers!' he cried, adrenalin suddenly pumping through his veins, charging him full of new energy. Next instant he was pelting down the slope towards the strange object. Already a faint whirring to the left told him another one had already started on its lethal progress, and judging by Hawkins' startled yell behind them, the sergeant had seen it too.

Corrigan and Wolfers kept their heads down low. The troopers were giving covering fire, and the slugs were now beginning to fly in both directions. Zig-zagging madly, with the German fire now ripping up the earth all around them, Corrigan and Wolfers slammed into the side of a wrecked German half-track, chests heaving.

'Here it comes,' Corrigan choked, sobbing for air and fighting to control his breathing. 'It's powered by two electric cables trailing behind it. Wait till it passes and then grab the bloody things!'

Wolfers nodded, eyes round and wild with fear. 'What do I do then, sir?'

'Pull – pull for all you're bloody worth!

Here it comes!'

From beyond the blunt nose of the half-track, they could see the little tank churning its way up the slope, its cables slithering and sliding behind it like two grey snakes.

'*Now!*' Corrigan yelled, and dived forward. Grabbing his cable, he fell full-length in the mud Wolfers following suit. Now, with the German small arms fire intensifying, they began to be dragged through the mud by the strange, silent monster, packed with enough explosive to send the whole of what was left of the Assault Troop to their deaths.

Struggling violently, and trying his best to ignore the hail of slugs all around him, Corrigan ripped and tugged desperately at his cable. The strain was tremendous. His shoulder muscles were aflame with agony. His palms burned unbearably. With all his strength, he heaved.

'Done it, sir,' Wolfers cried, and fell behind, clutching the severed cable, bullets whipping up vicious little spurts of mud inches from his face.

Corrigan gave one last, mighty tug. There was a rending of metal, and suddenly the soft whirring was silenced. Corrigan fell face-down in the mud, sobbing for breath, as the Goliath ground to a halt. At that moment he could have lain there for ever, but already the electric whirring of another of the mini-monsters was goading him into action yet again. With a groan, he raised his head.

A hundred yards or so to Wolfers' left, another Goliath was climbing towards the troopers' stronghold, with Hawkins' fire howling harmlessly off its steel sides. 'Come on, Wolfers,' cried Corrigan, 'let's get it.' Wearily he staggered to his feet, head swimming with fatigue, his limbs feeling like lead. Wolfers followed dutifully, heaving himself out of the mud, dripping wet, too exhausted to notice the bullets stitching a lethal seam along the length of useless cable that still dangled from his hands. There was a look of utter helplessness on his face – and Corrigan knew why. Even if they overtook the second Goliath, which was already well up the hill and crawling inexorably toward the Assault Troop's positions, there was a third down below, followed this time by a crouched, determined huddle of SS infantry. Number three would never stop – *never.*

Gasping like ancient asthmatics, they started to stumble upwards towards the Goliath. Bullets pattered off its sides like heavy hailstones, but they were as ineffective as the rain itself. With inhuman determination it ploughed on to its target. Helplessly, hopelessly, the two men slithered after it towards the twin smears left by the cables.

Desperately summing up the last of his energy, Wolfers dived forward and grabbed the left-hand cable. It dragged him to his knees. Frantically he held on, like a rider trying to restrain a runaway horse, while Corrigan slithered up the slope after him.

'Hold it, Wolfers,' Hawkins screamed.

*'Hold it!'* went up the cry from a score of fear-choked throats.

*'For God's sake – HOLD IT!'*

'I can't ... I can't!' Wolfers sobbed, tears streaming down his ugly face, as he felt the cable being wrenched from his muddy, slippery grasp. *'I can't, lads...'* At last he let go and collapsed there on his face in the mud, while the little monster churned ever upwards towards the men.

Nothing could save them now.

Then it happened. The great, round-engined silver shape barrelled down straight out of the rain. One moment there was nothing; the next, there it was, filling the rain-sodden heavens, machine-guns chattering frantically, deadly white rockets streaking towards the little monster like a swarm of furious hornets.

As he knelt there, weeping in the mud, Wolfers felt the searing heat of the missiles as they whizzed over his head straight for their target. The Goliath disappeared in a tremendous blast of startling scarlet flame. A huge, hot wave of blast slapped him across the face, dragging the air from his lungs, threatening to burst them at any moment.

Behind him, Corrigan was whipped off his feet and flung backwards into the mud, as more and more of the silver shapes came roaring in at four hundred miles an hour, drowning the wild cheers of the men they had saved and the screams of those they had come to slaughter.

Colonel Bremer shrilled his whistle in a desperate attempt to rally his men, but he already knew in his heart of hearts that the counter-attack had failed. The Battle of France was lost. Now the Armies of the Reich would soon commence that great retreat to their homeland, whence they had started on this last Germanic migration westwards four long years before.

As the Allied *Jabos* screamed overhead, he, too – Colonel Gerd Bremer, holder of the Knight's Cross with Oak Leaves and Swords – joined the frantic, panic-stricken mob of youths who had once been his pride and joy, running for his very life. The men of Morthomme had won.

# TEN

There was a sinister yet awe-inspiring majesty about the scene. The night shadows were already beginning to race across that shattered lunar landscape. The sky itself was a startling electric blue. But the long line of bombers which stretched back as far as England was still in the dying sunlight to the west, the planes' metal sides twinkling like fairy lights.

Beside the long column of tanks grinding up to the height and its smoking ruins, the infantry spread out in lines to left and right. The commanders opened their turrets to view the great silver armada heading for Caen. At last they had broken through. They were off the beaches at last. They were moving inland.

Above them the pathfinders were dropping their great clusters of glittering flares and breaking to the left in slow curves. They cascaded down in ever-widening arcs like clusters of brilliant, sparkling jewels. Puff-balls of brown smoke started to dot the sky, for the gunners around Caen knew what was coming.

Now the bombers began to sail in in

majestic grandeur, weaving in through the puffs of flak as if through the meshes of a giant net. Here and there one staggered visibly and the men heading for the silent village groaned as the bomber broke formation, streaming smoke.

Already their huge bombs were beginning to fall on the doomed city. Huge mushrooms of smoke began to ascend into the darkening sky, as below cherry-red fires broke out everywhere.

Slowly the horizon was transformed. The night shadows fled to be replaced by a great crimson burning landscape that coloured the faces of the liberators a glowing, unnatural red as they plodded towards that silent summit.

There was the hooting of a car in a hurry. A ragged cheer rose from the files of heavily laden, plodding infantry. It was Montgomery's Humber staff car, Union Jack flying proudly at its bonnet. 'Monty!' they cried, their tiredness forgotten for a moment at the sight. 'Good old Monty!'

Standing bolt upright in that eerie red light, Montgomery, the victor again, saluted and waved and at regular intervals threw out green packets of Woodbines. A strict non-smoker himself, he knew his soldiers kept going on coffin-nails and char. The Humber rolled on towards the new front. The Germans were pulling back, slowly but surely, everywhere. The Battle of the Beaches had been won and the new battle for Caen had commenced. Montgomery was going up to supervise.

Grunting steadily under their loads, the first company plodded on through the gaping shellholes and the dead. The smell of death and decay was everywhere. Tanks and half-tracks lay drunkenly, half across the ditches and holes where they had been knocked out, their plates already beginning to rust. Clouds of greedy flies buzzed around the open turrets.

Doggedly, awed to silence now, not even grunting with the effort of the climb, the infantry threaded their way through the dead of Bremer's *Hitlerjugend*. His 'Babies' lay everywhere in their camouflage tunics, faces a waxy white or mottled green in that eerie glow. The last feverish gestures of their fanatical devotion to their cause was evident even in death. One had been caught attempting to set up his machine-gun. Another was kneeling in a gap in the hedgerow, hand arrested in mid-air: he had been about to throw a stick grenade. Another young SS man had been killed as he crawled from behind a wrecked half-track, a cunning, almost triumphant look on his pinched young face. All of them looked like waxworks in some hideous tableau at Madame Tussaud's.

Now they were almost there. Still, an awesome silence hung over that dread summit. No movement came from the shattered ruins of Morthomme. The leading infantrymen stumbled to a ragged halt. They looked in bewilderment at each other. Were they all dead up there? What was going on? Had they fought all this way to relieve dead men?

A young officer, as nervous and as awed as his men by this sombre place, pushed his way through the hesitant infantry. He raised his hand, changed his mind, and cupped both hands around his mouth. 'Ahoy there!' he called, his young voice barely under control, 'Ahoy there, Recce Assault Troop!'

His call echoed and re-echoed among the ruins. No answer. He hesitated, feeling the sweat of fear begin to break out unpleasantly all over his body. But he knew his men were watching him. He had to go through with it. Alone, he stumbled forward a few paces and cupped his hands to his mouth again. 'Hello there, Recce Assault Troop! Hello, are you there? Answer please...'

One hundred yards to his right a solitary figure, a stark black against the blood-red glow over Caen, rose from behind a shattered wall with infinite weariness like a corpse from the grave and stood there absolutely silent. A moment later another rose to the left – and another. One after another the survivors came slowly to their feet, swaying

313

violently as if they might fall at any moment.

The young officer's innocent, boyish face blanched. It was as if he were rousing the ghosts of soldiers long dead. He swallowed hard and turned. 'All right, chaps,' he cried in a broken voice, 'they're coming down now...' His words trailed away as silently, like sleep-walkers, the survivors of the Assault Troop started to make their way down that desolate, scarred slope, looking neither to left nor to right. Noiselessly he counted them as they filed unseeingly by him. At twelve he stopped and waited. But no more came. Blood Beach had taken its final toll.

# ENVOI

**21 ARMY**  **GROUP**

# PERSONAL MESSAGE
# FROM THE C-IN-C

*(To be read out to all Troops)*

1. After four days of fighting the Allied Armies have secured a good and firm lodgment area on the mainland of France.

2. First, we must thank Almighty God for the success we have achieved and for giving us such a good beginning towards the full completion of our task.

3. Second, we must pay a tribute to the Allied Navies and Air Forces for their magnificent co-operation and support; without it, we soldiers could have achieved nothing.

4. Third, I want personally to congratulate every officer and man in the Allied Armies on the splendid results of the last four days.

   British, Canadian, and American soldiers, fighting gallantly side by side, have achieved a great success and have placed themselves in a good position from which to exploit this success.

5. To every officer and man, whatever may be his rank or employment, I send my grateful thanks and my best wishes for the future.

   Much yet remains to be done; but together, you and I, we will do it, and we will see the thing through to the end.

6. Good luck to you all.

B . L . Montgomery

General,
C.-in-C.,
21 Army Group.

France,
10 June, 1944.

'Prisoner and escort – *quick march!*'

Swiftly the hard-faced major of military police flung open the door of the schoolhouse. The escort, an embarrassed captain of infantry armed with a pistol, dug Corrigan in the side. 'Off we go, old chap,' he hissed. Marching smartly, arms swinging level with their shoulders, the two of them advanced on the waiting court.

'Prisoner and escort – *mark time!*' the MP commanded harshly.

As one, the escort and the shaven-headed prisoner, minus his belt and cap, started marking time where they stood, knees moving up and down with rigid precision, the stamp of their highly-polished boots making a hollow, echoing sound on the stone-flagged floor of the Bayeux schoolhouse which was being used for the trial.

The MP major let them sweat it out. Corrigan knew the score: this sort of technique was used quite deliberately to intimidate prisoners. But he was not intimidated – he was too angry at the whole bloody silly business.

'Prisoner and escort – *halt!*'

Like automatons, they stamped to a halt and stood staring at the panel. They were gathered round a simple Army trestle table covered with a grey issue blanket: the brigadier, wearing his purple-ringed cap and looking very pleased with himself, Stirling, who could barely conceal his delight at the position in which Corrigan now found himself; the adjutant, who was clearly embarrassed by the whole business and was looking studiously at the table, trying to avoid Corrigan's hard, contemptuous gaze. The fourth member of the panel, Corrigan did not recognize. He was a middle-aged, swarthy-looking lieutenant colonel with horn-rimmed glasses and a bald pate which he touched constantly with the tips of his splayed fingers, as if hoping to find that his hair was beginning to grow again. He was the legal officer from the Judge Advocate's Branch, and he had a self-satisfied, cunning look about him, as if nothing had ever gone wrong in his life – and never would.

Now a heavy silence hung over the court, broken only by the muted sound of the convoys outside, heading for the front. Corrigan waited, knowing that this, too, was part of the treatment – that same campaign of harassment to which he had been subjected ever since his arrest a month before, one day after the Iron Division had finally linked up with the battered survivors of the defence of Morthomme.

He had become accustomed to it. He was

no longer even bitter – just contemptuous of these pathetic attempts to break his spirit. These men facing him across the table wore the same uniform as he did, spoke the same language, were fighting the same enemy. But the looks on their easy, complacent faces told him that they hated him; hated him more than they did the Germans. He had become a threat: a threat to their security, their lazy amateurish way of running the war. And they were going to punish him for it. Oh yes – there was no doubt about that. Today they were going to break him once and for all.

'Prisoner.' It was the colonel from the Judge Advocate's Branch, his voice insidious, full of cynical menace. 'Tell the court, your name, rank, unit and appointment – please.' He glanced at the brigadier in his purple cap, smiling softly and knowingly at the word, as if to say: *We won't have to say "please" to the cocky little bugger much longer, sir, don't you fear.*

Corrigan supplied the information, his gaze fixed on some distant spot behind their backs.

'I hear you wish to defend yourself, Corrigan,' the colonel said.

'Yes, sir.' Still Corrigan's eyes remained fixed on that distant horizon.

The colonel made a note on his pad and cleared his throat angrily. 'Very well. Captain

Smythe-Smythe, please begin.'

Reluctantly the adjutant rose to his feet, his too-long blond hair escaping from beneath his cap and giving him the air of an overgrown schoolboy – which, indeed, he had been only a year or so before. 'Captain Corr ... er, *prisoner,'* he began, flushing hotly and hastily correcting himself, conscious of the brigadier's angry look, 'you are charged on three counts: taking away government property without permission; deliberately disobeying the order of a superior officer–'

Next to him, Major Stirling, wearing the pip and crown of a lieutenant colonel now, smirked knowingly and gave Corrigan a triumphant look.

'...And refusing a further order from the same officer – in a highly insulting manner.' The adjutant flashed a quick look at the legal colonel, as if seeking approval. The latter nodded, and the adjutant asked quickly, 'Prisoner – how do you plead?'

Corrigan took his time. His career was over. He had nothing to gain by attempting to go along with them. They were his mortal enemies now. They would cashier him, he knew that. If he was lucky, they might not sentence him to prison, but that was about all he could hope for. He cleared his throat and said very quietly, 'Gentlemen, I shall not plead.'

'What the devil is that supposed to mean?'

the brigadier barked. Stirling's self-satisfied smirk disappeared suddenly and he looked cheated. The adjutant flushed a deep shade of red.

'But you *have* to plead, man!' the colonel from the Judge Advocate's Branch snapped angrily, still fiddling with his thinning hair.

'Do I?' Corrigan said coldly, apparently unmoved, but with his thoughts racing wildly. Suddenly his eyes blazed with fury. 'In order to please *you*, gentlemen, perhaps? No, I shall not plead. All I shall say is this: I did what I did because *I* thought it was right. I did it to save the lives of the men on the beach, which were being thrown away for nothing. I did it to end this damned war quickly. I did it because I couldn't stand this nine-to-five kind of battle you gentlemen seem to wish to conduct. I did it—'

But suddenly the brigadier was on his feet, his face as purple as his cap, spluttering frantically, beating the trestle table with his cane, '*Stop it! Stop it! At once!*'

The escort grabbed Corrigan's arm. He could hear the major of the military police running down the corridor. The bald colonel was making excited signs to the escort to draw his revolver. Suddenly the schoolroom seemed to have become a whirl of noise and movement, with Corrigan in the midst of it all, pale, silent and smiling in cold triumph. He had said his piece. Now they could do what they liked with him. His role in World War Two was over.

But for once Captain Corrigan was wrong.

Suddenly, rather absurdly, all of them froze in their positions, the brigadier in purple anger, the bald colonel with his hand in the air, the escort, fingers clutched to the butt of his revolver. Behind them, the running major came to a sudden halt. Corrigan heard him stamp to attention and felt the draught of air as the door was opened. Then they were all snapping to attention and the escort, with a swift glance over his shoulder, was gasping, 'Oh, holy Christ, it's *him!*' Finally there came the sound of many feet advancing hurriedly up the long passage.

Hastily, the escorting officer pushed Corrigan to one side to allow the procession to pass. For the first time he saw the procession of high-ranking officers and the little man at its head. Now it was his turn to gasp.

He was dressed carelessly, even sloppily, for a general officer: suede desert boots, a baggy pair of civilian corduroy trousers, shabby battledress blouse and he was even carrying a faded green umbrella! But there was no mistaking the authority of that fierce, hawk-like gaze under the black beret of the Tank Corps. It was the Army Commander himself. It was Montgomery of Alamein!

General Montgomery halted, propped

himself up on his umbrella, and taking his time, stared up at the panel standing rigidly to attention, their faces revealing all too clearly just how startled they were by his unexpected visit. Behind Montgomery, a brigadier and a colonel, both bronzed and wearing the white 'Y' patch of the 5th Infantry Division, presently fighting in Italy, took up their positions, as if they, too, had some part to play in the events to come.

'Brigadier,' Montgomery said, in that crisp upper-class voice of his, 'I have the War Office's permission to quash the trial of this officer.'

'But, sir,' the brigadier began. 'I do not think...'

Montgomery shot him a quick glare from his startlingly blue eyes, and the brigadier immediately fell silent.

'Furthermore, I am relieving you of your command as of this moment. Brigadier Roberts–' with a wave of his skinny hand he indicated the bronzed, bemedalled officer behind him – 'will take over your brigade with effect from twelve hundred hours. You will be returned to the UK for reassignment.'

Hearing the note of absolute, overwhelming finality in the little Army Commander's voice, the brigadier bowed his head in resignation. He knew instinctively that there would be no appeal.

'Colonel Douglas will take over the command of the Reconnaissance Regiment immediately,' Montgomery continued, indicating the other bronzed officer from Italy.

Stirling's face fell. Like the new brigadier, Douglas had all the appearance of a fire-eater. The typical new broom. Suddenly he was afraid. How long would he last, even as a lowly squadron commander, back in his old rank of a major, with a brigadier and a commanding officer like *that* in charge? Not very long, he guessed.

Montgomery gave the standing officer a flash of those penetrating blue eyes and then Stirling and the rest of the panel were dismissed with a wave of his hand as if they had never existed. They filed out by the little general, saluting as they did so. He deigned not to notice. Silently and sternly he waited till they had gone.

Now he turned and gave Corrigan a hard look, face fierce and imperious as he stared at the tall, lean officer, eyes revealing nothing. Even Corrigan, as hard-bitten as he was, felt uneasy under that unblinking scrutiny. Abruptly, as if he had just made up his mind, he crooked a skinny forefinger at Corrigan. Smartly Corrigan stepped forward and snapped to attention, towering above the bird-like little man in whose hands lay the destiny of Britain's armies in this fateful summer of 1944.

'So you are Captain Corrigan,' he said in his high-pitched upper-class voice.

Corrigan waited. He knew Montgomery expected no answer from him.

'Captain Corrigan, you have been dreadfully insubordinate. If I had been your brigadier, I would have seen to it that you were cashiered forthwith.'

Suddenly his blue eyes twinkled and the severe look vanished. Deep wrinkles of good humour spread from the eyes. 'Fortunately for you, Corrigan, I wasn't. However you did the wrong thing for the right reason, and you *did* help materially to stop the Boche push. If they had captured that height at Morthomme well, let's say it doesn't bear thinking about.' Montgomery breathed hard. 'It is because of that that I have ordered this court-martial to be quashed.'

'Thank you, sir,' Corrigan spoke for the first time. He desperately wanted to stay in the Army and see this thing through to the end. 'Thank you very much, sir,' he repeated with more humility than he thought he possessed.

'Don't thank me, Corrigan,' Montgomery snapped, the twinkle vanishing as quickly as it had appeared. 'Thank the fact that I need more officers of your kind. Men who don't just sit around on their fat bottoms and bellyache, but get up and *do* something. There has been far too much pussy-footing about already. It must be stopped!' He rasped the words, as if he were laying down the law to a meeting of his senior officers instead of a lowly captain.

Montgomery went on, resuming his normal tone. 'Your trial has been quashed, but I have ordered that your personal file be duly marked. You're bolshy, Corrigan, a notorious trouble-maker. You made trouble in Italy, I see from your records, and you have made trouble here. See that you don't make trouble again. Next time you won't find me so lenient. Good-day to you.'

'Good-day, sir,' Corrigan heard himself say, as if from afar. The next thing he knew he was following the procession of red-capped staff officers outside in a kind of daze, only dimly aware of the escorting officer's parting, 'good luck for the future, old chap', and blinking suddenly as he stepped out into the slanting rays of the July sun.

For a moment Captain Corrigan stood there, bewildered by the tremendous flow of traffic which clogged the ancient streets, heading nose to tail to the front, urged on by sweating, angry, red-faced military policemen, their uniforms caked in white dust, the stuff swirling around their feet so that they looked almost as if they were floating there.

Corrigan shook his head. He still could not quite take in the fact that after a month's close arrest he was free again by some miracle; that he was part of the great push eastwards once more. Open-mouthed, he stared like some country yokel at the tremendous spectacle of Britain's might surging past before him: tanks, trucks, half-tracks, artillery, jeeps, one long khaki stream heading for the new front beyond the River Seine. Nothing could stop Britain now, it seemed at that moment, as he stood there in the dusty sunshine, face pale after a month's imprisonment. Suddenly he felt proud, very proud, to be British and belong to this great army.

'Got a light, sir, for my fag?' a well-remembered Australian voice rose above the roar of the traffic and cut into his daze. 'Old Monty's been handing out fifty cigarette tins of coffin nails like they was ready money. But he forgot the matches, sir, see. Fair dinkum, eh?'

Corrigan spun round.

It was Sanders all right. His bronzed cunning face cracked into a big grin and he raised his hand in a lazy attempt at a salute. On his wrist, as his sleeve rolled back, Corrigan could see five wristwatches. Obviously the little rogue hadn't been wasting his time since he had last seen him.

'You ... you...' Corrigan stuttered. He was too surprised to be angry at the little Australian's lack of military courtesy.

'Yes,' Slim Sanders replied as cockily as ever, 'me. Mrs Sanders' handsome Aussie son, the pride of the bleeding outback. Before your very eyes, sir.' He paused and waved to one of the passing three-ton trucks, laden with pale-faced youths obviously going up to the line for the first time. 'Good luck, lads! Give old Jerry a kick up the arse for me!' he called.

A couple of tins of some sort of ration came flying his way as thanks and Slim caught them neatly. 'Fall for it every bleeding time,' he said with a wink, shoving them in his pack. 'Mugs!'

'But what,' Corrigan stuttered, 'what … the devil are you doing here, you little rogue?'

'Just doin' a little tradin', sir.' He indicated the watches with a mighty, knowing wink. 'Before we go up again.'

'Go up again?' Corrigan echoed helplessly.

'Yes, sir.' With an eloquent sweep of his hand, Sanders indicated the line of new half-tracks, which Corrigan now saw for the first time, standing to the right of the schoolhouse where his trial had ended so suddenly and so unexpectedly. 'Sergeant Hawkins and the lads thought we'd come and fetch yer – that new CO from Italy said it was okay. This way, sir.'

Like a butler escorting a guest, Sanders led a dazed Corrigan through the packed traffic, ignoring the red-caps' shouts and shrill whistle-blasts and offering a crimson-faced sergeant an obscene gesture as he went.

Corrigan paused. For the first time he was aware that his troopers were assembled by the roadside – and they seemed to be cheering. Before he had not been able to hear the sound above the roar of the traffic. But now there was no mistaking it. There they all were: the handful of bronzed veterans of the Battle of Morthomme, and many white-faced replacements sent out from England to fill the gaps in the ranks of the Assault Troop – and they were cheering *him!*

For a moment Corrigan felt overcome by emotion. Tears flooded his eyes. What had they to thank *him* for? In the past he had led them to death; and in the dark future, soon to come, it would be no different. Yet there they were – cheering at the top of their voices.

And there was Sergeant Hawkins, large as life, hair freshly dyed, wizened face set in a broad grin – and Wolfers, huge corned-beef sandwich in his free hand! Together, they helped him into the cab of the first brand-new half-track, where Sanders was already gunning the engine impatiently. Then they were easing their way into the khaki-coloured stream of traffic heading for the

331

new front.

Half-track after half-track followed, aerials gleaming and whipping a bright silver in the breeze, the yellow-and-green pennants of the Reconnaissance Corps fluttering bravely, the men's faces bold and excited as they stared to the east for the first signs of the new battle.

Corrigan's Assault Troop was going to war again.

The publishers hope that this book has given you enjoyable reading. Large Print Books are especially designed to be as easy to see and hold as possible. If you wish a complete list of our books please ask at your local library or write directly to:

**Magna Large Print Books**
Magna House, Long Preston,
Skipton, North Yorkshire.
BD23  4ND

This Large Print Book, for people
who cannot read normal print,
is published under the auspices of

**THE ULVERSCROFT FOUNDATION**

... we hope you have enjoyed this book.
Please think for a moment about those
who have worse eyesight than you ...
and are unable to even read or enjoy
Large Print without great difficulty.

You can help them by sending a
donation, large or small, to:

**The Ulverscroft Foundation,
1, The Green, Bradgate Road,
Anstey, Leicestershire, LE7 7FU,
England.**
or request a copy of our brochure for
more details.

The Foundation will use all donations
to assist those people who are visually
impaired and need special attention
with medical research, diagnosis
and treatment.

Thank you very much for your help.